Try Like You've Never Been Grounded

Smoke and Laura - Summer Lake Book 4

SJ McCoy

A Sweet n Steamy Romance

Published by Xenion, Inc

Published by Xenion, Inc.
First Paperback edition 2017
www.sjmccoy.com

Cover Design by Dana Lamothe of Designs by Dana
Editor: Kristi Cramer of Kristi Cramer Books
Proofreaders: Aileen Blomberg

ISBN 978-1-946220-10-3

Dedication

For Sam. Sometimes life really is too short. Few xxx

Prologue

Smoke shut down the engines and ran a hand over his eyes. He needed some time to catch up with himself. He loved his job, but sometimes he longed to be still for a while. He'd spent the last six months based in Houston, the six before that in Miami, but even being based somewhere meant he spent maybe a week out of every month there. The rest of the time he was flying folk around. Shuttling Jack and Nate between Miami, New York and Houston, spending time out here on the West Coast, getting Pete from LA to San Francisco and Seattle.

He removed his headset and unbuckled his seatbelt. He seemed to spend more time in this cockpit than he did anywhere else. He grinned as he stood to make his way into the cabin. The three hot chicks back there reminded him that he really had nothing to complain about. Most guys would give anything to live the life he was living. Flying a jet, having time to kill in some of the greatest cities in the country. It was looking like his new home base would be Santa Monica—how bad was that?!

He smiled to himself as he let down the steps. Hell, ferrying three hot women around wasn't exactly a hardship! He almost lost his grip on the handle when he spotted another, even hotter woman standing on the tarmac grinning and waving. He felt his throat go dry. Damn! Long dark hair, bright blue eyes, and that smile! He was barely aware of Missy and then Emma thanking him and then making their way down the steps to greet her. He had to drag his eyes away from her and try to focus when he realized Holly was speaking to him.

"...Pete said we should let you know an hour before we head back to the airport, is that enough time for you?"

Smoke stared at her, forcing his mind to make sense of what she was saying. All he wanted to do was turn his head to look back at the woman on the tarmac. "That's great, thanks. It gives me time to file our return flight plan and be ready to go." He couldn't believe how normal his voice sounded. He was surprised he could even hear it over the thundering of his heart in his chest.

Holly waved down at the others who were waiting, then she raised an eyebrow at him. "Could I introduce you to Laura before we leave?"

Smoke grinned. Could she ever?! He'd already decided Pete's new girlfriend was cool. As he followed her down the steps towards Laura, he upgraded that opinion to awesome. He looked at the beautiful face that was turned towards him. It seemed he mostly dated blondes, but the idea of long dark hair with bright blue eyes had always appealed. And here she was.

"Laura," said Holly, "This is Smoke, Phoenix Chief Pilot and an old friend of Jack and Pete's. Smoke, this is Laura Benson, Jack's cousin."

She held out her hand, he shook it as her gaze met his. Hot damn! She was gorgeous. Her bright blue eyes sparkled with fun and laughter as she smiled at him. Her long slender fingers, wrapped around his, made him want her long arms wrapped around his neck—and her long slender legs wrapped around him too, for that matter!

He was vaguely aware that the girls were getting on the waiting golf cart. He should let go of Laura's hand, but all he could do was keep staring at her beautiful face. She wasn't letting go of his hand either. He heard Holly saying "Go, go, go." The spell was broken as Laura turned away from him.

The golf cart pulled away with three giggling women on it. "Sorry, sweetie, no room." Missy waved happily at them.

Smoke grinned as Laura turned back to him and rolled her eyes. "No-one could ever accuse that bunch of being subtle, sorry!"

He laughed. "Subtle no, perceptive, definitely. And I for one am grateful." More than just grateful. He couldn't believe his luck. She was smiling at him. Damn, she was beautiful!

"Oh, don't get me wrong. I'm grateful too. I'm just not quite sure what to do with it."

"Well, the way I see it, we could miss an opportunity because we're both taken by surprise, or we can think on our feet and make the most of the few moments we have."

A touch of color appeared on her cheeks as she looked up at the plane and then back at him. Damn, she had a dirty mind! She looked surprised, but definitely interested. But no, he'd want more than a few moments in the back of the plane with this woman. He'd want a whole night in a big bed.

He pursed his lips and gave her a knowing smile. "When I say we can use these moments wisely, I mean you can give me your number, so I can call you and we can see where this goes."

She laughed, looking a little embarrassed. "Of course you do." She reached into her purse and took a business card from her wallet. As he tried to take it from her, she held on to the corner, not letting go. He met her gaze. "You only get it if you really want it, Captain. Don't take it if you don't."

He flicked his wrist and pulled the card from her grasp. He held it up with a smile. "I really want it, Laura." He was gratified to see the little pink stains on her cheeks deepen when he added. "And I will take it."

She put her hands on her hips and smiled, the sexiest smile he'd ever seen. "I want it too, Smoke." His throat went dry again when she asked, "So, are you going to give it to me?"

He was glad that the black slacks of his pilot's uniform were loose fitting, otherwise she'd see how much he'd like to give it to her!

She threw her head back and laughed. "Get your mind out of the gutter and give me your number, Smoke!"

He laughed with her as he took his wallet from his back pocket and handed her his card. "I will call you, but I need to warn you, my schedule is a little crazy. I don't know when I'll be able to get back here, but it will be as soon as I can."

She nodded. "That's okay. My life is a little hectic too. I'm sure we'll get around to it."

Smoke intended to make damned sure they did. "Do you ever get up to Summer Lake?" he asked.

"I'll be going back and forth until Jack and Emma get married, since I'm one of the bridesmaids. Will you be going to the wedding?"

Smoke nodded. "I will." The golf cart was approaching. Her friends would be waiting. He took her hand again. She smiled. "I'm so glad to meet you, Laura."

She gave his hand a squeeze. "You too, Smoke." She climbed onto the golf cart. "I'll see you at the wedding if not before," she called as she rode away.

Smoke stared after her.

~ ~ ~

Laura smiled to herself as she walked back out to the limo where the others were waiting. Sweet Lord above! That was one hot man. And that uniform? Wow, just wow! He wasn't exactly her usual type, but good grief! She could certainly make an exception, and it wasn't as though her usual type had been working out too well. So she usually went for guys with brown hair? She'd take his gray over any of them. So she was a sucker for green eyes? Who knew gray eyes could be so mesmerizing? When she reached the limo, the others stood smirking at her. She should be mad at them for running away like that. "Oh my God, you guys! How could you?"

"How could we what?" asked Emma sweetly.

"Sorry sweetie," laughed Holly. "Had to get to the bathroom."

"How about a thank you?" asked Missy with a grin.

Laura grinned back. It was hard to believe that she'd only met the three of them a couple of weeks ago. They were becoming real friends. She clasped her hands together. "Thank you. Thank you. Thank you! Where did you find him, and can I keep him?"

Holly herded them all into the limo so they could get going, but Laura's mind was still on Smoke. She took the glass of champagne Missy handed her. Laura wasn't used to being affected like this by a man's physical appearance. She normally went for brown haired, bookish types, more serious and studious than studly. She found herself attracted to men for their minds, not their muscles. She had no idea what Smoke's mind might be like...but holy hell, those muscles! "Did you guys see him? I think I might still be drooling!"

"I know I am," said Holly. "But he only had eyes for you. He lit up the moment he clapped eyes on you!"

Laura buzzed with excitement at having her own impression confirmed. She knew, just knew, that Smoke had been as bowled over by her as she had by him. Still, hearing Holly say it made it even better. She didn't want to admit it though, so she said, "But you guys were sooo mean, running off like that." She couldn't even pretend she wasn't happy about it. "And I am sooo grateful!"

Missy gave her a shrewd look. Laura had already noticed that she didn't miss a trick. "So did you get his number?"

She tried to keep a straight face as she remembered the shocked look on his face when she'd asked if he was going to give it to her. "We exchanged cards."

They were all looking at her expectantly.

She didn't want to admit just how brazen her conversation with Smoke had been. These girls were becoming real friends, but they were still new friends. "It was a little awkward, you know? But he said he'd be at the wedding, so I'll see him then if nothing else." She smiled at Emma. "Will you hurry up and set a date, Em, and make it soon?"

For some reason, Holly went quiet after that. Missy moved the conversation on to shopping, and shoes, and dresses. Laura's mind kept straying back to Smoke, hoping she wouldn't have to wait 'til the wedding before she'd see him again.

Chapter One

A few months later.

Smoke sat in the FBO building watching the parking lot, hoping she'd arrive soon. He'd spent the last couple of days hanging around San Francisco. As always seemed to be the case with him and Laura, their schedules hadn't worked out. He'd found himself wandering the city alone while she was tied up with some diamond people from London.

His head snapped up as he spotted her Audi pulling in. He jumped to his feet and headed out to meet her. Damn, she was beautiful! Her long dark hair fell around her shoulders as she got out of the car. Her beautiful face and smile full of fun had his throat going dry as she greeted him.

"Hey, Smoke. I am so sorry I couldn't get away any sooner."

Smoke smiled, the frustration of the last few days forgotten. "You're here now."

She nodded and reached into the back to get her bag. He drew in a deep, calming breath as he took in the longest legs, perched on sexy-as-hell heels, with the greatest ass at the top. The frustration was back, in his pants at least. He had not been able to get this woman out of his head since he'd met her. Just the thought of her made him hard. Now she was finally here, he could feel the blood rushing in his veins. Man, she was hot.

She turned to face him with a smile. "I am, but all we've got time to do is head to Summer Lake for Missy's party. I really wanted to show you round San Francisco before we had to leave."

Smoke stepped towards her. She was tall, and in those heels her eyes were almost level with his. "It's you I want to get to know, Laura, not San Francisco."

She smiled and took a step towards him, too. "We'll have to see what we can do about that, won't we?"

He wanted nothing more than to pull her to him and kiss her. From the way she was smiling at him, he got the impression she was hoping he would. Damn. He couldn't though. He was working. He reached down and took her bag. "We will," he said. "Once we get to Summer Lake."

A look of disappointment crossed her face before she followed him into the building.

He let her climb the steps of the plane ahead of him, his gaze fixed on her perfect ass. Did they really have to go to Summer Lake? Smoke would rather stay here, take her out to dinner, just the two of them—and see where the night went. He secured the door ready for takeoff. Laura sat in one of the big club seats.

"Wouldn't you rather sit up front with me?" he asked. It was only a short hop up to the lake, but he'd waited so long to be able to see her again. He wanted her close, not back here.

"Would that be alright?" She looked thrilled.

"Seems like it's the only way I'm going to be able to get you alone."

She smiled and stood up. "Hopefully not the only way, but it'll do for starters."

He let her into the cockpit. Once she was settled in the right seat, he pulled the seat belt down over her shoulder and clasped it to the lap strap before buckling her in. He watched her breasts rise and fall, pleased to see that their proximity was clearly affecting her in the same way it was him. He placed the headset on her and tucked a strand of hair behind her ear. Her gaze was fixed on him as he deliberately brushed her cheek before adjusting the mouthpiece for her. He closed his eyes and forced himself to sit down, buckle in to his own seat, and focus on the job at hand. It may only be a short hop, but he needed to focus. Fly the damned plane, Smoke!

~ ~ ~

Laura kept quiet until they were up in the air. Fascinated, she listened as first the tower then Air Traffic Control gave him instructions, and watched as he input numbers and adjusted settings. She found it incredibly sexy to watch his big, capable hands working the instruments. She hoped that someday soon she'd feel those hands on her.

He turned to her. "You okay?"

She nodded. "Just admiring a cool, calm professional at work." He smiled as the ATC's voice came through the headset and he turned his attention back to the instruments to adjust course.

She'd been starting to think that Smoke was destined to be just a fantasy for her. Ever since they'd met, that day the girls came shopping, it seemed that events had conspired to keep them apart. There had been plenty of opportunities, but all they'd managed were a few snatched moments here and there. A quick hello with the whole gang around, or a plan to meet that got messed up by one of their schedules changing. She'd been so grateful to her cousin Dan when he'd arranged it so Smoke would be spending a few days in San Francisco before flying her up to the lake for Missy's birthday party. Yet again it had been another missed chance. The people from Levy had shown up on Thursday morning and she'd spent every waking moment of the last three days with them. It was a huge honor that they wanted to work with her. They were one of the few remaining family-held diamond companies and they wanted her to design an exclusive line of jewelry for them. It was a fantastic opportunity, and one that would give her chance to travel to London. She'd get to meet their design team and spend some time in their flagship store there. She just wished they could have arrived next week, instead of coming to town on the only couple of days Smoke could be there. It couldn't be helped though. She'd just have to make the most of the chance they had now. She smiled to herself, glad that she'd decided to spend the week at the lake instead of just the weekend. She hadn't mentioned that yet, though; she'd see how tonight went first.

She listened to Smoke talk into his headset as they made their final approach to Summer Lake. The water sparkled and the mountains huddled together as the sun sank behind them. It was so beautiful up here. However things went with Smoke, it would be great to spend the week here to relax and let her creative mind get to work on design ideas for this new line. She looked across at Smoke, who was concentrating on making the landing. She wondered how much she'd get to see of him while she was here.

He shot her a smile as he taxied the plane towards the FBO building. "Are you okay with getting changed into your costume here?"

She nodded. She wasn't normally one for costume parties, but she was excited to wear the angel outfit she'd picked up—she knew how good she looked in it. And Smoke, in cowboy gear? Yes, please! Though she doubted it could be any hotter than his pilot's uniform. "Yeah. Em and Jack will probably be waiting so it'll be a quick change and off to the Boathouse, I expect."

Smoke grinned. "I hope you're going to dance with me."

"You bet I am." She held his gaze. "As long as nothing else comes up. It seems every time we try to do anything together, something else comes up to stop us."

The look Smoke turned on her as he shut the engines down set Laura's heart racing. "Something might come up, Laura. But nothing is going to stop me from dancing with you tonight."

That look made her think the dancing he was talking about was the horizontal kind. Although that wouldn't be happening tonight, she hoped that it would happen at some point in the not too distant future. The way his gray eyes were boring into her, all she could do was nod. No, it wouldn't happen tonight.... That would be too soon...wouldn't it?

"Come on," he said, nodding through the window to where Jack and Emma were standing outside the building. "We can't keep them waiting." He rested a hand on her thigh as he unbuckled her belt. "Much as I would like to. Let's get in there and get changed."

She nodded up at him.

"Be warned though. Once I'm out of this uniform, I'm off duty. My ability to remain cool, calm and professional may just evaporate."

"Oh, I hope so," she said with a smile.

~ ~ ~

"So, tell me about the diamond people," said Emma. "It sounds so exciting, but it's a pity they had to show up this week."

Laura nodded. It was. "It wasn't the best timing," she agreed, "but it is a wonderful opportunity. They want me to design a new line for them, and it will mean at least one trip to London."

They were sitting at one of the big picnic benches out on the deck, where Emma had dragged her so she could meet Missy's

brother, Chance. Dan was out here too, but Laura kept
glancing back inside to where Smoke stood talking with Jack.
She hoped tonight wouldn't be yet another missed
opportunity. She looked up as a hand came down on her
shoulder.

"Hey, Laura. Glad you could make it."

"Hey, Ben. How are you?"

"I'm great." He handed her an envelope. "Your key is in there
and I had the guys take your bag down to your cabin. I think
you'll like it. I gave you one of the ones down by the water."

"Aww, thanks, Ben. You didn't need to do that." Laura was
thrilled; she'd booked a room at the lodge, not a cabin.

"I didn't need to, no. But I checked when you called about
staying the week and there was one available. I thought you
might enjoy it." He gave her a mischievous grin. "You can
thank me when you leave. If I did the right thing."

She looked at him, puzzled, but he just gave a shrug before
heading back inside.

"You're staying the week?" asked Emma.

"Yeah, sorry I didn't tell you. I just decided after talking to the
Levy guys. It's a good week for me to take a little break, start
thinking about this new line and catch up with you guys." Of
course she was also hoping she'd get to see some more of
Smoke too.

"You could have stayed with us."

"I know. Thanks, Em. I wanted some alone time though. I've
been under a lot of pressure these last few weeks. You don't
mind, do you?"

Emma smiled. "Of course not. I understand. This is a great
place to decompress. As long as you know you're welcome at
our place any time."

"I do. Thanks." Laura's attention had drifted back to Smoke.
Was he ever going to come out here?

Emma dug her in the ribs. "Can you at least pretend to be listening to me?" she said with a laugh. "He'll be out here soon enough."

"Sorry, am I that obvious?"

"'Fraid so, but I can't say I blame you. You still haven't had chance to spend any time with him, and now Jack's got him cornered. Tell you what, I'll go and get Jack and bring them out here."

She was up from her seat and gone before Laura could reply.

~ ~ ~

"So, it didn't work out for you this week?" asked Jack.

Smoke shook his head. He was treading carefully around Jack when it came to Laura. Jack was a good friend, had been since college, but he was also Laura's cousin. Smoke knew he was very, perhaps overly, protective of the women in his life.

As if reading his mind, Jack grinned. "Well, you get to see her tonight. I'll do my best to leave the two of you alone and not hang around and chaperone. You know what I'm like, though."

Smoke nodded again as Emma appeared at Jack's side and put a hand on his arm.

"Will you leave the poor guy alone, Jack. Laura's sitting out there all by herself."

Smoke laughed as Jack turned to scowl at Emma.

"You dragged her out there so you could see Chance!"

Emma hung her head. "I thought you'd follow us."

Jack wrapped his arms around her. "And why would I follow my wife just to watch her throw herself at another man?"

Emma wriggled and laughed, but Jack wouldn't let go as he laughed with her. She looked at Smoke. "I'd make a break for it if I were you. I think I can keep him distracted for a while."

Smoke grinned and left them to it. He quickened his pace when he saw the guy they'd called Chance lean in to talk to

Laura. That was all he needed—to have some good looking cowboy make a move on her now!

He reached the table and stuck his hand out in front of Chance. "I'm Smoke. Nice to meet you," he said as he slid onto the bench next to Laura and put an arm around her shoulders.

While Laura's smile was filled with surprise, Chance's was one of understanding. "You too, Smoke," he said with a nod. "Nice talking to you Laura." He stood up and disappeared into the crowd.

Laura shook her head. "Smooth, Smoke! Not subtle, but smooth."

He laughed. "I can't afford subtlety at this point. No way is some guy making a move on you tonight."

She raised an eyebrow at him.

"Not unless it's me, anyway."

"Less smooth." She laughed.

"Tell you what, how about you come dance with me. I'm real smooth on the dance floor." He was relieved when she stood to join him. All he wanted to do was hold her against him, feel her gorgeous body moving with his. The dance floor was as close as he was going to get. For now.

His throat went dry when she reached her arms around his neck. He placed his hands on her waist, holding her just a little away from him as they swayed to the music.

"Are you keeping me at arm's length?" she asked, her smile teasing.

"I think I have to." If he held her to him the way he wanted to, she'd know the dance floor wasn't where he really wanted to be. The angel costume she was wearing barely covered her ass and her endless legs seemed even longer in another pair of sexy heels.

"What are you afraid of, Smoke?" Damn, she really enjoyed teasing him, her eyes sparkled with mischief. She knew damned well what she was doing.

He chose to ditch subtlety completely. "The only thing I'm scared of is scaring you off before I get into your panties."

She arched an eyebrow. "I don't scare easy."

"Good," he breathed as he closed his arms around her. He drew her closer until they were touching from knees to chests. God, she felt so good!

The little pink stains appeared on her cheeks, but she tightened her arms around his neck. Lifting her chin, she pressed herself against him. "And this is supposed to scare me?"

"Hell, no! It's supposed to make you want me."

She was tormenting him as she moved to the music, rubbing her hips against his. She brought her lips up to his ear and whispered. "It's working."

~ ~ ~

By the time they made their way back outside the gang had grown to the point where they'd had to pull two picnic benches together. Smoke enjoyed hanging out with these guys. It was a good thing he did since it was looking like Summer Lake was now going to be his new home base, not Santa Monica. Jack was already living up here and Pete was spending most of his time here too, even though his house wasn't finished yet. If he stayed with the Phoenix Corporation, Smoke could see himself living here quite happily.

He watched Laura jump up to join the other girls. Where were they off to? He'd been lost in thought. He watched as the guys followed them. Seeing the girls climb up on the bar to dance, he grinned and headed over there too.

How the hell could she dance in those heels, and on the bar too? He envied Pete, who was pawing at his girl's legs. Smoke wanted to paw at Laura. What he really wanted to do was get

her down from the bar and take her back to his cabin. He tried
to get a grip as the song came to an end. Dan was lifting Missy
down. Pete and Jack had their girls. Hell, he wasn't going to
miss a chance like this. He stood in front of Laura and reached
his arms up to her, and she let him lift her off the bar. He held
her up high for a moment, then loosened his grip so that she
slid down his front 'til her feet hit the floor.

The way she smiled at him, he didn't care where they were, or
who they were with, he needed to kiss her. He lowered his
head, but a hand on his collar dragged him away. Dan and Jack
were up on the bar now and Ben was pushing Pete and pulling
Smoke to join them. As he danced and clowned around up
there, Laura's eyes never left him. When the song ended and
Dan and Jack started line dancing to some country song,
Smoke jumped down. All the girls watched, transfixed as
Chance joined the Benson boys. Hmm, maybe that country
stuff wasn't as corny as he'd thought. It certainly seemed to do
it for the ladies.

~ ~ ~

Laura watched her cousins dance. They were quite something.
Missy's brother was something else! She stole a sideways
glance at Smoke. Even just standing there watching, he was
still a whole lot sexier than any of the guys dancing on the bar.
He caught her eye and leaned a little closer. "Are you having
fun?"

"I am, but I think I'm leaving soon."

His face fell, but before he had chance to say anything Laura
heard raised voices and turned to see what was happening. She
was surprised to see Dan's ex, Olivia—what the hell was she
doing here? She was making quite a scene.

~ ~ ~

After all the fuss around Missy and Dan had died down, Smoke appeared at her side. "Are Jack and Emma leaving early?" he asked.

"I don't know. Why?"

"You said you were leaving soon."

She smiled, waiting to see what he had to say.

"I could give you a ride out there later if you want to stay a while. I've got the crew car from the airport."

She smiled again. He really was keen. She couldn't resist playing with him. "That's okay. Thanks though." She was curious to see how cocky and confident he really was. She usually liked her men a little more timid, but she was enjoying sparring with Smoke as an equal.

He gave her a sexy smile and stepped closer. "At least dance with me one more time?"

She nodded and let him lead her out onto the dance floor. This time he immediately pulled her to him and held her close against his hard body. She slid her arms around his neck and let herself go soft in his arms, allowing him to lead her. She'd intended to tease him, but it felt like he was teasing her. One hand rested at the top of her butt, holding her against him as his hips moved. His other hand was between her shoulder blades, pressing her against him so her breasts pushed at his broad chest.

His smile was still cocky, sexy-as-sin as he looked into her eyes. "Is it still working?"

She had no clue what he meant. She was too distracted by the feel of his body owning hers. It didn't matter that they were on a crowded dance floor. It didn't matter that they were fully dressed. His body really was owning hers.

"What do you mean?" she asked.

Heat was building between her legs as he held her against him. His hand strayed lower onto her butt. His smile grew wider.

"You asked if this was supposed to scare you, remember? I said it's supposed to make you want me." He brought his lips to her ear and nuzzled it before he said, "I need to know it's still working."

Damn, him! He was too good at this. "It's working," she breathed.

"But you have to go home with Jack and Emma?"

She shook her head. "I never said that."

His arms tightened around her. "Then where are you staying?"

"Here. At the resort."

His smile was victorious. "So. Can I walk you home?"

"Yes, please."

Chapter Two

As they made their way off the dance floor, Holly appeared out of the crowd.

"Hey, sweetie. We're about to leave. You're not supposed to be staying at Missy and Dan's are you? I doubt they'll want any company tonight. I just wanted to check that you're all set."

Laura smiled as Holly eyed Smoke. "I'm good, thanks. I'm staying at the resort." She had to laugh at the way Holly's eyes widened.

"Oh! I see." Holly looked back at Smoke. "Well, you two have fun. We'll all be out here for breakfast...if you're not too busy," she added with a saucy grin.

Laura shook her head. Holly was terrible! "My plan was to stay out here to get some alone time. I need a break."

"Yeah, alone time, right! I think you'll find Summer Lake has this weird effect on people's plans. Just ask Pete! I'll see you when I see you, sweetie. Call me though. I need to talk to you about the plaza."

"Will do. Good night."

As Holly turned away, Jack and Emma came pushing their way through the crowd. Laura looked at Smoke. "So much for making a quick exit."

He made her knees go weak with the heat of the look he gave her. "We've waited for months. I can stand another few minutes, but not much longer."

"Are you sure you want to stay here?" asked Jack when he reached them. He gave Smoke a dark look before turning back to Laura. "Why don't you come up to North Cove with us?"

She had to laugh. "Because, Jack, you're my cousin, not my dad! And besides, my plan in coming here was to get some me-time. Things have been crazy the last few weeks and I need to just chill out. You of all people know how that feels."

Jack's glare softened. "Okay then." He looked at Smoke. "Sorry, bro. Make sure she gets to her room safe though, huh?"

Smoke nodded. "You can count on it."

"And breakfast? Here? Around ten?"

Laura rolled her eyes. "Maybe."

"Only if you want to," said Emma. "Come on, Jack. "I'm tired. I want to go home."

At that Jack seemed to forget everything but taking care of his wife. As he led her away, Emma looked back and winked at them.

Smoke laughed. "She certainly knows how to handle him!"

"She does. I think I need her to give me lessons. I swear he thinks he's my dad sometimes. I wouldn't mind, but he's only a year older than me."

"He's just looking out for you. You've got to respect that."

~ ~ ~

Smoke was glad when they finally got out of the Boathouse. "Are you all checked in?" he asked.

"Yes. Ben took care of it and had my bag sent down, too."

As they crossed the square, Ben came down the steps from the lodge. He nodded at them. "It was a good night, huh, guys?"

"Great," said Laura. "I'm so happy for Dan and Missy."

"Me too," said Ben. "And you're happy with your cabin?" He raised his eyebrows.

Ben seemed to be acting strange. Smoke liked him, but he still wasn't sure about him and Laura. They'd been paired together in Jack's wedding and seemed to have become friends. Smoke wasn't convinced there wasn't more to it than that."

"I haven't been out there yet," said Laura. "But thanks again. It's really good of you."

"Oh," Ben gave Smoke a smile he didn't understand. "I hope you'll think so," he said. "Anyways, I'll see you tomorrow. I need to get back to it. Good night guys."

"Good night."

Smoke frowned to himself. He didn't know what Ben was trying to get at, but he didn't think he liked it. He shrugged. He had more pressing matters to get to. Like getting Laura safely home—and into bed. He put an arm around her waist as they walked on.

"So, where is your cabin?" he asked.

She laughed. "Down by the water somewhere. I don't even know." She opened her purse and took out an envelope. Opening it, she took out a little map and a key. The tag on the key read 11B. Smoke had to bite back a laugh. Now he understood Ben's weird smile. He said nothing as Laura held up the map and tapped it.

"Wonderful," she exclaimed. "Cabin Eleven is down on that little beach in the pines." She smiled at him. "Come on. Let's go see."

They followed the road through the resort and down to the lakeshore. Laura gasped when the road rounded a bend and she saw the cabin in the pines, the moonlight reflecting off the water behind it. "Isn't this perfect?"

Smoke nodded. It couldn't be more perfect as far as he was concerned. He laughed as she ran the rest of the way to the cabin, then stopped dead.

She turned back to him, disappointment etched on her face. "Look," she whispered once he'd caught up to her. "I have neighbors!" The cabin was a duplex, one door at either end of the building. "I thought I was going to have this whole beach to myself." Her disappointment was almost comical.

"You don't need to whisper."

"I don't want to wake them up!"

He laughed. "You won't."

"How do you know?" she hissed.

He took the key from her hand and unlocked the door. "Trust me, you won't."

She eyed him suspiciously as he ushered her inside.

"Come on. I promised Jack I'd see you safely to your room. My job isn't done until you're inside."

She smiled and stepped past him. He closed the door behind him and followed her into the great room. A stone fireplace was set into a wall of windows looking out onto the lake. Smoke stood close behind her and put a hand on her shoulder as she looked out at the lake.

"Alone at last."

She stepped quickly away from him. "Finally we get chance to get to know each other," she said, once she was on the other side of the room.

Smoke nodded. They could play this however she wanted. He reckoned they'd know each other pretty well by morning. "Are you going to offer me a drink, then?" he asked. She looked flustered. This was going to be fun.

"I didn't bring anything."

"Let's check the kitchen shall we?"

He wasn't surprised when she found a bottle of champagne with a bow on it in the fridge. He'd stayed at the resort often enough to know that was standard.

"Look!" she held it up with a grin.

"Great." He took it from her and popped the cork while she went through the cupboards and returned with two glasses.

"Want to take these out on the deck?" he asked. "It's a beautiful night."

She hesitated. "I'd love to, but I really don't want to disturb whoever is next door. I know there must be someone staying there. Ben said the resort is full this weekend."

"I told you," he grinned. "You will not disturb your neighbor."

"How do you know?"

Smoke couldn't keep it to himself any longer. "Because I am your neighbor. That place next door is my temporary digs 'til I figure out where I'm going to be living."

She threw her head back and laughed. "So that's what Ben was acting so smug about!"

"Apparently. I couldn't figure out what he was up to. I'd never have guessed he'd thought to put you out here."

She bit her lip and smiled at him. That was so damned sexy. It made Smoke want to bite her lip himself.

"What?" he asked. She was evidently quite happy about something. "Are you glad he put you out here for the night?"

"He didn't."

Smoke didn't get it. "No?"

"No. He put me out here for the week!"

This was getting better and better! "You're staying the whole week?"

"Yep. I wanted to get some peace and quiet. Spend some time relaxing while I start work on this new line of jewelry."

She was leaning back against the kitchen counter as she spoke. Smoke came to stand in front of her. He put his hands on the counter either side of her, caging her in. He leaned his weight against her, satisfied to feel her tremble as she looked up at him.

"It is peaceful out here, and it's really quiet."

She nodded and moistened her lips with her tongue.

Damn, she made him hard. "I think I can probably help relax you a little, too." He thrust his hips against her, making perfectly clear what he had in mind. He smiled as her arms came up around his neck.

"And how might you do that, Smoke?"

He lowered his head. "Like this," he murmured before brushing his lips over hers. "Open up for me, Laura."

She lifted her lips to him. He covered her mouth with his, slowly at first, exploring gently. Once she was eagerly returning his kiss, he stepped his feet between hers. He edged his knee between her thighs and pushed out, spreading her legs as he thrust against her heat. It wasn't just her lips he wanted her to open up and let him inside. He kissed her deeply as he ran his hands down her sides. Her body was perfect, just the way he liked his women, long and lean. When his hands reached the hem of her angel costume he pushed it up around her waist. She was still clinging to his neck, lost in his kiss. He pushed her panties down and found her heat. She pressed herself against his fingers. She moaned when he slipped a finger inside her, and bit his lip as he slid it deeper. He needn't have worried if she was ready for him, she was hot and wet—and so damned tight.

He withdrew his hand and unbuckled his jeans. Her hands joined his. He moved fast, grabbing the foil package he'd had ready in his pocket, while she unzipped him and pushed his pants down. Seeing the condom she arched a brow while he put it on.

"Confident I was a sure thing?"

He smiled. "The day we met, lady. I told you I want it, and I will take it."

"We'll see about that."

She closed her fingers around him, guiding him towards her. He looked down to watch as she stroked herself with the very tip of him. This was driving him crazy; he needed to be inside her. He looked into her eyes and closed his hands around her ass, pulling her away from the counter and onto him. He buried himself deep inside her.

"Oh, God, Smoke!" she gasped. She began to move with him. He thrust hard and fast. She was so tight, he was losing his mind as he lost himself in her.

"Wait!" She was pushing him away.

Damn! What was she doing?

Her neck and cheeks were flushed, she was breathing hard. He needed to be back inside her. She pulled the costume up and over her head. "I'm obviously no angel," she said with a smile. "I want to get naked with you."

No way would he argue with that! He kicked out of his pants and unbuttoned his shirt without taking his eyes off her. She was fabulous! Her panties were gone and she unfastened her bra, pushing the cups to the sides before she slid the straps off her shoulders. He shrugged out of his shirt and reached for her, needing to feel her slender body under him, needing to taste her small, round breasts. She smiled as she put a hand to his shoulder to stop him.

"Take a seat, Smoke."

He frowned, puzzled.

She pulled out one of the dining chairs and pushed him back to sit in it. His cock strained to be back inside her as she stood beautifully naked before him. He grabbed her hips as she straddled him and thrust up as she lowered herself onto him.

"Smoke!" she moaned as he pulled her down and thrust deeper. He clamped her to him as he rocked his hips. Seemed she wanted to be in charge. Well, she needed to know that this was his show. He slid down so he could fill her more deeply. She grasped the chair either side of his head. He knew she was hanging on, trying not to lose it, but she had exposed another weakness—he could tease her nipples with his lips and tongue. Now he was losing it. He had to come, and he had to take her with him. He firmed his grip on her ass and filled her determinedly as he got closer and closer to the edge. She tightened around him.

"Oh, God, Smoke!"

He could feel her orgasm take her. It took him too as their bodies melted into one. A blinding rush of pleasure swept through him and he crushed her to his chest as it exploded deep inside her. Her body strained with his, flying high together. Her hands had dropped from the chair to his shoulders, clinging desperately to him as she rode him hard, clenching around him.

When they finally slumped together, he held her slender body to him as he recovered. "Jesus!" he breathed against her shoulder. She quivered in his arms, clinging to him as she returned to earth. Jesus! She was good!

She lifted her head and smiled down at him.

"How's that for a start?" he asked.

"At making me relax, or getting to know each other?"

He chuckled. "Both."

Her smile was gorgeous, blue eyes full of fun. "It'll do for starters," she said and slid off him.

~ ~ ~

Laura sat on the deck, sipping her champagne. It was a beautiful evening, if a little chilly. She snuggled under the blanket Smoke had brought out for them. He was quite something! She'd told herself she wasn't going to sleep with him tonight. This was the first time they'd been out together. But when it came down to it, she hadn't been able to resist him. He was so incredibly sexy! And anyway, it wasn't like they'd just met. She'd known him for months, and the chemistry between them had been obvious from the get-go. She didn't regret having sex with him this quickly. In fact, it had been so good her only regret was that they hadn't found a way to do it sooner! She smiled. She had a feeling they might be making up for lost time this week. Ben was a superstar for putting her in this cabin, with Smoke on her doorstep and no one else around. For a whole week!

Smoke stepped back out onto the deck. She took a deep breath as she ran her gaze over him. That was some man. She may have never been into muscly guys, but Smoke was making her rethink that one. He was a wall of muscle. He was quite a bit taller than her, which must put him well over six feet. Broad shoulders, broad chest, huge arms, narrow waist, muscled thighs...wow! She slowly lifted her gaze when she realized she'd been staring. That was one confident, cocky smile. He knew just how gorgeous he was. Whether it was in his pilot's uniform for work, a cowboy outfit for the party, or best of all, completely naked like right now, he was panty-dropping gorgeous—and he damned well knew it.

He smirked at her. "I was going to ask if you wanted some more." He waved the champagne bottle in the air, "Of this. But maybe," he turned around and wiggled his ass, "you'd sooner have some more of this?"

She laughed. "And here I thought you were the shy, serious type."

He came and joined her under the blanket, snuggling up on the big wicker sofa. "Maybe you're right. Maybe I am shy and serious and you bring out the best in me. Or maybe...." He wrapped his arms tighter around her and nibbled her neck. "Maybe, it's just because you've never seen me out of the uniform before." He ran his hand down to her waist and drew her closer. "I'm never going to be shy, but we can get down to serious if you're ready." He walked his fingers down over her stomach 'til his hand was between her legs, stroking, drawing a little sigh from her.

She pulled herself, and her legs together. "We've already figured out we're seriously good at that. How about you tell me about yourself. I'd like to know more about the guy who just screwed my brains out."

He chuckled. Such a sexy sound. "I think, technically, you just screwed my brains out, lady. Tied me to the chair and then climbed all over my stuff!"

She laughed. "I did not tie you to the chair!"

He winked. "No, but maybe next time?" He rolled her nipple between his finger and thumb. "If I'm a really bad boy?"

"Smoke! Be serious."

His hands were wandering all over her now. "I'm trying to." His gray eyes bored into her as his fingers found their way back between her legs and began to work her.

Oh, God! His lips came down on hers. Her arms came up around his neck. She'd hoped to feel his capable hands on her, now they were she was completely at his mercy. Somehow he'd maneuvered her underneath him. He was still stroking her. Still kissing her. Using his knees to spread her legs. How the hell had he done it? She'd wanted him to talk. She put her hands against his chest.

"Smoke!"

"Yes?"

She tried to bring her legs together. She liked to be in charge in bed; she decided when.

He grinned at her, keeping her legs spread with his knees. His cock was hot and hard, and despite her protests, she wanted him inside her.

"What, Laura?" The glint in his eyes told her he knew damned well what.

"What are you doing?"

"I'm doing what you want me to do. I'm showing you what it's like when a man takes charge." He rocked his hips against her, throbbing at her opening.

"What makes you think I want that?" she breathed.

"The look in your eyes. The way say you want to just talk, but you're hot and wet for me. The way you took charge in the kitchen. You're used to pushing men around in bed, aren't you, lady?"

She swallowed and nodded.

"You wouldn't normally sleep with a guy like me, would you?" She shook her head now. How the hell did he know that? She hadn't even been fully aware of it herself until this moment!

He rolled off her and sat up, drawing her into his arms. "I wouldn't normally sleep with a woman like you, either."

She turned to look up at him, but his face was giving nothing away. He reached for the champagne and poured two fresh glasses. "So," he said with a smile, "what do you want to know about me?"

It was as if the moment had never happened. But it had, and it had wormed its way into Laura's mind. Why didn't she like a man who took charge in bed? Why had she panicked when Smoke had been about to? And why was she so disappointed that he had respected her and stopped? He had stopped though.

He was still smiling at her. "Go on, ask away."

She asked the question that was burning in her mind. "Why wouldn't you normally sleep with a woman like me? And what does that even mean?"

His chuckle was a low, deep rumble. "You are trouble, lady. That's what it means. You're damned hot—and you know it. You don't need a man. And when you take one it's on your terms only."

She stared at him. He certainly had her figured out. "But that doesn't answer my question, why wouldn't you normally sleep with a woman like me?"

"It does answer the question. Like I said, you are trouble. Trouble with a capital T." He was caressing her thigh, making it hard to concentrate on his words.

"And you don't like trouble?"

His lips curved up in a sexy smile as his hand worked its way up her inner thigh. "I want to be in trouble."

His hands really were so very capable. She pushed him back against the cushions. "Have you got a condom ready?" He was so damned cocky, she wasn't at all surprised when he fished one out from under the cushions and handed it to her. She shook her head. "When did you stash that?" she asked as she rolled it onto him.

He just smiled as he lay back. She closed her fingers around him and watched him close his eyes. He thought he could tease her? Now he was at her mercy. She knelt above him, enjoying the pleasure on his face as she stroked him. He was growing harder in her hands, she needed to feel him. She lowered herself on to him, slowly. God he was so hard. She rocked her hips, gasping as he slid deeper. He opened his eyes and grasped her hips as he thrust up.

"Is this where you want me?"

She bit her lip and nodded as she rode him.

His smile was sinful. "You're the boss."

Damn, he was right. She'd taken charge again. Oh, so what? He was enjoying it. She lowered her breasts to his face and moaned as he mouthed her nipple and thrust deeper. She knew how to take them both over the edge. And she did. She felt him tense and grow bigger; she clenched around him, holding him deep as she felt the heat build and explode, tearing through her in an orgasm that had her gasping. His release carried her away as they strained together. God he was so good. She slumped down onto his chest and lay there, spent.

Eventually his hands came up to stroke her hair. "That's two to zero now."

She lifted her head to look at him. "Huh?"

"Twice you've taken me and we've done it your way. Zero times you've let me take you."

She shrugged. "You can't tell me you didn't enjoy it."

"No, but I can tell you you'll enjoy it even more when I take you." He closed his arms around her. "And I will take you."

She shuddered in anticipation. He was so sure of himself. "Is that a threat or a promise?"

There was that gleam in his eye again. "Both."

"Really? And when do you plan on doing that?"

"Whenever I want to." His lazy smile gave her the impression that they were already doing everything his way.

Chapter Three

Laura woke to the sun streaming through the window. She glanced at the clock on the nightstand and was surprised to see it was after nine. Maybe the clock was wrong. She hadn't slept this late in years. She got up and padded through to the kitchen where she'd left her purse. She pulled out her phone to check. No, it really was a quarter after nine. She smiled. Well, it had been quite a night. After the kitchen, and the deck, she and Smoke had finished off the champagne and then headed for the bedroom. She'd taken charge in there too. And he really was good. There was no sign of him now, though. He'd left at some point before she woke. She was kind of relieved. She wanted to take a shower, get some coffee and relax out on the deck. She jumped as her phone buzzed in her hand. A text from Jack.

You coming for breakfast?

She chuckled to herself and replied.

Maybe

Perhaps she would take a wander up there if she was ready in time. She checked the cupboards. There was coffee, but nothing worth eating and she was hungry. It seemed last night's workout with Smoke had given her an appetite. She started the coffee pot and headed for the shower.

Sitting out on the deck with her coffee, she stared at the lake. This week would be just what she needed. She could kick back and relax. Start thinking about this new line and just have some time to herself. Life in San Francisco had been crazy for far too long. Her jewelry store was doing wonderfully, and now she'd finally gotten everything set up so that she wasn't needed for the day-to-day running of things, the design side had really taken off. She'd made a couple of exquisite pieces for one client and her reputation had spread like wildfire. Now she had a high-end clientele who were prepared to wait—and pay—for her to design the exclusive pieces they wanted. She'd done so many engagement rings recently that she was starting to get sick of them. She took a sip of her coffee, then blew out a big sigh. It was almost a year now since she'd given her own engagement ring back to Dale. Her phone buzzed again, interrupting her thoughts. Jack again.

Want us to come get you?

She shook her head with a rueful smile.

NO, Mr. Persistent! I'll walk up.

She may as well go join them. If she didn't they'd only come down to see her after they were done with breakfast.

She climbed the steps to the deck of the restaurant and waved when Jack called to her. The place was crowded and she had to weave her way between the tables.

Emma stood to hug her. "Sorry. I tried to make him leave you in peace."

Holly and Pete greeted her. Ben waved from the end of the table. One of the guys from last night was there too. He smiled and nodded as she took a seat opposite him. She was surprised how disappointed she felt not to see Smoke. She'd assumed he'd be here.

"I'm glad you came." said Holly. "I need you to help me talk some sense into these guys."

"Talk sense into guys?" asked Laura with a laugh. "Never going to happen, Holly. You may as well face it."

Holly laughed. "We have to try, sweetie. You need to see what they want to do with the Plaza at Four Mile."

Laura had tentatively agreed to take one of the spaces in the retail side of Jack and Pete's new development over on the Eastern shore of Summer Lake. "Why, what are they up to?" She frowned at Jack, knowing he was probably ignoring the practical for the sake of some architectural design detail.

He grinned at her and held his hands up. "Don't blame me!"

"Yes, do blame him!" said Holly. "He's going all Mediterranean features on us. Which, I admit, would make for beautiful buildings to look at, but will not do anything to draw customers into stores, because he's not giving us big enough display windows and storefronts."

Laura looked at Jack. "Are you being a brat about design details?" she asked sternly.

He looked up at her, putting on big, sad puppy-dog eyes. "But it'll be the perfect little village!" he pouted.

"Is this Plaza about you building your perfect little village or about you building a viable shopping center?"

Jack scowled, but said nothing.

Laura looked back at Holly who shook her head in amazement. "I've been arguing with him for weeks!"

"Yes, and you've no doubt been using reasonable arguments and trying to appeal to his business brain, right?"

Holly nodded.

"Forget it, girlfriend. All you need to do is call him out on being a brat!"

Pete laughed loudly. "Looks like she's got you figured, partner."

Jack nodded and smiled. "Yeah, she does. I just like my details."

Emma pecked his lips. "Don't worry. I appreciate your attention to detail."

Jack pulled her into his lap and wrapped himself around her. For the first time, seeing Emma and Jack like that irritated Laura. They were always a little over the top with their lovey-dovey stuff, but today it just seemed like too much.

"Well, since you dragged me out here for breakfast, can you at least put your wife down for a minute so we can order some?" she asked, picking up her menu.

Jack shot her a puzzled look while Emma slid back into her own seat. Laura felt bad. Where the hell had that come from? Never mind. She really was hungry. She ordered the full Boathouse breakfast.

"Not you as well?" asked the guy sitting across from her. Michael, was that his name? "I thought Missy was the only tiny female around here that could put away that much breakfast."

She raised an eyebrow at him. "Tiny? I'm five feet nine!"

He smiled at her. Nice eyes, hmm, green eyes. Her favorite. He deliberately ran those green eyes over her before meeting her gaze.

"I said tiny, darl'. Not short."

Wow! Another cocky, good-looking guy. Did they breed them out here or something? And that accent, sexy! What was it, Australian?

"Quit it, Michael," said Ben. "Let's get this order in, can we?"

Michael shrugged. "Just sayin'." He smiled at Laura. "Anyone up for a ride on the boat this afternoon?"

"No," Jack cut in.

God, he really was trying to be her dad!

She shot him a look, but he gave her a hard stare and continued. "Laura's coming up to North Cove with us, and Pete and Holly are heading back to LA."

Laura didn't have chance to argue before Ben said, "I'll come out with you, bud. I've got a quiet afternoon for once."

She had to laugh at the look on Michael's face. Ben winked at her. It seemed they all thought they were saving her. This was small town life as she remembered it—and one of the reasons she'd been so eager to leave it behind her in Texas and move to San Francisco. For a moment, her stubborn streak was tempted to say she'd join Michael and Ben, just to push back against having other people make her decisions for her. She bit her tongue though. No way was she going with Jack and Emma, and it sounded like Smoke would be working this afternoon, taking Holly and Pete back to LA. So, she could do what she really wanted, kick back at the cabin and hang by herself, doing a whole lot of nothing.

~ ~ ~

"Em, will you tell him I'm not coming with you?" They were standing in the square. Everyone had gone about their day and Laura had walked with Emma and Jack to his truck.

Jack smiled. "I know you're not, sweetie." She looked at him and he shrugged. "You already told me that. It's just, I'm having a hard enough time backing off on you and Smoke, no way was I going to start worrying about Michael trying to get you alone on his boat!"

Emma slapped his arm. Laura had to laugh. "Seriously?"

Jack gave an exaggerated nod. "Seriously! Work with what I'm giving you. I'm backing off on you and Smoke, isn't that enough? Where is he anyway?"

Laura shrugged. "I haven't seen him today."

Jack raised his eyebrows disbelievingly. "What, not even this morning?"

"Jack!" Emma slapped his arm harder this time.

Laura just shrugged again. "No, not even this morning."

Jack frowned at her.

"Oh, for God's sake!" Laura laughed. "Will you two get going and leave me to enjoy my day in peace? If you keep this crap up I may just head home instead. My business is my business and you of all people know that."

Jack hugged her. "Sorry. I'm just looking out for you."

"I know and I appreciate the intention, but the reality is getting to be a bit much. Give me some space, huh? That's what I came here for."

"Okay. But call if you need anything."

"I won't!"

Emma laughed. "Come on hubby, take the hint." She hugged Laura. "You know where we are. I'm sure we'll all be getting together to celebrate with Missy and Dan sometime this week. Is it okay if I call you for that?"

Laura hugged her back. "Of course it is. I do want to see you guys, I just want a little chill time first. I'll call you."

She waved them off then went into the resort's little grocery store to get some supplies. Once she had what she needed, she took the path that led down to the water's edge. She needed a walk after that huge breakfast.

Back at the cabin, she stocked the fridge and cupboards, then wandered around checking things out. It was a great little place; she'd have a good time here. She stepped out onto the deck and smiled at the sofa. Now that had been a good time! She wondered if Smoke would even be back tonight or if he'd be staying in LA waiting to bring Holly and Pete back.

It was warm. The days were getting cooler, but the sun shone brightly today and the deck was a perfect sun trap. It had been a long time since she'd had chance to lay out in the sun. One of those loungers would be perfect. They might technically be on Smoke's side of the deck, but she doubted he'd complain. Once she'd dragged the lounger into the perfect spot on her side of the deck, she settled down to read. It really was warm.

She wished she'd thought to bring a bikini, but she'd hardly expected to be sunbathing. Maybe she should walk back up to the resort and buy one? No, she was enjoying this too much, and knowing her luck it'd probably cloud over if she did.

There was no one around, and no one likely to come out this way. She stripped down to her underwear—it was no different than wearing a bikini. Well, perhaps a little more revealing than your average bikini, hmm and lacier too, but hey, it worked. She smiled to herself—it was a pity Smoke wasn't around, she was quite sure it'd work for him. Maybe he'd be back? She pulled her purse closer and checked inside, just in case. Yep, she had some. She pulled her hair up off her neck and tied it into a ponytail, then settled back into her book.

Smoke waited for the hangar door to roll back into place. Once the motor whirred to a stop he checked to make sure it was secure. He hadn't really needed to wash the plane this morning, but it was a job he enjoyed. It was one of those mindless tasks he could get lost in for a couple of hours, and feel a sense of satisfaction when it was done. It was his go-to whenever he needed to occupy his hands while his mind sorted itself out. And man, did his mind need sorting out! What the hell was he playing at? He'd fantasized about getting Laura in the sack since the first time he'd laid eyes on her. She was his kind of sexy. What he hadn't banked on was her being his kind of smart, with a sassy mouth too. She was everything that turned him on about a woman. Worst of all, she was a challenge. A challenge that would take time to conquer. He badly wanted that conquest. He'd told her the truth. He wouldn't normally sleep with a woman like her. He normally went for women who presented no challenge. They weren't hard to find. The ones who were wanting and willing to please him. He liked his women to look to him for their lead. He was used to taking it, especially in bed. It made it easy to walk away afterward.

Laura sure as hell wasn't one of them. She was just like him. The same kind of animal. She expected her men to roll over and do as she pleased. He'd left her sleeping this morning because he'd needed to get away from her before he tried to end the game too soon. Lying there with her, watching her sleep, he could have woken her. Had her under him. But something made him want to see how this played out. She'd give in to him—give it up to him—he had no doubt, but he believed they had a lot more fun in store before they got to that point.

The trouble was, he shouldn't even be considering it. She was Jack's cousin. Jack his friend. Jack who owned Phoenix. Jack who would tear a guy limb from limb if they hurt someone he cared about. Not that Smoke intended to hurt her, but women could get weird about that shit. Laura seemed like the kind of girl who could play the game and then move on, but the smart move would be not to even take the risk. He smiled as he walked back into the FBO. Too bad he was a risk taker then, huh?

There was no one at the desk, so he went into the back. "You around, Rochelle?" he shouted. Rochelle's family ran the airport, and he needed to talk to her about hangar fees. She wasn't in the back either, though. He'd catch her another day. He picked up the keys for the crew car and left a note. It seemed he was the only one that used the old pick-up, but he didn't like to take it without letting her know.

It was supposed to be fall, but it was a beautiful day. He rolled the windows down as he drove back to the resort, glad to have the day off, even if it was unexpected. He'd thought he'd be flying today, taking Holly and Pete to LA and dropping Laura back in San Francisco. As so often happened in his job, everything had changed. Holly had decided to drive back to the city so she'd have her car there for some fashion show later in the week. And Laura...well. He smiled. Laura was staying the week, staying right next door to him. He stepped on the gas. She probably wouldn't be there this afternoon, but still. And she'd be around tonight, even if she was going out, she'd be back by bedtime.

By the time he pulled up in front of the cabin, his head was full of images of what they might do later. He ran up the steps and knocked on her door, hoping maybe she'd be here and he wouldn't have to wait 'til tonight. He waited and then knocked again. Nothing. Ah well. He'd go take a shower and then maybe sit in the sun a while. It was such a beautiful day.

He emerged from the shower and toweled himself down. Fastening the towel around his waist, he tried to decide whether to sit out or go for a hike in the hills. He wasn't one to sit around doing nothing, especially on a day like this. He slid the door open and stepped out. The lake sparkled in the sun and a light breeze whispered through the pines. No way. It was too good a day to sit out here.

Then he noticed that one of the loungers had been moved. Was Laura out here? He walked over to the screen that separated her end of the deck from his and peered around it. Jesus! His cock sprang to life under the towel and his throat went dry. She was asleep on the lounger, one arm flung above her head, the other hanging down at her side. She was in her god-damned underwear, and man was it sexy. Purple, and lacy. Her bra plunged between perfectly round little breasts and her panties were just a scrap of lace covering the place he needed to be. Her legs were parted slightly, just enough to look like an invitation, and one that he was not going to turn down. He walked around the screen and over to the lounger, making no effort to be quiet. Part of him hoped that she'd hear him and wake. She didn't.

He stood over her, heart pounding. She was so gorgeous. He sat on the edge of the lounger, expecting her eyes to open. They didn't. He traced his fingers over her ribs. Her eyelids fluttered, but still didn't open. He let his hand travel up and close around her breast. She gave a little moan and her hips rose up. He let his hand slide back down over her soft skin 'til his fingers met lace again. He slipped his fingers inside her panties, all the while watching her face. Her hips rose up to meet him, she moaned and writhed, but her eyes still didn't open. His fingers worked their way down, she was already wet. He smiled and slid her panties down. He couldn't decide if she was only pretending to be asleep, but either way, she was ready, and he couldn't wait any longer. He covered her body with his own, losing the towel as he positioned himself above her. He took hold of her wrists and pinned her hands above her head. Her eyes fluttered open and filled with surprise as he spread her legs with his knees.

"Smoke?"

She really had been asleep. He smiled. "Were you expecting someone else?"

Her smile reassured him that she wanted to play along, even as she tried to pull her hands away. He held them fast. She wriggled underneath him. She could escape if she wanted, but she wasn't really trying, just tormenting him, making him harder.

"What are you doing?" she breathed.

He pushed at her slick entrance. Her heat reassuring him that she wanted this as badly as he did. "You, unless you say no."

She smiled. "What took you so long? I've been waiting for you." She spread her legs wider.

"Really?" he breathed. "You're going to claim that this was your idea? That you set me up?"

Her pink tongue darted out and moistened her lips as she nodded.

Smoke grinned. She did not want to be beat in this game they were playing. He'd let her have the victory if he could have her body. "Okay. Then you've got me where you want me. Now what?"

Her smile was triumphant as she pulled her hand away from his and reached under the lounger and into her purse. "Now you put this on."

Damn! She was good at this game. He may have lost this round, he admitted as he rolled the condom on, but he'd won anyway. She held her arms up to him. He lowered himself to her, and did as she pleased.

Chapter Four

"What do you think?" asked Smoke. "Do you want to get out of here for a while?"

What the hell was he saying? He should get out of here himself, not ask her to come with him. He didn't hang around after sex. Women got too clingy, it made him feel claustrophobic. He looked at Laura. She wasn't exactly clingy, sitting there staring out at the lake. Messy hair, kiss-swollen lips...the freshly-fucked look suited her!

"Where do you want to go?"

"I'm heading for the hills." Wasn't that the truth!

She raised an eyebrow with a knowing smirk.

"No!" Dammit! He wasn't going to prove her right. "I'm saying, how about you come with me. Take a hike instead of wasting the afternoon sitting around here."

"Okay, I'll go and get changed."

She disappeared inside, leaving Smoke wondering why he'd asked her along.

He was surprised when she knocked on his door five minutes later. Surprised she was ready so quickly and even more surprised that she was actually dressed for a hike. He'd been taking his time, expecting the typical female thing...her taking at least half an hour to fix her hair, or makeup, or whatever it was they did that always took them so long.

As he'd pulled his boots on he'd been cursing himself for asking her. They'd just gone one round, so she wasn't likely to have sex with him out there. What else did he want her along for? Now she stood at his door waiting for him. He ran his gaze over her body appreciatively. Damn she was hot. From her ponytail all the way down her long, long legs, to a pair of well worn hiking boots that had evidently seen a few trails.

"Are you ready?"

He nodded and grabbed the keys for the pickup.

"Where are we going?" she asked as they pulled out of the resort.

"Four Mile. I went up with Pete a couple of weeks ago to check it out. I've been going back and exploring a few of the old trails."

"Oh, good! I've wanted to get out there and take a look around."

Smoke shot her a grin. "There's no country club out there yet, lady. Just a couple of old trails. Think you can handle it?"

She put her feet up on the dash and tapped them together. "Do these boots look like they belong in a country club?"

"Just checking. There are no bathrooms or viewing points on these trails."

She threw her head back and laughed. "Your only worry about me, Smoke, should be whether you'll be able to keep up with me."

Smoke shook his head. There she went again. She was competitive about everything, not just in bed. "No worries there."

~ ~ ~

As they followed the road up the East shore, Laura looked out the window at the mountains. It really was so beautiful here.

She was glad to get out and explore. She hadn't had chance on her other visits. She was a member of a hiking group in San Francisco and tried to join at least two hikes every month. She wouldn't admit it to Smoke, but there were usually viewing points and well kept bathrooms on those trails. Still, she got off the beaten track whenever she could, to feel some real mountain air. This was more like her idea of hiking.

Smoke pulled off the road and left the truck running while he got out to unlock a gate. He got back in and pulled through. As soon as he stopped, Laura jumped out and went to close the gate behind them.

"Thanks," he said when she climbed back in.

"No problem, I do better as part of a team than being chauffeured around like the little lady."

Smoke smirked. "I'll try to remember that."

She was under no illusion that him doing everything himself was some kind of chivalry. It was just that he was totally self-sufficient. The thing was, so was she. If they were going to hang out together, he'd do well to remember it.

The dirt road wound its way up into the foothills, following the twists and turns of a dry creek bed until it reached a plateau.

Smoke brought the truck to a stop and cut the engine. "Welcome to the country club. This is where your plaza is going to be."

"Oh, cool! Do you mind if we take a look around?"

"That's what I stopped for."

Laura climbed down from the truck and took in the view. Below them the lake stretched away into the distance. She could see the resort, away to the left on the opposite shore. A few boats lined the blue water with white wakes. It was breathtaking. She looked at Smoke. "Wow! It's beautiful."

"Isn't it? I'm just glad I get to enjoy it before they build all over it."

"You don't like the idea?"

"I don't dislike it. I just like to be able to get away from the crowds. Get back to nature, back to my roots."

"Where are you from?" Laura realized she didn't know the first thing about his background.

It seemed he wasn't too keen to tell her, either. He shrugged. "My family is in the valley. I grew up there. Come on." He pointed up to where the land rose again at the edge of the plateau. "We can pick the creek up back there and follow it up a ways." He grinned. "There's a clearing up there where you can see for miles." He set out without waiting for her to reply.

She lengthened her stride to catch up and fell in beside him. The valley? He must mean the Central Valley. There was a lot of farm country there. She wanted to ask, but needed to concentrate on just keeping up with him.

They walked on in silence. Laura was pleased that after a while Smoke slowed his pace a little. She prided herself on being in shape, able to keep up on any hike, but she was glad not to have to push so hard. She didn't know why, but it was important to her that Smoke shouldn't think she was anything less than his equal.

They followed a path alongside the creek bed that led them into the trees. It was cooler in here, and the pines smelled wonderful. Smoke was a good hiking partner. He picked out a path, and once he'd dropped the breakneck speed, he matched her pace intuitively. He pointed out squirrels and birds that she would never have noticed. He turned to look back at her.

"You doing okay?"

"Great thanks." As she spoke her foot caught a rock and she stumbled forward.

Smoke turned and caught her arm to steady her. "Careful," he said.

She looked up at him, about to pull her arm away, but bit back the I'm fine! she'd been about to spit at him. She'd been expecting mocking, or at least his condescending smirk, but his face was full of concern.

"Are you all right?"

Wow! This was a new one. He actually looked like he cared. She smiled. "I am, thanks to you."

His face was even more handsome when the cockiness was gone. When his smile was soft like it was right now. Instead of letting go of her arm, he pulled her toward him. She went willingly. He wrapped his arms around her waist, she reached hers around his neck. God, this new-to-her smile was so sexy. He lowered his head to her. She closed her eyes. His lips came down on hers in a sweet, tender kiss. She relaxed against him as she kissed him back, letting a strange feeling sweep through her. She felt safe, like she could finally let her guard down and relax, sheltered in the circle of his arms. When the kiss finally ended he hugged her close and rested his forehead against hers, smiling that new, sweet smile. She didn't want to speak, afraid to break the spell. She just smiled back, getting lost in his eyes, loving the feel of his arms around her, holding her to his hard chest.

He shook his head slowly.

"What?"

"Trouble, lady. I told you you were trouble."

"I didn't do anything!" she protested.

He chuckled. "You didn't need to."

He tightened his arms around her, hugging her to him for a moment before letting her go and heading on up the trail. "The clearing isn't far now," he called back. "Wait until you see the view."

Laura followed, trying to figure out what was going on with him. She hoped he wasn't just taking a different tack in whatever competition they were in, getting her to lower her defenses. If he was, it was working! But whatever was going on with him, she was more concerned about what was going on with her. The way she'd felt back there, all wrapped up in his arms? That had felt way too good! She'd have to be careful. She didn't need to be enjoying his kisses that much either.

The trees thinned as they walked on and soon they emerged into a clearing. It was a small meadow that sloped up to where the tree line began again.

"Race you to the top," said Smoke, breaking into a run.

Laura ran as fast as she could and was soon neck and neck with him. He grinned and put on a spurt of speed, his long legs easily carrying him ahead. Knowing she wouldn't be able to overtake him, Laura caught up as much as she could and flung herself at him, wrapping her arms around his waist and tackling him to the ground. They rolled over and over, laughing as they went. When they finally lay still, he pulled her closer and stroked her hair away from her face.

"You just can't stand to lose, can you?"

She shook her head. "Nope. I don't deal well with losing."

"Me neither. But, you know we can't both be winners Laura. Someone always has to lose." His face was serious, eyes wistful. This was a different Smoke again.

She didn't know what to do with this. "We could say we both won?"

"We could, but would it be true? Neither of us got where we were going, let alone got there first."

She shrugged and pecked his lips before standing up and pulling him to his feet. "We will. We just took a little detour. Had some fun. Now we'll go up there together."

He held her eyes for a long moment, then took her hand and started walking up the meadow.

Once they reached the top he turned and swept his arm out over the view before them. The lake looked smaller from up here. "Didn't I tell you, you can see for miles?"

Laura nodded, it was breathtaking.

Smoke sat down on a fallen tree and stared off into the distance. She went and plonked herself down beside him.

"You're good to hike with," he said after a while.

"You sound surprised."

He chuckled. "I am. You're a woman."

She pushed at him. "And what's that supposed to mean?"

"It means women usually ruin hikes by not being able to keep up and by wanting to talk the whole time."

She let out a short laugh. "So why did you ask me along?"

He met her gaze. "I have no fucking idea!" He looked confused. Lost for a moment. Then the cocky grin was back and he laid his hand on her thigh. "I'm sure we could come up with a good reason though."

Laura's breath caught in her chest as his hand moved higher. He slipped his fingers inside the hem of her shorts. But no. She stood up. "I think just finally getting to spend some time together is reason enough, don't you?"

Smoke got up and came to stand behind her. He put his hands on her shoulders and rubbed her neck with his thumbs. Oh, that felt so good!

"I'd say it is, lady." He planted a little kiss behind her ear, sending shivers racing down her spine. His arm snaked around her waist and pulled her back against him. She could feel how hard he was as he nibbled her neck. She relaxed against him, willing now for whatever he wanted to do. She let out a little sigh as his warm breath fanned her ear. Maybe it was time to

just give in. Let him take charge. Do whatever he wanted. Her
body was coming alive at the thought of giving in to him.
"Smoke," she breathed.

He let her go and stepped away with that god-damned smirk
on his face. "Sorry. Yeah. Just spend some time together.
That's all you want, right?" His eyes gleamed with mischief,
knowing the effect he'd had on her.

She wanted him badly right now. But she'd be damned if she
was going to ask! She stared at him for a moment. No! No way
was she going to ask. That would be admitting he'd won. She
pulled herself together. "Yeah. That's all. Let's follow the trail
shall we?"

His smile told her he knew he'd won this round...if not the
whole game. Yet.

~ ~ ~

Smoke paced the cabin. It had been a good afternoon. The
first time he'd enjoyed a woman's company on a hike. She was
fun. He smiled to himself, remembering the way she'd tackled
him to the ground, just so she wouldn't lose the race. His smile
faded. What he'd told her was true though: they couldn't both
win this game they were playing. It didn't work that way
between a man and a woman. If someone got what they
wanted it was always at the expense of the other. He knew that
only too well. Maybe he should stop this now—call it a draw
and walk away. He would never put himself in the position to
be the loser again. And much as he liked the idea of
'conquering' Laura, it would mean making her the loser. That
thought didn't appeal much either.

He'd walked her to her door when they got back earlier, but
had refused her offer of a drink. This was weird though. He'd
wanted to get away from her, straighten his head out. But she
was just on the other side of that wall. And his head sure as
hell wasn't getting any straighter. He needed to eat and he

wanted a beer. Maybe he should walk up to the Boathouse? He
didn't feel like cooking. He could ask her to come. He shook
his head. He'd already spent more time with her in the last
twenty-four hours than he'd spent with any woman in...years.
Any woman since.... No. He wasn't going there. Except to
remind himself that that was how it worked. The more time he
spent with a woman, the more they wanted—and the sooner it
got old. The novelty wore off and the need to escape, to fly
away, kicked back in. So that's what he could tell himself,
right? That was why he was heading out of his door to go
knock on hers. It was simply to reach the inevitable end of this
sooner. It had nothing to do with the fact that he couldn't
focus on anything but laughing blue eyes, long dark hair and
sweet plump lips. Nothing to do with the fact that she was on
the other side of that wall and he needed her closer. Nah,
nothing to do with any of that at all.

Her eyes were laughing as she opened the door. "Yes?" She
raised an eyebrow. Evidently seeing some small victory in the
fact that he'd come knocking not two hours after his gruff,
"See you tomorrow, maybe."

He pursed his lips, conceding this one with his smile. "I'm
heading to the Boathouse to get some dinner. Do you want to
tag along?"

She grinned. "Thanks, but I'm not really a tag along kind of
girl." She was laughing at him. Reveling in her victory and they
both knew it.

He reached an arm around her waist and crushed her to him.
"Okay. So how about, I'm begging you to please come have
dinner with me?"

He felt her breath catch in her chest as she looked up at him.
Felt her soften in his arms. "I'd love to," she breathed, and
they both knew the advantage had shifted back. She visibly

gathered her thoughts, then the sassy smile was back. "Since you asked so nicely, it'd be rude of me to say no."

They sat out on the deck; the restaurant was quieter tonight. Sunday saw the weekend visitors leave. Smoke liked the place better this way.

"How long are you staying in the cabin," asked Laura after the server had taken their order.

"I don't know. I've got it 'til the end of the month. Ben says I can have it for the winter season if I want. But since it looks like I'll be living here, I'm thinking of looking for a place of my own." He smiled at her. "Besides, I have this new neighbor, and I'm afraid she may lower the tone of the neighborhood."

"I wouldn't worry. She'll be gone soon. I'd just make the most of it if I were you."

"I intend to," he said. What he didn't say, because it surprised the hell out of him, was that he wished she wouldn't be gone so soon. Where had that thought come from? He'd be glad to see her leave by the end of the week, wouldn't he?

"Well don't get too many ideas. I understand your new neighbor has a lot of work to do this week. She's in high demand, you know. There's international interest in her talents."

That bothered him. He wanted her talents all for himself, even though they weren't the ones she was talking about. He brought himself back to the moment. "I believe so, and I understand why."

She didn't quite blush, but those faint pink stains appeared on her cheeks. Good, he was getting to her, too. Point scored, he came back to her work. "So what kind of jewelry are you working on?"

Her eyes lit up as she began to talk about her work. He didn't have the first clue about diamonds or karats or cuts, but he smiled as he listened. What he did know was that here was a woman who truly loved what she did. With a passion. And that was something he could relate to.

"...and I can't wait to go to London," she was saying.

"London?" Did he know that? Had she mentioned it? Surely he would have remembered. "What exactly will you be doing there?"

"Meeting their design team. Seeing the flagship store." She grinned. "I'm sure it won't mean much to you, but it's a huge honor. And...." She looked around as if someone might be listening. "I haven't told anyone yet, but they mentioned possibly buying my store!"

Smoke wasn't sure why this might need to be kept a secret, but she did seem excited by the idea.

"And what would you do then?"

"I don't really know, but it would mean more freedom. I'm a designer, not a retailer. I need some kind of base, but the store feels more like a ball and chain, you know?"

Smoke nodded. He knew that feeling only too well.

"If I sell, I won't have to deal with the day to day responsibilities," she continued. "I'll be free to travel and meet high-end clients."

He raised an eyebrow, not understanding that and trying to repress a smirk at the thought that she made herself sound like a high class hooker.

She shook her head, apparently seeing where his thoughts were going. "Get. Your. Mind. Out of the gutter!" she said, with a smile that only pinned his mind firmly in the gutter...or to a chair...or a lounger.

He grinned. "Sorry." He really wasn't. "What else would you need to meet high-end clients for?"

He listened as she explained how she was building a clientele, by word of mouth. People who wanted exquisite custom pieces designed just for them.

He thought about Jack and Dan who had both asked her to make engagement rings. Now that was scary stuff. He brought his attention back to what she was saying.

"I love San Francisco, but I don't think I want to be there anymore." For the first time since she'd started talking about her jewelry, her eyes weren't shining. "It's been good, but I've finally figured out it's not for me."

What was all that about? He gave her an inquiring look.

She shrugged. "I thought I could settle down, build a normal life, you know? But it turns out I'm not too good at it."

All the light had gone from her eyes now. Smoke wanted to see her smile again—and to steer her away from what looked like heavy stuff if he asked her what she meant. He gave her a grin. "If you ask me, normal is over-rated. Especially for people like us. A career that you love wins hands down over normal."

She smiled at that, seeming to agree. Good. Away from the heavy stuff. "So what do you design most of?" He had no clue about jewelry but he wanted to see her animated and happy again. Steering her back to her work should do it.

Unfortunately, his question brought the sadness back to her eyes. "Lately it's been engagement rings."

Damn, he should have thought of that. "Yeah, I saw the ones you made for the guys. What else? Is it all kinds of rings, or necklaces and earrings too?"

She wasn't going for it; she was still caught up in her thoughts. She smiled, but it didn't reach her eyes. "Yeah. The ones for Dan and Jack were fun to do. Dan especially. All he knew was that he wanted something with three diamonds, so Missy would know it was about the three of them—about her and Scot becoming his family.

Smoke nodded. Even he knew how great Dan and Missy were together and how much Dan loved the kid.

Her smile was more genuine now. "Jack was different." She laughed. "In fact he was a total pain in the ass."

Smoke laughed with her, knowing the feeling. Jack was a good friend, but he had his ways. "He is pretty big on his 'crucial details'. I don't envy you that job."

"Yeah, I can't really say it was a design job, more a case of making his design a reality. And detail? He even provided the stone and told me how I needed to cut it!" Something about that had her shaking her head, lost in thought again.

Dammit. Heavy stuff or not, he needed to know. His curiosity was piqued, if he didn't ask he knew he'd only keep wondering.

"So, you design a lot of engagement rings, but you don't wear one?"

She shook her head and ate the last bite of her burger. He waited, sipping on his beer, wondering if he wanted to hear the story. There no doubt was one, he could tell.

Eventually she looked at him. "I used to."

"But?"

"But like I told you, it turns out I'm no good at that kind of thing."

Smoke nodded, knowing to leave well enough alone. He surprised himself by reaching across the table to take her hand. He gave it a squeeze and smiled, "Like I told you, normal is over-rated. You're too good for it, lady. You had a lucky escape."

She nodded.

"And I'm glad you did," he added.

She looked confused, no doubt wondering what he had meant by that.

He squeezed her hand again and called for the check, feeling a little confused himself—what had he meant?

~ ~ ~

"Jack!" Emma poked him in the ribs.

He turned to look at her. "Sorry, baby."

Emma shook her head at Ben, who was grinning at them from behind the bar. "Honestly, Ben! He says he's bringing me out for a drink and then spends the whole time spying on Laura and Smoke. I'm glad you're in here tonight. At least you still pay attention to me."

That had Jack giving her his sad puppy dog eyes before pulling her against him. He'd never quite been able to ditch the last remnants of gnawing jealousy when she was around Ben. He knew it was stupid, but he just couldn't shift it. "You have all my attention, baby. And I wasn't spying. It was you that told me they were out there, and you that wouldn't let me go say hi."

Emma laughed as she snuggled in his arms. "Because I don't want you scaring Smoke off, and because we told Laura we'd leave her in peace!"

"I wouldn't scare him off!" Jack feigned innocence.

Emma just gave him a knowing look.

"I'm surprised you're being like this," said Ben. "I mean I know you're Mr. Protective and everything, but it's Smoke, you know him. He's been a friend since college, hasn't he?

Jack nodded. "Yes, he is my friend." He gave Ben a dark look. "And I do know him."

Ben raised his eyebrows questioningly, obviously surprised.

"Oh, ignore him," said Emma. "You know what he's like."

Jack hugged her to him. "Yeah, but baby, you don't know what Smoke's like."

A little crease appeared between her brows. Dammit! He shouldn't have said that! He forced a laugh. "Sorry. You're right. Ignore me. I'll tell you what though. I need to go to the office for a couple of hours tomorrow, do you want to come to the city?"

"I can't. You know that."

Jack did know that. She was going to see her Gramps. Truth was he didn't really want her along, and he didn't really need to go to the office either. What he did need to do was have a talk with Smoke.

Chapter Five

Laura opened her eyes. She was too warm. The sun was streaming in through the windows. That wasn't what was making her so warm though. Smoke was wrapped around her, his face relaxed in sleep, his head resting on her shoulder. His arm was tight around her waist, holding her close. One of his legs was wrapped around both of hers. She smiled and nestled against him. He felt so good—warm, but good. He was so big he made her feel small—not something she was used to. She liked it. He most definitely wasn't her usual type. Dale had been more like her, her height, her build, slender. When he'd tried to wrap himself around her in any way, even putting an arm around her shoulders, she'd felt suffocated, needed to escape. Which was weird—shouldn't she feel like that with Smoke? He was so much bigger than her. His arm lay heavy across her middle, holding her close, but she didn't want to escape.

She trailed her fingers along his muscular forearm. It didn't feel like too much, or too close. If anything she wanted him to be even closer. She wanted him. What was really weird was that she didn't want to wake him up and take him, ride him as she knew she could. What she really wanted was for him to wake up and take her. Out on the trail yesterday, she'd willingly have done whatever he wanted. Last night, when they'd come back after dinner, he'd sidestepped the competition over who was taking the lead by asking her to do whatever she wanted with him. And she had. Out on the deck. On the sofa in the moonlight.

Now though, now she wanted him to do as he pleased with her. Her body was fully awake, coming more alive by the moment at the thought of him pinning her down, spreading her legs with his knees and taking her—because he wanted her.

She touched the light stubble on his cheek. He was so gorgeous. The corner of his mouth curved up. She smiled, not sure now if he was still sleeping or not. She ran her hand over his chest and on down over hard abs. Oh, he was awake alright. He was huge, hot and hard in her hand. He opened his eyes and smiled his lazy smile. "Are you taking me while I'm sleeping now?"

She shook her head. Hoping he would see in her eyes what she really wanted. Understanding spread across his face. His expression softened and he gave a small nod as he propped himself up on his elbow. With his other arm he drew her towards him so that her upper body was underneath him. Her whole body was wide awake now, screaming for him. Yes. This. He put a hand to her shoulder and pinned her to the bed as he lowered his lips to hers. He explored her mouth, slowly, possessively. His hand strayed down to her breast, closing over it. Oh, this was so good, so different. He wedged his knee between her thighs and spread them, shifting his weight on to her. She made a quick decision.

"Are you clean?"

He stopped, looking puzzled for a moment. Then understanding and delight dawned on his face.

"I am. Regular check just done. You?"

She nodded, not quite believing she was doing this, but wanting it too much to take the sensible route.

"And you're on birth control?"

She nodded again as all the muscles in her belly, and lower, tightened deliciously.

He grinned and shifted so his body was covering hers. He supported his weight on his elbows and smiled down at her. "Are you sure about this?"

She smiled back. She was damned sure—she couldn't remember ever wanting anything more than she wanted this, wanted him in this moment.

"You're not going to try to escape?" He raised an eyebrow. "That could be fun—for both of us."

She brought a hand up to his chest and pushed. "Actually, I changed my mind."

He caught her hand and pinned it to the bed with a grin. She wriggled underneath him, deliberately tormenting him to see what he'd do. He was right—this could be fun!

He caught her other hand, pinning it down and spreading her legs. He was going to take her. Her whole body was on fire, begging him, needing him to do just that.

At that moment Smoke's phone rang. He frowned and let go of her hands. Springing from the bed, he picked it up and walked from the room.

"This is Smoke."

Laura lay staring after him, her breath coming slow and shallow. What the...? He couldn't have just let it ring? Her heart was still racing, she was aching with need for him, and he answered the god-damned phone? She closed her eyes and blew out a short sigh. Damn him! They'd been so close. She got up from the bed. She'd wanted him to take her because he wanted to. Because he couldn't resist, couldn't stop himself. But apparently answering the phone had been more important to him. He couldn't want her that much. She went in the bathroom and started running the shower.

"...Sure thing, Jack. I'll see you over there."

Jack? Ooh, she could throttle her cousin right now!

Smoke appeared in the doorway, looking apologetic. "Where we were—can we take a rain check on that very moment?" He smiled, but his cockiness wasn't quite on full beam.

She shook her head. "Wherever we were. We're not there anymore."

"I'm sorry, Laura." He stepped towards her. "It was Jack's ring tone. I had to get it."

Damn Jack! Throttle him? In this moment, Laura could quite happily castrate him!

Smoke was coming closer, his presence invading her senses. He was smiling, knowing the effect he was having on her.

It seemed she could forgive his gorgeous naked body anything. "I'll forgive you this once." She raised an eyebrow. "As long as you'll make it up to me, right now."

He looked pained. "I have to go. I've got to get Papa Charlie ready."

She wasn't going to be rebuffed twice—once for her cousin, once for a plane. No way. She stepped towards him, smiling now, reaching for his still impressive erection. "Let's deal with this before you go, shall we?" She closed her fingers around him and watched his eyes close as he let out a low moan. "There, see. Work can wait."

At that his eyes opened and he stepped out of her reach, face set. "No, Laura. Work can't wait." He grabbed his clothes from the bedroom and stalked out. Laura stared after him, open-mouthed. She heard the deck door slide open and then slam to.

"Well, screw you!" she said.

~ ~ ~

Smoke sat in the cockpit, running through his pre-flight checks. What a disaster this morning had turned into. Laura had been so mad at him. Not as mad as he'd been at Jack. What a sense of timing that guy had! He took a deep, calming breath. Maybe it was for the best? He was breaking all his own rules with Laura. Where would they be now if Jack hadn't interrupted? Hiking yesterday, dinner last night. Sleeping the whole night with her? No. That wasn't what he needed to be doing. It wasn't part of the game. And this morning? That hadn't even been the game. That was honest to goodness want and need. She'd wanted him badly, and he'd needed her. But if they had? What then? There'd be nowhere left to go after that. It'd be game over. He checked the cabin then ran back down the steps and over the tarmac to the FBO. Jack should be here in ten minutes. And perhaps Smoke should be thanking instead of cursing him.

Rochelle was at the desk this morning. "Hey, Smoke. Have you got everything you need?"

"Yeah. Thanks, Rochelle. My passenger should be here any minute and we're filed for ten thirty. I expect we'll back late afternoon and I'll need refueling then."

Rochelle smiled at that. "Thanks, Smoke."

He nodded. He tried to manage his fuel so that he could buy it here in Summer Lake. It was slightly more expensive than at the big airports, but at least here he knew he was helping a family stay in business. "I need to catch up with you about the hangar fees, too."

"Whenever. I know you're good for it." Her eyes lit up as a man appeared in the doorway beside her.

"Smoke! How you doing, man?"

Smoke grinned and went to shake the other pilot's hand. "Jason! I'm good, thanks. And you? How long are you back for?"

"I've just had a couple of days. I'm leaving this afternoon. The Seoul run again."

"Yeah," Rochelle was smiling at Jason. "Just a couple of days. I have to make the most of him while I've got him."

Smoke laughed. "I'll leave you to it then. My guy's here." Jack's truck was pulling into the parking lot.

"I won't see you before I leave, but talk to Rochelle will you?" said Jason. "We've got a couple of ideas we want to run by you."

Smoke nodded as Jason pulled her into the office in the back. He smiled, knowing full well what they were up to. Jason was a lucky guy. He and Rochelle had been married for years, had a couple of kids, and she still lit up whenever she talked about him. Practically glowed whenever he was home. She was so proud of him. He flew for a big corporation based out of San Jose. Their executives traveled to Korea a lot and Jason was gone most of the time. He seemed to have hit the jackpot. He had the freedom to fly and a woman who loved him when he was home. She supported his career, didn't try to ground him like most women did once they hooked a pilot. But then she knew the deal. She'd grown up in the world of general aviation. Her family had run the airport since it was nothing more than a grass strip on their land.

Smoke shook his head as he went to meet Jack. Rochelle was rarer than a winning lottery ticket.

He met Jack at the doors. "All ready to go whenever you are, boss."

"Great." Jack handed him a cup of coffee. "Thought you might need one. I know I do."

"Thanks." Smoke took a sip, straight cappuccino with two extra shots. Just as he liked it. Sometimes he appreciated Jack's attention to detail.

"I'm all set if you're ready," said Jack.

Smoke led the way to the door and swiped his pass.

Jack looked over at the desk. "Is there no one around today?"

"Rochelle's in the back. Something came up that she had to take care of." It made Smoke smile that she was obviously so eager to make the most of every moment with Jason. In his experience, women were more likely to ruin the time they could spend with a guy by sulking and whining about the times he couldn't be there.

Once Jack was settled, Smoke pulled the steps up and secured the door. "Is everything okay at the office?" he asked. Jack rarely went to the city anymore, and when he did he usually booked it and grumbled about it at least a week in advance.

Jack gave him a funny look. "Yeah, no problems there. What are your plans for the day?"

Plans? As if Jack had given him time to make any! He raised an eyebrow at his friend, sensing some kind of tension, but not understanding it. "I figure I'll stop by and clear the apartment. It shouldn't take long. I already brought most of my stuff up here. After that I'll just hang at the airport and wait for you. You got any idea what time you'll be done?" Smoke was starting to think that maybe, if Jack didn't take too long, he could get back in time to persuade Laura that she didn't need to stay mad at him. Despite all the reasons not to, he really wanted to finish what they'd started this morning.

"I won't be long," said Jack. There was still that odd tension about him.

"What's your deal, Jack?" They knew each other too well, and had done for too long for this kind of shit. Smoke was starting to think he wasn't the only one who had Laura on his mind, but he wanted to hear it from Jack.

"I think you know what my deal is. And I'll be honest, I don't even need to go to the office."

"Oh, for fuck's sake!" Smoke was pissed. "So what the hell are we doing?"

Jack shrugged. "Let's go anyway. I can check in with Lexi while you go collect your stuff. I'll meet you at that place near the airport for lunch, yeah?"

Smoke nodded. "You're the boss."

Jack had settled in one of the big club seats, which was unusual. But then Smoke didn't think he wanted him sitting up front today.

~ ~ ~

At one o'clock Smoke sat in the burger joint across the road from the airport. He was agitated. He knew Jack was going to warn him off Laura, and he understood why. He'd be doing the same in Jack's position. But Smoke had been thinking about it while he'd collected the few things he still had in the Santa Monica apartment, and he wasn't willing to back off. Even though, after this morning, that might not be his choice to make. She'd been ready to give in to him, even been ready to go back there after he'd left her high and dry. But she'd been madder than a scalded cat when he left. Maybe this little chat with Jack was a pointless exercise. He pursed his lips. But no matter what Jack said, no matter what Laura might say, no matter even what the better part of himself knew to be the wise thing to do, there was a stubborn little voice in his head that wasn't about to quit.

He nodded as Jack came in and made his way over to the booth where Smoke was sitting. He slid in opposite Smoke and gave him a rueful grin. This morning's tension was gone. This was the Jack of old, his college buddy, his partner in many ways.

"Sorry, bro. I feel like an asshole, but she's my little bitty baby cousin."

Smoke laughed, glad to release the last of his own tension. "She's no little bitty baby anything, Benson! She's a fine woman who knows her own mind and can hold her own with anyone, if you ask me."

Jack nodded, "Yeah, she can that."

"So what's the problem? I mean, I know I wouldn't want a guy like me around my sister, but Laura's nobody's fool."

Jack sighed, but said nothing as the waitress came to take their order. She smiled at Smoke and leaned a little too close as she refilled his water. "You were right, Smokey. Your friend is handsome, but I'd still rather have you. Maybe we could bring him along for Ashley?"

Smoke shook his head at her. "Leave it, Vicky."

She put a hand on his shoulder. "I'll wear you down one day, Smokey." She turned her smile on Jack. "I know what Smokey wants, how about you, handsome?"

Jack laughed. "I'll take the Swiss burger, thanks, with everything but pickles."

"Coming right up." She walked away, her backside swaying with every step.

Jack watched her go then looked back at Smoke. "That's more your style. Why not stick with something like that? Nice and easy."

Smoke frowned. "Maybe I've had enough of nice and easy?" As he said it he realized it might be true. Yeah, Vicky was hot, blonde and curvy, wanting and willing, and Jack was right, she was more his style, but looking at her now, she did nothing for him. He wanted the tall, slender, blue-eyed, dark-haired challenge that was Laura. "You know damned well Laura can take care of herself. What are you worried about?"

"Honestly?" Jack was always straight up honest, when he asked permission first it usually meant he was about to slam home a particularly hard truth.

Smoke nodded warily, not knowing what to expect, but knowing that he wasn't going to like it. "Yeah, your honesty is always useful—if mostly painful, too."

Jack shrugged, "The truth is like that, bro. It can be a bitch."

"Go on then, lay it on me."

"Honestly, I'm as concerned about you as I am about her."

Now that was unexpected. "Why?"

"Because last night Em and I were at the Boathouse for a beer and I saw the two of you having dinner. Alright, I didn't just see you, I sat there and watched you for a while. And do you want to know what I saw? I saw my old buddy, Smoke, Mr. Fuck 'em and Forget 'em, go through a whole range of emotions as my little bitty baby cousin talked. I saw Mr. Don't Care start to care. And I saw my closed off, men-are-as-disposable-as-vibrators cousin start to open up. She poured something out to you and you didn't turn and run. You didn't even lighten it with a joke and a laugh. You reassured her. You took her hand and you took her home." Jack gave him a meaningful look. "And it scared the shit out of me—for both of you. I know you and I know her. I've helped patch both of you back together over the years. I know where both of your flaws and your weaknesses lie and I'm scared that if you try to bring them all together, it might just shatter you both."

Smoke just stared at him for a long time, not knowing what to say—or what to think.

Vicky returned with their food. Looking at their faces she simply said, "Enjoy, boys," as she slid the plates onto the table and left.

"But I don't let women get to me," said Smoke eventually.

"That's what I thought 'til I saw you with Laura last night. You can't tell me she's not getting to you?"

Maybe he couldn't, but he wasn't about to admit that she was
either—especially not to himself. Jack let him mull it over
while they ate in silence.

"What's her story anyway?" he asked when his burger was
gone.

Jack shook his head. "I'm not telling you her story, and I'm not
telling her or anyone else your story. I'm wading in way deeper
than I should already, and I know it."

"So what was the point in today then? You're warning me off
her—for her sake, for my sake, either way?"

"No. Part of me wants to lay down the law, go all badass on
you, but no. I'm just asking you to stop and think. Is it worth
it?"

Smoke thought about it as he picked at his fries. Apparently it
was. Maybe he was being stupid, pig-headed, but he wasn't
ready to walk away. Vicky waved at him from behind the
counter, giving him her come-on smile as she leaned forward
on her elbows, her pose deliberately showcasing her
impressive cleavage. He looked away. He'd had way more than
his fair share of nice and easy.

"I don't want to walk away yet, Jack."

Jack nodded. "I kinda knew that last night. I just feel like I'm
watching a train wreck about to happen and I needed to try to
warn you."

"You don't think we can just play the game for a while then
shake hands and leave as friends when it's done?"

Jack shook his head slowly. "Before last night I would have
thought that of all the people I know, the two of you were the
most likely to be able to do that. But seeing the way you were
together? Nope. Sorry. It's a train wreck waiting to happen."

Smoke blew out a sigh. He had a feeling Jack was right, but he
still didn't want to change tracks. "So what are you
suggesting?"

"That if you're going to keep seeing her, you might want to be up front with her and ask her to do the same. Tell her what your deal is, ask her to do the same. It won't ever work if you don't."

Smoke shook his head at that. How could it ever work if he did? And what did 'work' mean anyway? All he wanted to do was sleep with the woman. Didn't he? Not get into all this heavy stuff. Even if he wanted more than that it was pointless anyway. He could hardly say that to Jack, though.

"Just think about it, that's all, and if you want to talk to me, talk to me." Jack grinned now. "She may be my little bitty baby cousin, but you're my bud. That's mostly what I needed to tell you. Whatever goes down, that doesn't change, okay?"

"Okay." Smoke was glad to hear it. He had no idea how this might go down, but however it did, he'd hate to lose Jack's friendship over it.

Chapter Six

Laura couldn't concentrate. She'd thought she'd be able to distract herself by getting down to work. She usually lost track of herself and everything else when she was designing, but not this morning. The way Smoke left had rattled her. She kept telling herself it was all for the best. She must have been crazy to think about having unprotected sex with him. It just went to show that she was as stupid as the next woman when she got around a big, muscly—she pursed her lips—sexy-as-sin guy. She'd do better to stick with her brown haired bookish types. The ones she could push around and never consider being vulnerable with. If it was all for the best though, why could she not stop thinking about the damned man, and his gray eyes— and his damned muscles?!

Her cell phone buzzed, interrupting her mental ramblings. She didn't recognize the number.

"Laura Benson."

"Hey, Laura. It's Ava from Levy."

"Oh, hi Ava. What can I do for you?"

"Colin, Mr. Levy Jr., is going to be in San Francisco tomorrow and he'd like to stop by your store. Mr. Levy Sr. has talked to him about the possibility of buying it. Since Colin didn't get the chance to meet you last week he's hoping to introduce himself and take a look around. Is there a time that would work for you?"

Laura frowned. "How long is he going to be in town?"

"Just tomorrow, he's on an early evening flight back to London."

Oh, crap! She didn't want to go, but she couldn't afford not to. "Would late morning work?"

"It would. He had suggested eleven if that will work for you."

"It will." It'd have to.

"Thanks. I'll let him know."

"Great."

Laura ended the call. Just great! Now she'd have to rent a car and get her ass back there by tonight. She picked her phone back up to call Missy.

Dan answered. "Hey, Laura!"

"Hey, Dan-o. Is Miss around?"

"No, she's out with her brother. Shall I get her to call you? Anything I can do for you?"

"No, it's okay. I just wanted to say hi. I'd hoped to be around whenever you two have your little engagement bash, but I've got a meeting I have to get back for."

"I thought you were staying all week?"

"So did I." She sighed.

"So why not have Smoke take you and bring you right back?"

Laura rolled her eyes. "I don't think so. I'll rent a car."

"I'll pay for the fuel if you want to fly?"

"Thanks, but no thanks, Danny. I'd rather drive."

"Are things okay between you two?"

She laughed. When did Dan get so perceptive? "I don't know and I don't have time to think about it. Just call me, or have Miss call me when you figure out your engagement party, okay?"

"Sure, but if you're going to come back for it, why don't you take my Jeep? It'd save you renting something."

"Oh. Now that could work."

Dan laughed. "Yeah and it'll make sure you come back too, if you have to return my Jeep. I know you. If I don't make you come back you may disappear for months, go into hiding again."

Laura smiled. He was right. "Thanks, Dan. I will if you really don't mind."

"Don't mind at all. Want me to come get you? You're at the resort, right?"

"I am. Cabin Eleven B. How about I call you when I'm ready?"

"Perfect. Hopefully Miss will be back soon and I'll bring her with me."

"Great. See you later then."

~ ~ ~

Laura was surprised to see Emma when she answered the knock at the cabin door. "Hey. Come on in. I'm afraid I can't chat for long though, I have to leave."

Emma stepped inside. "It's okay, I know. I talked to Missy, she's bringing Dan's car over. I said I'd meet her here so we can have a girly half hour before you have to go. I'll give her a ride home so you can hit the road."

Laura smiled. She wasn't used to having girlfriends around who would just show up for a 'girly half hour', or for anything else. She liked it. "Come on through. I'm all packed and ready."

Emma looked around the cabin. "It's nice, isn't it?" she said, walking over to the windows. "And great views."

"It is beautiful. I'll tell you what, I'll just go leave the door open for Miss then we can sit outside if you like."

Emma opened the sliding door and stepped out onto the deck. Laura went and wedged a shoe in the front door so Missy could come straight in when she arrived. Out on the deck, Emma looked at her wide-eyed and pointed at the partition on the deck.

"Is anybody staying there?" she asked in a comical stage whisper.

"Yes, but don't worry, he's not home."

"He?"

"That's where Smoke is staying."

"Oh." Emma's face fell. "I'm sorry Jack had to go to the city. I guess that ruined your day, huh? And now you have to leave. You two have the worst luck."

Laura shrugged. "Maybe it's good luck. Maybe fate or the universe is trying to tell me something. We've been trying to get together for months and it just never works. I think it's time to take the hint and give up."

"Nooo! You mustn't give up! What if the universe is just testing you to see how much you want it?"

Laura laughed. "I don't really think the universe has anything to do with it, Em. He's a good-looking guy, actually he's gorgeous, so it was worth giving it a try, but we can never make the time to see each other, so there's not much point." She was telling herself more than telling Emma, that it was time for her to forget about Smoke. A heavy weight settled in her chest at the thought, but it was true.

"Hey, ladies." Missy poked her head around the screen door.

"Hey, Miss. Come on out."

Missy came and gave her a hug. "It's such a shame you have to leave." She smiled. "But wasn't Danny clever, lending you his Jeep so you have to come back?"

Laura was so happy for Dan, that he and Missy had gotten together—and gotten engaged! She'd never in a million years have put the two of them together, they were polar opposites, but they couldn't be more perfect for each other. She grinned at Missy. "He is clever, but then we all knew that. What I can't get over is how head-over-heels in love with you he is."

Missy smiled. "Me neither! And you know it's a two way street."

"I do. I'm so happy for you both."

"Well you can show me that you mean that by making sure you come back for our engagement party."

"I'd like to, but when is it?"

"When can you get back?"

"Oh, you mustn't wait for me!"

"Yes, we must. We both want you there. And besides it's not going to be anything big, we're just having everyone over to the house, since we haven't done that yet."

"When are you thinking?"

"We were thinking tomorrow night, but I know you can't make that." Missy wrinkled her nose. "Unless you get Smoke to take you and bring you right back?"

"No. No can do."

Missy gave her a hard stare. "What's going on with you two?"

"Nothing. Nothing at all."

Emma looked at Missy. "We need to work on this, sister."

Missy laughed and looked at Laura. "You need to watch this one. She has a pretty good track record on making predictions—and helping things along too."

"Not in my case," said Laura.

"I'm two to zero so far," said Emma with a laugh.

Laura's pulse quickened at the way Emma's words echoed Smoke's. "Well, enjoy your successes, but I won't be joining your list of victories." She wouldn't be joining Smoke's list either, close as it had been this morning. "Anyway," she looked back at Missy, "I could be back by Wednesday night."

"Wednesday and Thursday are out, because Holly is gone. So how about Friday?"

"That works," said Laura. And it would mean she didn't have to rush back too. The idea of spending the week here had lost its appeal. "I'd better get going for now though. If I get on the road soon I can be home before it's dark.

~ ~ ~

It was dark by the time she got home. She let herself into her apartment and dumped her bag in the hallway. That was one long-ass drive! Tired and hungry, she rummaged in the kitchen drawer for a takeout menu and fished her phone out of her purse. There were three new texts—all from Smoke. She forced herself to ignore them and call for the food first—that was more important. Call made, she opened them up and smiled.

> *14.17: Sorry about this morning. I'll make it up to you :0)*
> *17.30: I'm home. Where are you?*
> *20.22: Call me?*

Wow! She'd wondered if she might get a text from him. She'd never have expected three of them. She pictured him sitting out on the deck at the cabin. Ah well. He had been a nice idea, but it really was best to quit while they were both still ahead. She took a quick shower while she waited for the food to arrive. When it did she ate quickly. Once she'd cleared the dishes she wandered around the apartment, wondering whether she should call him. There really wasn't much point, but then it would be rude not to. She smiled and picked up her phone. That was it. She was just being polite.

He picked up on the second ring. "Hey, lady. I've got a really nice Cab Franc waiting for when you get back."

He sounded as cocky—and as sexy—as ever. Missy was right, his name suited him. Smokin' hot and even his voice was smoky. Ah well. Too bad. "I'm not coming back."

"What? Where are you?"

"I'm back in San Francisco."

He was silent for a long moment. "I'm sorry, Laura. You didn't need to leave, though."

She laughed. "Don't flatter yourself. I had something come up at the store I had to get back for."

"Really?"

Oh, my God! He didn't believe her!

"That's quite an ego, Smoke, if you think I'd up and leave, just because you'd rather talk to Jack on the phone than have sex with me."

When he spoke again his voice was low, controlled—angry? "It was about doing my job, Laura. Not about talking to Jack."

"Whatever, Smoke. It doesn't matter."

"It does matter. I'd rather have sex with you than do just about anything else."

What was it about his voice? Low and smoky, it wrapped itself around her, vibrating through her body. She didn't dare respond, not trusting what she might say.

"So, if that's not why you left, when can we get back to where we were?"

She pulled herself together. She couldn't go there. "We can't."

"Yes we can, and you know we will. So why not just tell me when?"

Damn him! He was sure of himself, and of her! She stared at the phone, not knowing what to say.

"Call me. Let me know. I'll be waiting."

She nodded, then felt stupid—he could hardly hear that, could he? "I have to go."

He chuckled. "Sleep well, lady. Dream of me."

She hit the end call button. What an arrogant prick!

~ ~ ~

Smoke sat out on the deck watching the moonlight reflect off the lake. Another beautiful night in Summer Lake. Only now there was no beautiful Laura to share it with. Why the hell hadn't he ignored his phone this morning? What man in his right mind would have climbed off her for any reason? Let alone to answer his phone. He shook his head. No point thinking like that. It was how he was. It was who he was. His job defined him. In the air he was responsible for the lives of his passengers. That wasn't something you could just shut off when the wheels touched down. When Jack or Pete called, he answered. Every time. Immediately. Women couldn't understand it. Women expected to come first. They were miserable when they realized they didn't. And then they made his life miserable, too. That was why he stuck to the 'nice and easies.' They were grateful for some fleeting attention—and the sex. He should just forget about Laura. He went inside and poured a glass of wine, which reminded him—he really should call his folks soon. Returning to the deck, he stared out at the lake, still unable to shift Laura from his head. Maybe she'd call him?

Chapter Seven

Laura turned the Jeep onto South Shore Road. She was glad to be back in Summer Lake. This place was growing on her. It had been a productive week, the meeting with Colin had gone well, and it looked like they really did want to buy her store. She was pleased she'd gone back, but still more pleased to have the weekend in Summer Lake. She jumped in her seat as a truck headed in the opposite direction honked its horn. Emma's Gramps was behind the wheel, smiling and waving. She waved back with a grin. He was a great old guy. That was another thing about this place; she actually bumped into familiar faces around town. That never happened in San Francisco. As she turned onto Main Street her grin faded as she spotted a very familiar figure. It wasn't the pilot's uniform or the gray hair, but the familiarity of the broad shoulders and narrow hips that told her who he was. A shudder ran through her. He was walking arm in arm with a woman. A woman with short brown hair who was chatting away to him. She looked vaguely familiar, but Laura couldn't place her. Maybe she'd been at Missy's party? Well, wow! Just, wow! He didn't waste any time, did he?

She'd intended to go straight to Missy and Dan's, but after seeing that, she needed a drink! She pulled in to the square at the resort and headed straight for the bar. Ben was chatting with some customers at one of the high top tables. He smiled and waved when he saw her. She waved back and took a seat at the bar. She ordered a Jack Daniels and took a big slug.

"I hope whiskey nights don't mean the same to you as they do around here?" Ben climbed on to the stool beside her.

It really was a pity he wasn't her type. He was certainly good looking, and he was such a great guy. "Hey Ben. What do they mean around here?"

"That something serious just hit the fan." He smiled. "In fact the last whiskey night I can think of was when Em saw you and Jack on the beach and didn't know who you were. I guess it's a drown your sorrows kind of thing."

"No sorrows here, Ben." There weren't, were there? So Smoke had already moved on? So what? She'd done that herself when she left here on Monday. Hadn't she?

"Glad to hear it," said Ben, the concerned look he was giving her not quite matching his words.

She laughed, wanting to reassure him—and herself. "To me this is like a toast to my cousins."

Ben gave her a puzzled look.

She raised her glass. "Jack and Daniel!"

Ben laughed. "Damn, that had never occurred to me."

"Yeah, most people don't realize, and I wouldn't bring it up if I were you. You know about their dad, right?"

"Yeah. Mind if I join you for one, and then we'll go get your key. You could have taken it with you."

"Key?"

"For the cabin. You are staying for the weekend aren't you?"

Laura thought about it. She'd paid for the room before she came last weekend, but when she'd checked out so early she'd assumed she'd lost the rest of the week. She'd intended to stay at Missy and Dan's.

"It's yours if you want it," said Ben.

She smiled. Why not? It'd be fun to mess with Smoke's head. He could hardly start screwing his new friend out on the deck with her next door. "Thanks, Ben. I will. I'd rather not impose on Missy and Dan at the moment."

Ben gave her an odd look, but didn't question her.

"Are you going to their house tonight?" she asked.

"Course I am. I wouldn't miss that for anything."

"Good. So, how about I come look for you once I've dumped my bag and had a quick shower? We can head over there together."

"Sounds good. Come on, let's go get you that key."

~ ~ ~

Smoke pulled up at the cabin after dropping Rochelle back at the airport. She'd given him a lot to think about. He wanted to talk to Jason too, but in principle, it could really work. He'd agreed to have lunch with Rochelle tomorrow to start going over initial ideas, but he liked the possibilities she'd pitched at him.

He checked his watch before stepping into the shower. He'd need to get a move on if he was going to get to Dan's on time. He was still trying to find a balance between work and social life. He liked to keep the two separate. It had been easy when he was based out of Miami and Houston. Even the short while he'd been in Santa Monica, he'd have a beer with Jack and Pete now and again, but that was all. They were old friends, but he'd never wanted to become 'one of the gang', with all that entailed. He smiled as he soaped himself down—he'd kept his social life 'nice and easy'. That seemed to be changing up here, though. It was such a small town it would be hard for it not to. Breakfasts at the Boathouse, nights listening to the band, dinner at each other's houses, everyone hung out together and they were trying to draw him into the circle. Even Dan, whom he hadn't known that long, was becoming a real friend, and had insisted that he come tonight.

He stepped out of the shower and toweled himself down. All week he hadn't been able to take a shower without thinking about Laura. Standing there naked with the water running behind her. *I'll forgive you this once...If you'll make it up to me right now.* He would have done, too. If she hadn't said, *Work can wait.* That had pushed all his buttons, set alarm bells ringing. Taken him back in time. He could hear the echoes in his mind now.

Work can wait, Smoke. I won't.

I think you love that plane more than you love me!

He shook his head to clear it as he got dressed. No. It was for the best that Laura had left. That she hadn't called him. It just wasn't worth it—on so many levels. He wasn't capable of the kind of relationship a woman wanted. It seemed he wasn't capable of keeping it to strictly sex with her either. So it really was for the best. So why was part of him clinging to the hope that she might be at Dan's tonight?

~ ~ ~

Missy's son Scot answered the door. "Hey, Smoke! Are you going let me come fly with you again soon? I've been practicing on the simulator, I was making missed approaches at McCarran!"

Smoked grinned. He liked the kid. "Sure thing, Scot. You can come up with me whenever you like."

Scot looked warily over his shoulder. "Will you tell my mom that? She says I'm not supposed to bug you about it."

Smoke laughed. "Leave it to me," he said with a wink.

A big grin spread across Scot's face. "Awesome! Thanks, Smoke. Come on. Everyone's out back."

He followed the kid through the house. It was a nice place. They went through a big kitchen and out a set of French doors. All the gang were there, and a whole bunch of other people. He checked his watch. Was he late?

Jack came over and shook his hand. "No worries, bro. You're not late. It's just that we've all been dying to get invited over here and showed up way too early."

Smoke smiled, relieved. He was never late.

Pete came to join them. "S'up, partner? How you doing?"

"Doing okay. How about you?" As he spoke, Smoke's gaze traveled over the groups of people standing by the pool, sitting at tables on the brick patio.

"I'm good. I wanted to talk to you. We're coming up on the lease renewal. What do you think? Shall the three of us sit down sometime next week to go over it?"

This was typical Pete. He had no boundaries between the work and social aspects of his life! "Sure," Smoke replied. "I think it's best we get to it early. I've got a few ideas for some changes I'm thinking about making."

Pete's brows came down. "What kind of changes are we talking about?"

Smoke was still scanning, he couldn't see Laura anywhere. He looked back at Pete with a grin. "Don't worry. I'm not talking about charging you more." Pete looked so relieved, he couldn't help but add, "Well, not too much more."

Jack laughed at Pete's expression. "Come on, bro. You know he's only winding you up."

Pete glowered. "I can never tell with you, Hamilton."

"I know," Smoke laughed. "That's why I do it so much."

Pete shook his head. "At least give me a clue what we're talking so I don't spend the whole time fretting and wondering if we need to start leasing a plane from someone else."

"You'd soon find you wouldn't get half the plane for twice the money."

Jack gave him a worried look. "And we wouldn't want twice the plane for half the money. Leasing Papa Charlie from you works for all of us, doesn't it?"

"Yeah. It does. I'm just taking stock. I might hire another pilot, free myself some time up."

"To do what?" Jack was all over this.

Smoke shrugged. "That's what I'm figuring out."

"What are your options?" asked Pete. "I know I can be an asshole, but I don't want to lose you."

Smoke laughed. "You sound like I'm your girlfriend, Hemming! Don't worry, I'm not breaking up with you, honey."

They all laughed at that.

"So come on," said Jack, refusing to let it go. "What are you thinking?"

"I'm thinking I'd like to get back to doing some flight instruction." He watched the shock register on Jack's face. Even Pete looked surprised. "At the same time, part of me thinks I should get back in the long haul business. You know, bigger, faster planes, more exotic locations."

Pete nodded. "You getting itchy feet again? I suppose it's a bit different for you, limiting, now we're both based here?"

Smoke nodded. "It is...different. Like I said, I need to figure out what I want."

"Fair enough," said Jack. "How about you take some time? You let us know when you want to have that meeting?"

The way Pete frowned at Jack made Smoke smile. Jack was being all understanding because he thought this had something to do with Laura. But it didn't. Did it? He spotted Dan and made his excuses. He'd had enough of this conversation—and of this train of thought.

~ ~ ~

As he stood chatting with Dan, Missy came to join them. Smoke liked her, she was a little pistol. He leaned down to kiss her cheek. "Congratulations, Missy. I was just telling Dan what a lucky guy he is."

She smiled up at him as Dan wrapped an arm around her. "Thanks, Smoke, and thanks for coming. It's nice to be able to talk to you when I'm not scared stupid for once."

Smoke laughed. Missy was deathly afraid of flying, but she was a tough little cookie, she always braved it out. "The offer always stands. I'll take you up anytime you want to go. You can sit up front with me, see what goes on. It's a great way to get past the fear."

She didn't look at all convinced. "Thanks. I'm still thinking about it."

"Whenever you're ready, just say the word. I'll tell you what though, would it be okay if I took Scot up again soon? He really enjoyed it."

Missy wrinkled her nose at him. "Did he put you up to this?"

Smoke didn't want to snitch on the kid, but he didn't want to lie either. So he answered without answering. "Actually, I'm thinking about getting back to instructing. He'd be a good practice student for me. It's been a while."

"Hey, if you need students, you know I'm in," said Dan. He smiled at Missy, "And Scot will be too, right, Miss? It'd be good for him."

Missy groaned. "So I'm going to have to worry about both of you hurtling around the sky?"

"I'll keep 'em safe. I promise," said Smoke.

"Okay," Missy gave him a sly little smile. "Since I've decided I trust you." Smoke got the idea she was telling him something else too, but he didn't know what—until she added, "Have you seen Laura?"

He shook his head. "Not since last weekend."

Missy grinned. "Well, let's find her. She's around here somewhere."

Smoke's throat went dry. "She is?"

Missy scanned the crowd then her face fell. "Maybe she's not," she said a little too quickly. "Let's go get a fresh drink, shall we?"

Smoke checked the dock where Missy had been looking when her face changed. Laura was down there talking, flirting by the looks of it, with some guy. She was leaning back against the railing. The guy stood facing her, leaning towards her, one hand on the rail beside her. Smoke's chest constricted painfully as he stared at them.

Missy tugged on his arm. "Drink?" she asked apologetically.

He shook his head. "Thanks. I need to get going, I have a date. I just wanted to stop by and congratulate you both. I'll see myself out." He turned on his heel and left.

~ ~ ~

Laura walked back up to the house. Michael was fun, but she'd left him to it when some of his old school friends had joined them on the dock. He was a serious flirt—and quite appealing too. He wasn't exactly bookish, but he had the brown hair and green eyes. He was much more her usual type than Smoke was, but unfortunately nowhere near as appealing. Where was Smoke anyway? And why couldn't she get the damned man out of her head?

She found Missy and Dan on the patio. They'd know where he was. "Hey, guys." She smiled.

"Hey," said Dan. He looked troubled.

Missy was frowning.

Uh-oh. Not trouble in paradise already, surely? "Am I interrupting?" she asked cautiously.

"No." Missy's smile was unconvincing. "Not at all."

Dan shifted from one foot to the other and didn't look at her. She decided to ignore any tension—maybe that would help relieve it? "It's a great turn out and everyone is enjoying themselves." She took a sip of her drink and looked out at the lake. "Is Smoke coming?" she asked as nonchalantly as she could.

Missy sighed.

Dan looked at her. "He's been and gone."

"Oh."

"He saw you with Michael and left in a hurry."

Damn! "Did he say anything?"

Missy pursed her lips. "Yeah. He said he had a date."

See! What did it matter that she'd been flirting with Michael? He was off with his new friend anyway!

Missy took her arm. "Do you want a fresh drink, hon? I could strangle Michael!"

"Miss, it's not his fault."

Missy was mad. "It is! He's the world's biggest flirt!" She shot a look at Dan. "Isn't he?"

There was no mistaking the twinkle in Dan's eyes as he smiled at Missy. "He can complicate things, but he means well."

Missy huffed at him. "You're too forgiving!"

Dan just smiled at her some more as she led Laura back to the house.

What Laura wouldn't give to have what these two shared. And where the hell had that thought come from? She could have

had this. With Dale. This was what she'd run from. No. That
wasn't true, what she and Dale had shared had been nothing
like what Missy and Dan had. That was why she'd run.

"Seriously, Miss," she said. "Don't worry about it. It's all
good."

Missy stopped and looked up at her. "You're not saying you
like Michael?"

Laura laughed. "No, I am not. I'm just saying there's no point
me liking Smoke either. We could never figure it out to be able
to get together, and now he's dating someone else. It's cool.
No problem. I came back to see you guys, not to see him."

Missy wrinkled her nose. "Sorry, but I cry bullshit!"

Laura should have remembered. Missy was one shrewd little
lady. She didn't miss a trick. "Okay! So I can't get the damned
man out of my head! Satisfied? But we cannot get it together
and even if we could there's nowhere for it to go. So it's for
the best that he has a date with someone else."

"We'll see. Now, let's go get you that drink."

~ ~ ~

Laura slept late again. This was becoming a habit whenever
she was up here. She lay in bed, looking out the window. She
should feel relieved. She'd driven herself nuts all week,
wondering if she should call him, wondering if she'd see him.
Wondering if she'd be able to prove him wrong—how could
she prove that they weren't going to finish what they'd started
when she wanted to so badly? Now it was all moot. She
needn't wonder any more. He'd answered all her questions
with his little friend.

She groaned and rolled over, wondering if he was lying just the
other side of that wall right now. Lying naked with that
woman. That thought was too much to bear. She got out of
bed and padded to the kitchen to make coffee. What had she

been thinking coming back to stay here? She went to the bathroom and peeked through the little window that looked out on the parking spaces at the back. Eek! The airport pickup was there! He was on the other side of the wall. She tiptoed back to the kitchen and poured her coffee. She crept to the sofa and as she sat there sipping it she saw the funny side and started to giggle. This was ridiculous. He was just a man. Okay, a big, gorgeous, sexy-as-sin one, but even so just a dumbass man.

She was relieved a few minutes later to hear the cabin door slam and the truck start up. She flew back to the bathroom and peeked out. He was by himself. Relief flooded through her. But why? Knowing Smoke, it just meant he'd gone home with her, and sneaked out on her before morning. Knowing Smoke? Who was she kidding? She didn't know him at all. She took another sip of her coffee.

She just wanted to.

~ ~ ~

Smoke put his ladder away in the storeroom at the back of the hangar. Papa Charlie was the cleanest plane on the field thanks to Laura. He'd had to get out of the cabin this morning. He was sure she was there with that guy she'd been talking to.

He'd spent the rest of his evening sitting out on the deck. He hadn't exactly lied; he'd had a date with a bottle of Cab Franc. Seeing Laura with that guy had done a number on him, no question about it. But later on, hearing a car pull up at the cabin and hearing two doors slam before it pulled away again, had been the kicker. He'd gone to look out the bathroom window in time to see a cab leaving, but not in time to see who had got out of it. He hadn't expected her to come back here, but then Ben wouldn't have rented it to anyone else, so she must have. And two cab doors closing? There was only one conclusion to be drawn from that. Damn, if that was her way of telling him that it was game over, then she had won. Hands down.

He walked into the FBO. Maybe Rochelle would want to talk now instead of waiting 'til lunch. He needed to stay busy. Keep his mind away from Laura, and what she might be doing. The thought of her with that guy? Naked with that guy? He pressed his lips together. He couldn't go there.

Rochelle was at the desk. "Hey, Smoke. I can't wait to show you what Jason has drawn up. Do you want to start now?"

"I would love to."

Chapter Eight

Laura took the path up to the resort. She'd spent most of the morning in a fruitless effort to work on her new designs. She was getting nowhere. Maybe a walk and some lunch would clear her head. She spotted Ben coming out of the lodge and waved.

"Hey, Ben!"

"Hey, where are you off to?"

"I came to get some lunch, if it's not too busy."

"It is busy, but give me a minute. I'll check with the servers, see who's got a table coming free outside, if you like?"

"Thanks. Have you got time to join me?" She didn't feel like eating alone and Ben was always good company.

"Sorry. We're crazy with check-ins and check-outs today. Is Smoke flying?"

"I wouldn't know."

He gave her a puzzled look, but turned away when they heard someone shout, "Ben!"

Michael was striding across the parking lot towards them. "Who's up for lunch?"

Ben raised an eyebrow at Laura.

"You can join me, if you want," she said.

Michael grinned at Ben. "Aww, are you too busy, mate?"

Ben nodded, giving Laura a questioning look. "Want me to get you a table?"

"Yes, please." She gave him a reassuring smile. He was so sweet, looking out for her. And he didn't know that Smoke had already moved on to his next victim.

Once they were seated, Laura took a good look at Michael while he ordered. He was a good-looking guy, and that accent was sexy. He wasn't Smoke though, but she had to stop thinking like that.

Once the server had gone, he grinned at her. "Missy gave me a right good talking to this morning, for flirting with you."

Laura laughed. "I'm sorry."

"No worries, darl', I'm used to it, she's always giving me grief for something. Always has. I'm the one that's sorry. I didn't know I was treading on some guy's toes, did I?"

She shook her head. "You weren't, though."

Michael looked puzzled. "She said you were seeing that pilot guy."

She shook her head again. "We went out a couple of times, that's all."

Michael smiled. "That's not all though, is it? It's not over yet, darl'. It's written all over your face."

She looked at him. Was it that obvious? "Okay, if you're so good at reading faces, what does this look mean?" She rolled her eyes then tried to glower at him, despite her lips twitching up into a smile.

"It means...." Michael rubbed his chin, pretending to think hard about it. "I know. It means you think it's over, but you don't want it to be. It also means that you can't decide if you should tell me to wrack off because it's none of my business, or if you should pour your heart out to me because you need to talk about it to someone."

Laura threw her head back and laughed. "I wish I could deny any or all of that, but you really are good at reading faces!"

He smiled, a very genuine smile now. "I read people, darl'. Not faces." A shadow crossed his own face. For a moment he looked sad, lost. Then the smile was back. "So out with it. Let's hear your troubles, see if we can fix 'em. What's he done?"

"He's not done anything. At least, he's not done anything wrong."

The server returned with their food. Michael squeezed lemon over his fish before asking, "So, what's he done that's not wrong?"

"He started seeing someone else."

Michael looked up at her. "You sure about that?"

Laura nodded and toyed with her salad. "Yeah. I saw him in town with a woman yesterday. Then last night he told Miss he wasn't staying because he had a date."

"Ah. Do you know who she is?"

"Nope."

"Maybe I do. It's a small town. What's she look like?"

"Small. Short brown hair."

Michael's gaze flicked up at her, then returned to his food. "And when you saw them in town, what made you think she was a date and not just a friend?"

Laura thought about it. "Honestly?"

He grinned. "Not much point in anything else. I'm not asking for my benefit, I'm trying to help you figure it out."

She sighed. "Well, I suppose. If I'm honest. It was just the shock factor and a little jealousy. I was coming back here wondering if I'd see him."

"The two of you didn't have anything lined up?"

"No. The last time I saw him didn't end well, and the last time I spoke to him he told me to call him."

"And you didn't?"

"No."

"Because?"

Oh, what the hell? She'd told him this much and he really did seem to want to help. Like he'd said—she needed to talk to someone. "Because, with Smoke, it's like it's all a game, a competition. Neither of us wants to admit that the other might have the upper hand. Neither of us wants to lose."

Michael smiled. "So you'd rather lose him than lose to him?"

She pursed her lips, but said nothing.

"You might want to think about that one, darl'. Because I've got a feeling. This game the two of you are playing? It's a long way from over."

~ ~ ~

Smoke parked the truck in the square and got out. He waited for Rochelle to pull up alongside.

"I can't wait to talk to Jason," she said as she got out of the car. "He's going to be so pleased!"

Smoke smiled. "Yeah, I think this could really work."

"It will! Come on, let me buy you lunch to celebrate, then I need to get back for the kids. My mom can't keep them this afternoon."

"Do you want to leave it and get back to them? I'm not that hungry."

Rochelle laughed. "Neither am I! I'm too excited to eat, but I said I'd buy you lunch. Even if we just get a drink or something, we should celebrate. I really want to thank you."

Smoke nodded, he knew how much the gesture meant to her. Even though he'd rather go home and catch up on some of the sleep he'd lost last night, he didn't want to refuse her. "Okay."

Ben greeted them at the hostess station. He was looking shifty again; Smoke still couldn't figure the guy out.

"Hey! We're pretty busy today. There are a few high tops free inside though. Follow me." He started towards the bar, but Rochelle didn't follow.

"Look," she said. "There's a table free, right by the water, Ben. Can we have that? It's such a pretty day, I really don't want to sit inside."

Ben came back looking even shiftier now. What was his problem? Smoke looked outside to where Rochelle was pointing. Oh. That was the problem! The empty table was next to a couple—Laura and that Australian guy. Damn! Ben looked at him, giving him the choice of what to do. Smoke shrugged. He wasn't going to run a second time. Ben gave him an apologetic look then led them out onto the deck. Smoke's throat was dry, his heart was racing. He had to get a grip. She was just a woman he'd slept with. No big deal. He'd been in this situation before—many a time.

Laura had her back to them, he couldn't see her face. They were almost at the table before the guy noticed them. He surprised the hell out of Smoke by grinning and then winking at him! Jesus! Okay, so you got the girl! Ever hear of being gracious in victory, jerk? Smoke gritted his teeth and nodded curtly. The guy gave the tiniest shake of his head and shot a look at Laura then back at Smoke. What the hell was he trying to say? Laura turned, a smile lit up her face when she saw him, then faded away when she looked at Rochelle.

"Michael!" squealed Rochelle. "How are you? And how's Ethan? The kids are dying to have him over."

He stood up and greeted her with a hug. Did everyone know each other in this town?

"I'm just great, darl'. And you? And how about that husband of yours? Is he flying?" As Michael said that he gave Laura a meaningful look. What was he trying to do? Reassure her that

Rochelle wasn't competition? Dumbass! As if Laura would feel threatened by any woman!

Rochelle was rattling on about Jason. She turned and smiled at Smoke now. "And thanks to this guy, we'll have him home a whole lot more soon." She stopped herself. "I'm sorry, I didn't think. Do you two even know each other?"

"We've met a couple of times," said Michael, holding out his hand.

Smoke shook it politely, even though thoughts of it touching Laura had him wanting to crush it—and the guy it belonged to. What was this guy's deal? He was grinning at Smoke like they were old buds with some shared secret.

He turned to Laura. "Laura, this is Rochelle. Her family runs the airport." Smoke watched the two women shake hands. Laura looked put out for some reason.

"And," continued Michael with that same odd smirk on his face, "I believe you two already know each other."

Smoke finally allowed himself to meet Laura's gaze. She looked all kinds of mixed up, embarrassed maybe? The little pink stains were just visible on her cheeks.

"Hi."

Smoke nodded, not trusting himself to speak.

Michael put his arm back around Rochelle. "Are the kids free this afternoon? I'm taking Ethan out on the boat. Any chance your two might want to come? I know Ethan would love that better than being stuck with just his old dad."

"They'd love to! And I would!"

"Let's go do it then!"

"But I can't go now." Rochelle looked at Smoke. "We...."

"No worries, darl'," Michael was grinning at Smoke again. "These two will be just fine. Won't miss us one bit, will you guys?" He didn't wait for an answer; he was already walking

Rochelle away. He called back over his shoulder. "This one's on me. Enjoy!"

Smoke stared after him, then looked back at Laura. She seemed to have composed herself a little. He still had no clue what had just happened, but his feet were rooted to the ground. He couldn't bring himself to turn and walk away like the little voice of reason in his head was yelling he should.

"Are you going to join me?" she asked.

He stared at her. What for? She'd just spent the night with Michael. But Michael had just up and left, apparently trying to give Smoke an in. Why would he do that? It didn't make any sense. What made even less sense was that he himself was nodding and sitting down in the chair that Michael had just vacated. He waited for her to speak. This wasn't a conversation he wanted to start.

"So," she smiled at him then bit her lip.

Jesus! How could she still affect his body like this? He shifted uncomfortably in his seat. He wanted to bite her lips, kiss them, feel her naked body under him again. Dammit, Smoke, get a grip! Last night she'd been doing all of that with Michael.

"So?" He kept his face set. Not wanting to give her the satisfaction of seeing all the need and jealousy he felt. If this was her game, she'd well and truly outplayed him.

Her smile faltered. "I thought you might be pleased to see me?"

No. This was not a game he wanted to play. "I don't enjoy leftovers."

She looked at the plates on the table, confused. "We can order you something?"

He shook his head angrily. "I'm not talking about the food, Laura."

The pink stains on her cheek were back, her eyes widened. "What do you mean?"

"I mean, I saw the two of you at Dan's place last night. I heard you both come back to the cabin, and you're still with him at lunchtime. It doesn't take much guesswork to fill in what you've been doing in between!"

She did a good job of trying to look offended. If he didn't know full well he was right, he'd be taken in by her act of indignation. She was good.

"Seriously?! You think I slept with Michael? You think I'm the kind of woman who would kick him out of bed in the morning and be coming on to you by lunchtime? And you think I'm such a lousy lay that he would willingly walk away to give you another shot?"

Smoke's absolute certainty started to crack. No. Now she put it like that, he didn't think that was the kind of woman she was. And no man in his right mind would step aside for another guy after sleeping with her. "But I heard you both come back to the cabin last night."

"Both? I came back alone! In a cab. What makes you think Michael was with me?"

She must be lying. "You weren't alone! I heard two cab doors close." There, let her deny that.

She said nothing, apparently wondering what she could say next. Then her eyes widened in some realization. "You asshole! You heard one door slam twice. I got out and closed the door then realized I didn't have my purse. I opened the door, grabbed the purse, and closed the door again."

That was plausible. And if she had spent the night with Michael, would he have left like he did just now? Got out of the way? Oh, shit. His absolute certainty was crumbling all around him now. Still. "Even if that's the case. You didn't call me back last week. Didn't let me know you were coming or come see me when you got here. Why the sudden change that you want to play nice with me now?" Ah, that had hit a nerve.

She looked away, fiddled with her glass. "Go on. You explained how I was wrong about Michael. Explain how I'm wrong about this. Yesterday you didn't want anything to do with me. What's changed?"

Her blue eyes flashed with anger now. "Alright, you win! Yesterday, on my way back into town, I saw you with Rochelle. I thought you were with her. Last night I was just talking to Michael. He's a nice guy, and a big flirt. I thought flirting might cheer me up, especially if you were about to turn up with someone else. Then Miss said you left because you had a date. I was hardly going to come calling on you both when I got back—and certainly not this morning!"

Smoke was struggling to take all this in. "You thought I was with Rochelle?"

She nodded.

Wow! "And you were jealous?"

She bit her lip then nodded again, reluctantly.

Smoke pressed his own lips together, to stop the smile that was trying to break through. "And last night, at the party, flirting with Michael. You were hoping to make me jealous?"

"No! I was just...he was...I didn't...."

She stopped talking as Smoke reached across the table and took her hand. The pink stains deepened and her eyes flew up to meet his when he said, "Because if you were...it worked."

~ ~ ~

Laura stared at him. His gaze was intense—he meant it! He'd been jealous of her and Michael—just like she'd been jealous of him and Rochelle. And it was all just a big misunderstanding. She couldn't help the smile that she knew was plastered across her face. It was okay though, she was pretty sure it matched the one on Smoke's. He squeezed her hand and she squeezed right back.

"So, what now?" she asked.

"I think we have some unfinished business to take care of."

A ball of fire exploded in her belly and sent waves of heat through her whole body, eventually settling between her legs. He was still holding her hand, his thumb stroking back and forth across her palm.

"If you want to," he added.

This was no game. The question in his eyes was genuine. This wasn't cocky Smoke. This was the Smoke she'd seen out on the trail. This was for real—and as scary as that thought was, she did want to. She nodded and his face relaxed.

"Then let's get out of here." He called for the check.

"It's all taken care of," said the server. "Doc Morgan picked up the tab on his way out."

Laura smiled. Michael was a good guy. She owed him one—big time!

Smoke took her hand when she stood up, and led her back through the restaurant and out into the square. She liked the hand-holding Smoke. He led her to the passenger side of the pickup. Before he opened the door he lifted her hand to his lips. Holding her gaze, he kissed her knuckles one by one. "I don't want to let go."

Wow! Her body was melting in the heat of that look, it was full of need, lust...and something else. She didn't have chance to figure out what as his other arm snaked around her waist, pulling her against him. Her breath caught in her chest as she sagged in his arms. He was overpowering her senses, it was all she could do to stay upright. She was completely surrounded by Smoke; his muscular arm, his hard chest, the warmth and the scent of him. Yet she didn't want to run. All she wanted was more.

He lowered his mouth to her upturned face and nipped her bottom lip. She gasped as the message went zinging through her, alerting her breasts and the very core of her to expect

some Smoke. Soon. He gently pulled her lip with his teeth
then stepped back. "Let's go home, lady," he breathed.

When he parked at the cabin he came around and opened her
door for her. Taking her by the hand again, he led up her up
the steps on her side of the building. She fished the key out of
her purse with shaking hands. He smiled and took it from her.
Unlocking the door, he pushed it open, gesturing for her to
step inside. When she did, his hand came down on her
shoulder and he closed the door behind them. She turned back
to him and he took her face between his hands. The look in
his eyes was even more intense now—lust and...? Again there
was no time to wonder what else, before he was biting her lips.
He backed her against the wall, pinning her there with his
body while his hands raked through her hair.

He tilted her head back, giving himself better access to her
mouth. She surrendered to his kiss. There was no other way to
describe it. He was claiming her mouth, plundering with his
tongue. Owning her. All she could do was willingly,
desperately, surrender. His hands moved to her breasts as his
hips moved against her. She needed him to be inside her. She
fumbled with his buckle and zipper, needing to touch him. He
got rid of her top and bra and dropped his head to her breast.
She leaned her head back against the wall with a moan as his
tongue circled her nipple and his hand unzipped her and
found its way inside her panties. She reached for him, trying to
get him out of his shirt, wanting to see, to feel his muscular
body. He stepped back and shook his head. She felt bereft of
his warmth, his touch.

He shrugged out of his shirt and pulled her back to him. She
gladly wrapped her arms around his neck and pressed herself
against his naked chest. Running a hand over her ass and down
the back of her thigh, he lifted her leg and wrapped it around
his waist. With a wicked smile, he leaned back so her other

foot left the floor and she had no choice but to wrap that around him too. He carried her through to the bedroom where he climbed on the bed and lowered himself forward, pinning her underneath him, his erection pressing into her heat, tormenting her through layers of fabric that she needed to get rid of. She reached down, intending to solve that problem, but he caught her wrist and pinned it to the bed. He shook his head and continued to torment her, moving his hips against her. Her breath was ragged now. She needed him, wanted to undress him, ride him. He held her gaze and she felt herself getting wetter in the heat of that look.

"Remember where we were?"

She could hardly focus on where she was, let alone where they might have been. He took her other hand and brought it up above her head, transferring both of hers into one of his. She pulled and tried to get away, but he only gripped tighter and trailed his free hand down her cheek, then on down her throat.

"This time you're mine...." He thrust his hips, making her moan. His hand closed over her breast as he held her gaze, that other thing in his eyes outshining the lust. "...If you want to be."

Her breath caught in her chest as part of her screamed, yes. She did want to be his, in every way. His hand was back inside her panties, stroking, circling, tormenting her. Oh, God! Her hips moved of their own accord. She instinctively went to put her arms around him, but he kept her hands pinned to the bed above her. He slid a finger inside her and then another, flattening his palm against her, the pressure driving her crazy as his fingers slid in and out. She was no longer in control of her own body—he was. She struggled now, trying to get away, she was getting too close.

"Smoke, please?" she moaned.

"Come for me, Laura."

"But...." She wanted to come with him, not for him. She couldn't stop it, he really was in charge. The heat was building. He increased the pressure of his palm against her. She came undone, crying his name as the heat tore through her and he kept working her, sending her flying away in a haze of pleasure. When she lay still, he brought his lips down to meet hers in a deep, possessive kiss. She brought her arms up around him, clinging to him as she kissed him back.

He bit her lips, then her chin, then nibbled his way down her neck. He mouthed each breast in turn before carrying on, down over her stomach. He slowly pushed her jeans and panties down over her hips, following their progress with his tongue on her skin. He pushed them over her knees, then with a wicked smile, he somehow bound her ankles together with them. He ducked his head under her feet so her legs were wrapped around his shoulders, and she had no way to escape. His smile was even more wicked when her hands came down to his hair.

"Smoke, I...."

He took hold of her hands and held them under her ass with both of his, lifting her up so his mouth was inches from her. He spread her legs wider with his shoulders and blew into her heat.

"Now I want to eat."

"Smoke, no! I don't like...."

"Trust me, lady. You will."

She squirmed, trying to get away before.... His mouth closed over her. Oh, God! That felt so good! Why did she think she didn't like this? As his tongue trailed over her, she had no idea. When his lips teased her clit, she screamed. What was he doing to her? She tried again to free her hands, but he held them firm, sinking his tongue into her then sucking her hard, over and over again. She couldn't take much more, he was owning her again. The sensations were so intense. She let go, her orgasm wracking her body as his mouth demanded more, and more, 'til she was spent.

When he finally freed her hands, he pushed her jeans off her ankles, leaving her naked. He really was something else! Two mind-blowing orgasms before she was fully undressed, and before she'd even seen his cock. She reached for his zipper, needing to rectify that part of the situation.

He blocked her hand. "Lay back, lady."

She did as he said. Her limbs were still weak and shaky anyway.

He stood up with a satisfied smile on his face. Oh, no! This wasn't still some game to him was it, another victory? He seemed to understand what she was thinking. His face softened and he shook his head.

"No games, Laura. I'm deadly serious." As he spoke he unzipped his jeans. He pushed them down over his hips, freeing his cock which stood proud, looking like it was deadly serious too.

He came back to the bed and lay down beside her. She wrapped her arms around him, kissing him with all the need she felt. His big arm closed around her, holding her close to his hard, naked chest. They lay on their sides, facing each other, kissing, hands wandering over each other. She felt like they were kids, exploring each other for the first time.

Smoke propped himself up on one elbow, his other arm drawing her closer, drawing her underneath him. He shifted his weight onto her and spread her legs with his knees. She ached for him now. He was pressing at her entrance. This time he didn't pin her hands, but kept one arm underneath her, around her waist. His other hand tangled in her hair. Pulling her head back so she was looking up into his eyes. He lowered his lips at the same time he thrust his hips. She moaned into his mouth as he filled her. He was so hot and hard, moving inside her. She curled her legs around his as he crushed her lips in a deep, demanding kiss. He was entering and possessing every part of her, taking her deep and hard. She couldn't take much more, he was going to make her come again, she felt her legs stiffen in anticipation. He felt it too. He lifted his head and looked down at her. She felt him get harder and closer as their bodies moved together.

"You. Are. Mine."

He marked each word with a deep thrust and sent her hurtling away. With one last push, he gasped, "Laura!" His own climax exploding deep inside her as he buried his face in her neck.

They lay that way for a long time. He still filled her. She still clung to him. Even after their breathing had slowed back to normal. He nuzzled his face into her neck and she held him even tighter, not wanting the moment to end. She shuddered when he kissed her neck, sending goosebumps racing up her arms.

He brought his lips to her ear. "Mine," he whispered.

Chapter Nine

Laura stepped out onto the deck, not knowing what to expect. Smoke had been so sweet afterwards. He'd held her close for a long time. He'd been the gentle Smoke, not the cocky one. He'd even told her he'd missed her this week. But then he'd said he had some work to take care of, a few phone calls to make, and he'd see her on the deck in a little while. She'd taken a shower and pulled on some yoga pants and a t-shirt, then fiddled with her designs for a while. There was no point, though. She couldn't concentrate. She'd decided to come out to enjoy the air, and the view. The days were getting shorter now and the sun would be setting soon.

No sooner had she sat down than she heard Smoke's door slide open. He peeked around the partition. He was so damned handsome! He took her breath away. He took everything else away too as he stepped around the screen.

"Hey, gorgeous," he murmured.

"Who are you calling gorgeous, gorgeous?" Sexy-as-sin, unbelievably gorgeous in his case! He must have showered too, his hair was still damp. He wore only an old pair of faded jeans that hung low on his hips. His broad chest and shoulders were beautifully naked. Even his bare feet were sexy.

He came and squatted in front of her. Putting his hands on her knees, he pecked her lips. "You! Gorgeous. What are you up to?"

"I just came out to enjoy the view."

He smiled and fixed his eyes on her breasts. "Me too!"

She laughed. "Not much to see there. Definitely no mountains."

He scowled at her and cupped them in his hands. "How dare you! They're perfect!"

She closed her eyes enjoying the feel of his hands on her.

"And besides," he continued, "they're mine!"

That opened her eyes in a hurry. When he'd said it in bed, she'd thought it was something muttered in the heat of the moment. She raised an eyebrow at him.

He shrugged. "Okay, so they're yours. Can they dance?" He flexed his pecs. "Mine can."

She threw her head back and laughed. "Men and their muscles! Honestly!"

His face darkened and he stood, pulling her to her feet to face him. "So you're used to men with muscles are you?" He wrapped his arms around her, holding her so close she had to look up to see his face.

"As a matter of fact, I'm not."

His face relaxed as he nodded. "I didn't think so."

"Why?"

"It's another reason you wouldn't normally sleep with a guy like me, isn't it?"

She had to think about that for a minute. Damn, he was right! What did bookish really mean? If she was honest, it meant weak and weedy. But why? She looked up at Smoke, he seemed to have had her figured from the beginning. "Why do you think that?"

His face softened. "Because you're afraid to make yourself vulnerable. And the best way to avoid being vulnerable is to be the strong one." His eyes gleamed with mischief now. "So...you normally go out with little skinny guys that you can push around, right? Do you put 'em over your knee and spank 'em?"

"Watch your mouth, Captain, or I'll start pushing you around." She put her hand to his chest to give him a shove. Somehow though, before she knew what was happening, he'd scooped her up and thrown her over his shoulder. He had a firm grip on her legs and she was face to face with his ass.

"Put me down!" she laughed.

"Nope! You can't push me around."

She couldn't help laughing, this was ridiculous. She slapped his ass. "I said, put me down. Or you'll be sorry."

His whole body shook under her as he laughed. "We'll see who's going to be sorry, lady." He slapped her ass.

"Ow!" She wriggled to get down, but he just held her tighter. She giggled and paddled his backside with both hands now.

"That does it, lady! Now you're really going to be sorry." He tightened his grip on her legs and strode around the partition to his side.

She watched the upside down lake bounce by in wonder. This was a first. He'd never invited her to come in here before.

"How about I put you over my knee and spank you?" he asked as he slid the door open and headed for the sofa.

He wouldn't, would he? She wriggled for real now. "Smoke! No!" He was laughing. She was too, but he wouldn't really, would he? "Don't you dare!"

He stopped at the sofa and dropped his shoulder so she slid down his front to stand facing him.

"You!" She put both her hands on his chest and shoved as hard as she could, but he stood his ground, still laughing

"You'd better get used to it, lady. I told you, you can't push me around." He pulled her down to the sofa with him and somehow he was on top of her. Her hands were pinned and her legs were spread and he was still laughing. "I'm bigger than you and I'm stronger than you." The laughter faded from his face as he looked down at her.

His mouth came down on hers and her arms came up around his neck. It was the sweetest kiss that deepened into something so much more as their tongues danced in some ritual of permission sought and granted. Eventually he lifted his head, his eyes serious now.

"I'm bigger than you, and I'm stronger than you, and like I just told you, I will never ever push you around."

She knew he spoke the truth, but wasn't really sure what he was getting at. "I do trust you, Smoke."

He smiled and brushed his lips over hers. "And I trust you, lady." He sat up and pulled her into his arms. "So, say you'll have dinner with me?"

She frowned.

He tightened his arms around her, contradicting his words. "Of course, I'll let you go now, if you don't want to."

"I want to, but I said I'd go over to Missy and Dan's."

He grinned. "I bet they'd be happier to know you're with me."

She laughed. "You have a pretty high opinion of yourself, don't you?"

"Yes, I do. But I've earned it. And before long, you'll have a higher opinion of me too. I'm a great guy once you get to know me." His cocky smile was back to full beam as he swaggered his shoulders.

"Are you saying you're going to earn it?"

"Yep, right after you call Missy and tell her you're not coming, because I invited you for dinner and you couldn't resist." He picked his phone up from the coffee table and handed it to her.

"I'm not calling her from your phone!"

"Why not? If you don't you'll have to go all the way next door for yours and I don't want to let go of you for that long."

"You'll survive." She tried to stand up, but he held her tight.

"I might not. And wouldn't you feel terrible if I didn't?"

Why was it that all her life she'd felt claustrophobic—or just plain creeped out when a guy tried to hold on to her in any way, yet now that Smoke was doing it, she was loving every minute of it? Was it just because between the two of them it was only a game? She looked at his face; there was still something much more serious lurking behind the laughter. She wasn't sure it even was a game anymore—to either of them.

"I'll have to risk it. I'm going next door, I'll call them and get changed. Where are we going for dinner?"

He released her and leaned back to look at her. "Okay, go call them, but don't get changed. You look so hot just the way you are."

He wasn't playing. He meant it! The way he was looking at her proved it. She couldn't help but smile, knowing she was doing that to him. "I'm glad you think so. But I can hardly go out like this."

"Who said anything about going out? We can have dinner right here. That way I can have you all to myself." He reached out and touched her cheek. "How does that sound?"

She nodded. It sounded like the perfect evening. She stood up quickly, needing to break the spell. "It sounds wonderful, but I'm still going next door to call them. I'll be right back."

~ ~ ~

Smoke watched her step out onto the deck and disappear around the screen. Jesus! What the hell was he doing? He lay back on the sofa and blew out a big sigh. Whatever it was, he couldn't help it! When she'd told him she hadn't been with Michael, the relief had been overwhelming. When she'd admitted that she'd thought he'd been with Rochelle—and that she'd been jealous? That had blown him away. How the hell could she have thought that? She was so damned hot—how could she ever think she'd have any competition? But knowing that she had had softened something inside of him. He'd felt some instinctive need to reassure her, to tell her, show her, that he wanted her and only her. That he wanted all of her, all for himself. And that was the dumbest thought he'd ever had! He couldn't ask her for anything, because he couldn't give her anything. Not any of the things that women wanted anyway.

Damn! He'd come back in here to get away from her, knowing he shouldn't stick around too much. But all he'd done was make the few bookings he'd needed to for next week's travels, then sat trying to talk himself out of going back over there. He'd lost that battle as soon as he'd heard her step out on the deck. Then when he'd seen her sitting there looking abso-fucking-lutely gorgeous, he'd lost another battle with himself. No way was he going to be able to get out of here for the evening and stay away from her like he'd decided he needed to. He'd known the second he'd squatted down to look into her beautiful blue eyes that he was going to have dinner with her. Spend the whole evening with her—and the whole night too.

His phone rang—Jack! No way!

"If you need to fly tomorrow, I'll find you a pilot. I'm taking the day off."

Jack laughed. "Yo, bro. I take it that means you caught up with my little bitty cousin?"

"I'm saying nothing, Benson. What do you want?"

Jack laughed again. "Chill out Smokey! Em and I were talking about the fundraiser—our table is getting all kinds of crazy this year, and you never let me know if you're coming."

Smoke thought about it. "Is Laura going?"

"Yes. Does that mean you're more likely to come—or to stay away?"

"It means I'm coming. And...." Smoke made a decision. "It means I'm not working it."

"Huh? Now you're fucking with me, right? How are we supposed to get there?"

"I'll have another pilot on staff by then, Jason. He can fly."

"Oookay. Want to tell me what's going on?"

"No."

"Smoke! Talk to me, man? This is so not you, you're worrying me!"

He heard Laura coming out onto the deck. "I've got to go. We will talk soon, okay?"

"Is she with you now?"

"Yes. Not that it's any of your business."

She was coming around the partition.

Jack sounded serious now. "Talk to her, Smoke. Get her to talk to you."

"See ya, Jack."

He hung up as Laura came in. She arched an eyebrow. "Jack?"

He nodded.

"At least he waited 'til afterwards this time!"

He let out a short laugh. "Yeah, listen, Laura. About that...." What could he say? How could he explain to her?

"That was last weekend," she said. "This is this weekend. You just invited me to dinner. I just canceled my plans so I could accept. Clean slate, right?"

Wow! That was easy. "Thanks." No point going there if she didn't want to. They had the evening ahead of them. Why spoil it by getting into heavy stuff? He grinned and patted the sofa beside him. "Sounds good to me. Clean slate it is." As she sat down and he closed his arms around her, Jack's voice echoed in his mind. Talk to her, Smoke. Get her to talk to you.

Right now, all he wanted to do was hold her. He raked his fingers through her hair, tipping her head back as he lowered his lips to her. She tasted so damned good. Her kiss was so sweet, intoxicating. Soon they were lying on the sofa, legs entwined, bodies pressed together. Lips telling each other everything, without any need for words. His mind vaguely registered that she could only mean trouble. But trouble had never tasted so good.

~ ~ ~

She smiled as he handed her a glass of wine. "Are you going to make me dinner, or are you just planning on getting me drunk and taking advantage of me again?"

They'd made out on the sofa like teenagers until his need to have her again had become too much. He'd broken away, suggested a drink. He wanted her badly, but they had the whole night. He didn't want this to be all about sex. It wasn't, for him—as strange as that felt. He needed to know that it wasn't for her either. He met her gaze. "I'm not making you dinner."

She laughed. "So, just taking advantage of me, then? That's fine, as long as I know."

He took her glass from her and set it down. Leaning back against the counter, he drew her to him so she was standing between his legs. "Remember I told you I will never push you around? I need you to know I will never take advantage of you either, in any way."

She put her hands on his shoulders and planted a kiss on his lips. "Thank you, Smoke, but let's keep it light can we?"

Jesus! Maybe she was only in it for the sex—and he was the one going all heavy on her! What was she doing to him? He recovered quickly and squeezed her ass, playfully. "Okay, but I'm still not making you dinner."

A look of...something—what, panic, horror?—crossed her face. "You're not expecting me to make you dinner?"

"I am not. I thought we could order from that Italian place. They deliver."

"Oh, great." She was smiling again, but he wondered why she'd reacted like that.

~ ~ ~

They sat out at the table on the deck. The setting sun had turned the sky and the lake red and gold while they'd eaten. The food had been amazing. Giuseppe's had a wonderful menu once you got past all those pages of pizza.

Smoke went inside and returned with the Tiramisu, more wine and some candles. He lit the candles and refilled her glass.

She smiled at him. "Is this one of your standard moves? Do you do this with all the girls?" she teased.

"I do. I do it with every single girl I bring home."

She covered the disappointment quickly, but he saw it before her smile was back in place. Good! He was getting to her. He was going into all kinds of dangerous territory for her—he needed to know he wasn't going alone.

"You must go through a lot of candles."

"You'd be surprised."

She shook her head. "I doubt it."

Yep, definitely getting to her. She didn't like it. He didn't want to be an asshole about it though.

"Do you want to know how many candles I've used?"

She laughed, but it sounded too brittle. "You keep count? What do you do, buy them in bulk?"

He shook his head. "I have used a sum total of three."

She looked at the three candles on the table, then back up at him. "Three each time, right?"

He shook his head again and reached for her hand—what was it about her that made him do that? He'd never been a hand holder, even with.... Laura's long slender fingers closed around his, reminding him of the very first time they'd met. Maybe that was it? She was looking at him, bringing him back to the moment, waiting for him to answer. "No. Three ever. I've never brought anyone home before."

She laughed. "Now I do feel special. Don't worry, you haven't been here long. I'm sure you'll put up some good numbers soon."

He dug a spoon in the Tiramisu and brought it to her lips. She smiled and licked it seductively before taking it. Jesus! She was still playing with him! If her mouth was as talented as it seemed to be, she could win this game every time! He watched, transfixed, as he slid the spoon out of her mouth.

Damn, Smoke! Focus!

"I don't mean just here, Laura. I have never brought a woman home. Anywhere."

She couldn't speak with her mouth full, but her eyes widened in shock.

"Apparently you are special." He watched her swallow. "I keep breaking my own rules for you."

"Why?" she whispered.

He shook his head. "I'll tell you when I figure it out."

Chapter Ten

Smoke watched Laura step outside. She was so damned hot! Her hair was still damp from the shower—that had been fun. She was wearing one of his T-shirts and nothing else.

"Are you going to let me go next door now and get some clothes?" She put her hands on her hips and gave him that sexy smile.

She'd said she was going to get some earlier, but he'd blocked the bedroom door with his body—that's how they'd ended up in the shower.

"Nope." He grinned. "I made us some coffee. Come join me."

She took a step towards her side of the deck. "You can't stop me," she teased.

He was up from the table. "We both know I can...and I will!" he added, as she made a break for it.

He caught her easily. Closing his arms around her waist and lifting her off her feet. She beat her hands against his chest. "Put me down, you big Neanderthal!"

He laughed and went to the sofa, keeping hold of her so that when he sat she was straddling his lap. He was getting hard again. How did she do it to him? She'd ridden him hard before they got out of bed. He'd taken her against the wall in the shower not half an hour ago and now he wanted her again. He just could not get enough of her!

"I'll let you go soon," he said and planted a kiss on her lips. "Have coffee with me first, though?"

She nodded and wrapped her arms around his neck, planting a sweet little kiss on the end of his nose, making him smile. "Okay. Are you working today?"

He felt himself tense. He wasn't, but he didn't want to get into this one.

She took his silence as affirmation and planted another little kiss on his forehead. "Then we'd better make the most of the time we have. What time do you have to leave? Is it Jack?"

He felt the tension slip away. That wasn't the reaction he'd feared. No sulking, no pouting, no telling him it was the weekend and he shouldn't be working. He smiled. "I don't know yet. It's not Jack. The only flight on my schedule today is taking this hot chick back to San Francisco."

Laura frowned, "I thought she was doing a one way car rental."

"No. That got canceled. See, now she has her own private pilot at her disposal. So I'm just waiting for her to tell me what time. I'm hoping it won't be till tonight though."

Damn! That smile was making him harder.

"Oh. I see. Do you think she has plans here for today?" She arched an eyebrow.

Another game, huh? Well, he'd win this one. "Maybe. I understand she's met a guy here. She really likes him. She wants to spend the day with him and...she's hoping to get into his pants again before she has to leave."

She threw her head back and laughed.

Man, he loved it when she did that. It was such a carefree sound. But. Was she laughing at him? Suddenly he felt like she might be. What was he doing? He'd told her she didn't like to make herself vulnerable. Truth was, neither did he. "But, I could be wrong."

She tightened her arms around his neck and kissed him long and deep. The way her body pressed against his gave him all the reassurance he hadn't known he was so desperate for. When she finally broke away she smiled down at him. "You're not wrong. She does really like him. She would love to spend the day with him—and get into his pants again later. She's just not sure how all this is going to work. She's not used to making plans with a guy." She planted a little kiss on his lips. "And I don't think he is either."

Wow! That was laying it out there. Maybe he should do the same. "Yeah, I heard he's not too good at planning when it comes to women. Prefers to fly by the seat of his pants."

She nodded.

"But something's going on with him. I know he's hoping she'll spend the day with him. And sometimes he gets a crazy idea in his mind and he even wants to plan ahead."

"He does?" she raised an eyebrow.

"Yeah, I heard he wants to ask her if she'll be his date to the Phoenix fundraiser, but he doesn't know if he should. She might hate the idea."

Her smile was back. "She might love the idea! I think he should ask her."

A little rush of happiness settled in his chest. "I think he just did." She looked so happy it made him a little uneasy. "Maybe she should think about it before she says yes. I mean she hardly knows him. I hear he has a pretty bad rep when it comes to women. He's a bit of heart breaker, you know. Loves 'em and leaves 'em."

She smiled. "She already knows he has this huge ego. And she's figured out he has some demons in his past, she doesn't mind that. She has some too. She's prepared to take a chance. Isn't there some quote about how every saint has a past and every sinner has a future?"

"Oscar Wilde." He needed her to know the score, but wasn't willing to get into the heavy stuff, so he simply said, "I'm no saint, Laura."

She searched his face. Her eyes held a hundred questions, but she let it go with a laugh. "Then that must mean you have a future. And besides, I already told you. I'm no angel. So. You're taking me to the fundraiser. Subject closed." She climbed out of his lap and picked up her coffee. "What do you want to do today?"

He let it go too. He'd given her fair warning. "We have a few options. There are a couple of houses I was going to go look at today. You could come, if you like. Or we could go fly. I'm going to start instructing again, so I'll need to take one of the Cessnas up and get the feel for it. We could take a hike. Or...he put a hand on her thigh, we could just hang here. Whatever you like." He was finding it hard to believe, but he really didn't care what they did. As long as they did it together. If she weren't around, he'd go fly, no question about it, but she was.

"You're seriously thinking about buying a house here?"

He nodded. "The guys are making this their permanent base, so it will be mine, too. Plus, I've got a few plans in the pipeline with Jason and Rochelle at the airport."

She raised an eyebrow.

"Like I said, instructing and maybe taking on some other flight duties too. We'll have to see how it pans out. Even if I don't stick around here, I could always rent it out." That was what he kept telling himself. Property here wouldn't be difficult to rent. He'd already talked to Ben about it.

"I'd love to go looking at houses, if you don't mind me tagging along."

He couldn't resist. "I thought you weren't a tag along kind of girl?"

She looked at him from under lowered lashes. "You're not the only one breaking your own rules here, Captain Hamilton."

~ ~ ~

"Do they let you use this the whole time you're here?"

They were riding up the Eastern shore of the lake in the airport pickup. "They shouldn't. Most FBOs have a crew car. It's like a courtesy car for the pilots. On the busier fields you can use it for maybe a couple of hours, but out here there's not much call for it. So I use it. I am going to buy something though, now that I'm based here." He glanced across at her with a wicked smile. "Though Rochelle says I don't need to. She's happy to let me use this and she'll call if she needs me back."

Laura felt the heat in her cheeks. She had actually admitted to him that she'd been jealous of Rochelle! And now he was teasing her about it! Two could play that game. "Well, if you do need to go see her, you could always drop me off at Michael's on the way."

"Touché, lady, but I think that game is over. Rochelle is crazy about her husband and she's not my type anyway. And Michael? He's a good guy, I like him, but I think he must be blind, stupid or both."

"What do you mean?"

"He walked away from you to leave the way open for me. I would never have done that."

Wow! Smoke being open? They were still playing with each other, but the game had changed. Everything had more meaning now. Every jibe was loaded with a question, or laced with an answer. They were feeling each other out, but she wasn't sure what for. "Maybe he's just smarter than you and he knows how to stay out of trouble. Didn't you ever think of that?"

He glanced across at her. "All the time, lady. All the time."

He turned off the main road and headed up into the foothills. In just a few minutes they rounded a bend to see the cutest little house. It had a white picket fence around a flower garden and a front porch complete with swing. It was a two story, painted white with neat dark green shutters around the windows.

"Oh, Smoke! This is lovely!"

He smiled as he parked in the driveway at the back then came around to open her door.

"Are we meeting a realtor?" she asked.

"No, the place is empty. Has been all summer, apparently. The key is in a lock box".

He led her to the back door and tapped a number into the lock box that hung on the handle. The door opened into a big bright modern kitchen. It was filled with white cabinets and black appliances. Big windows looked out onto an orchard at the back of the house and an area with raised garden beds.

She looked at him and laughed. "I know you said you're from the Central Valley, but it's hard to picture you as a farm boy. I don't see you growing veggies out there."

"The Central Valley? What the hell makes you think that?" He seemed irritated.

"Sorry. I thought that was where you meant when you said you grew up in the valley."

He shook his head. "Napa Valley. Come on, let's take a look around."

She followed him through the dining room and into the living room. She gasped and looked at him, all her questions about Napa forgotten. He was grinning happily.

"Oh, my God, Smoke!" A wall of windows framed a magnificent view of the lake. "What an amazing view! I'll be honest, I wondered why you wanted to look at property up here and not down on the water. Now I get it! It's fantastic!"

"I like the water, but I'd rather be up high, see further. And this," he nodded through the window, "is why."

"Is that what you like so much about flying?"

"I suppose so. It's more than that, though. When you're up in the skies, you can see so much more of the world than when you're down in it, and you're not obliged to be a part of it. Or shackled to it either. At the same time it's like there is freedom and responsibility all rolled into one. You're responsible for your passengers, you brought them along and you need to make sure that you get them safely where they're going." He gave her an odd look. "You'll probably think it's my huge ego, but when I'm flying I'm responsible for their lives. I don't take that responsibility lightly."

That was an odd thing to say. She'd never thought about it like that before. "So, that's why your job comes before everything else, right?"

His face was set, lips pressed together, he nodded without looking at her. "Pretty much."

Why would he get pissy about that? She thought it was pretty cool and gave her new respect for him. Whatever his problem might be, she pressed on regardless, she was curious. "I imagine it must be weird when you're not flying?"

He raised an eyebrow, still staring out at the view, looking irritated—or something.

"Well, up in the air it's all in your hands. I'd never thought of it before, but it is isn't it? All the responsibility, all the decisions, all the lives, everything. Once you're back on the ground it's back to normal, right? I can see why you'd rather be flying than anything else."

He nodded, looking cautious now. He seemed to think it over before he spoke. "I love my job. It's not what I do, it's who I am."

"It suits you," she said with a smile. It seemed they were having two conversations with only one set of words. He was making some point that she didn't understand. "Can we explore the rest of the house?" she asked, wanting to lighten the mood, and also genuinely wanting to look around too. It was a lovely place, not too big, not too small, bright and airy with all the huge windows, but still cozy and warm feeling. Not waiting for him to answer, she wandered out into the hallway and headed up stairs.

~ ~ ~

"What do you think?" asked Smoke. They were sitting on the swing on the front porch, looking out at the fabulous view after touring the whole house, the grounds, and the outbuildings.

She grinned at him. "I don't think you should buy it."

He smiled through pursed lips. "And why's that?"

"Because...." She looked around as if seeking some flaw to the place. "Because it's got a picket fence, and you're not a picket fence kind of guy?"

"I could tear it down."

She looked at him, horrified.

He laughed, "Or maybe I could learn to be a picket fence kind of guy."

Oh, she doubted that!

"What else. Why don't you think it's for me?"

"Because, it's so perfect, I want it! And, it's far too cute to be a guy's house. And that little workshop by the orchard? I could turn that into my ideal workroom." The idea had been growing in her mind the whole time they were looking around. It was a ridiculous idea, but it felt so right. She could buy the place if she sold the store. She could escape San Francisco, have her own little workplace and a great group of friends all around her.

Smoke was staring at her. "You're kidding me, right? You moving out here is even crazier than me doing it!"

She nodded. "I know, but sometimes the crazy stuff makes the most sense." She laughed. "So be warned, we may need to get into a bidding war over this place. I love it!"

"Sorry, lady, but I love it too. Let's go see the other two, shall we? See if we can find one for you, because this one's mine."

She nodded, feeling thoroughly disappointed. She really could see herself buying this place, living here. But she could hardly argue if Smoke wanted it. She wouldn't even know it existed if it weren't for him.

"Okay, maybe you'll like one of the others better and I can have this one?"

He laughed. "I doubt it, but let's go see."

As they drove away, Laura watched in the mirror until they turned the corner and the house vanished from sight. It was such a lovely place. But still. It was just a crazy idea. She needed to drop it, whether Smoke wanted to buy it or not. What the hell made her want to move up here anyway? She looked over at him as he pulled the truck out, back onto the main road. There was her answer—he made her want to move here. And out of all the crazy ideas, that one had to be the craziest yet! There had to be something wrong with her head. She'd spent most of her life running from guys who wanted to pin her down. Now she'd met one who she knew would run— or more likely fly—a million miles rather than be pinned down himself, and she was thinking about moving her whole life to be closer to him? That really was crazy!

She had to keep reminding herself that she was probably only so attracted to him because he would never try to hold her

down. She couldn't help the smile that came at the thought—
except in bed!

"What are you smirking at?" he asked. "I hope you're not
scheming up ways to buy my house out from under me?"

She laughed, "It's not your house yet!"

~ ~ ~

"Are you sure you don't want to stay till morning?" asked
Smoke. "I could have you there by eight, or earlier if you
need?"

She shook her head and picked up her bag. She wanted
nothing more than to spend another night with him. And that
was exactly why she had to leave. "I can't, Smoke."

He nodded and took her bag from her hand. "We'd best get
going, then."

When they got to the airport, he drove up to the gates and
swiped his pass. Once the gates had rolled back into place
behind the truck, he drove out towards the hangars. Laura was
relieved not to have to face Rochelle. She still felt a little
embarrassed that she'd jumped to conclusions.

"Are you okay over there?"

She nodded. She was just sad to be leaving, and she wasn't
going to say that out loud.

"Want to watch me pre-flight?" he asked before he got out of
the truck.

She looked up at him, surprised. "I'd love to, except I don't
know what it means."

He laughed. "It means we're going to check old Papa Charlie
outside and in to make sure he's ready to fly."

"He?" she asked with a laugh.

"Yep," Smoke patted the side of the plane. "He's my old
buddy."

"Boys and their toys! How long have the guys had it?"

He frowned. "They've been leasing him for a few years now."

"Oh, I thought they owned it?"

"No, they just lease. Come on, I'll show you how to pre-flight, then maybe next time you can help me."

Her breath caught in her chest—next time? Oh, she liked that idea.

He was looking at her intently. "If you want to?"

His face relaxed when she smiled. "I'd love to."

~ ~ ~

Once they were up in the air, Smoke turned to her. "You're quiet, are you okay?"

"I'm fine," she said, but frowned when she couldn't hear herself.

He laughed and reached over to bring the mic on her headset down to her mouth. "Try again."

"Oh, thanks. I didn't think of that. I'm fine. I'm just trying to keep quiet and not distract you. You've got so much going on." And it was such a turn on for some reason, to watch him fly the plane—to watch his capable hands move over the instruments, listen to him talk to Air Traffic Control. He was in his element and she wanted to enjoy watching him, not disturb him.

He smiled, that soft smile that made her pulse race. "Thanks. You really mean that don't you?"

She nodded. Of course she did—why would she not?

His smile spread, then the controller's voice came through her headset, giving him a new heading. He adjusted course and then smiled at her again. As she smiled back, a terrible thought crossed her mind....

She was falling for him!

~ ~ ~

Smoke shut down the engines and took his headset off. Laura took her own off and tried to unbuckle her seat belt. He smiled as he watched, letting her struggle. This was another first—letting a woman he was seeing fly up front with him. He just didn't do that. Hell, he hadn't let very many stick around long enough to fly with him at all. But this had been good. He'd enjoyed her being there. He laughed as she yanked at the shoulder strap.

"How the hell do I get out of here?" she asked, frustrated.

He got up and leaned over her. "You can't until I let you." He'd meant it as a joke, but the look of panic on her face threw him. He undid the buckle quickly. "Just kidding. You do it like this." He slid the clip in and out to show her. "See, you can escape any time you like."

She met his gaze. "Thanks. That's good to know."

He stepped through to the cabin and opened the door to let the steps down, wondering why the relief in her voice bothered him so much.

The lineman met them with the golf cart.

"Evening, Captain Hamilton, Do you need any fuel or a tie down?"

"No, thanks. It's just a quick turnaround tonight."

The guy nodded and waited while they climbed on the cart.

Inside the FBO Smoke felt uncomfortable. This should be the point where he made himself scarce. The point where he would normally kiss the girl then, literally and figuratively, fly off into the sunset. But with Laura, nothing was going as it normally would. And when it came to her, he seemed to be incapable of doing what his better judgment told him he should.

"Well, I guess this is it, then," she said, with a smile that didn't quite reach her eyes. "Call me if you want to go to the fundraiser together." She reached to take her bag from him.

He snatched it away and held it behind his back with a laugh. "At least let me bring it to the car for you?"

She nodded.

He snaked an arm around her waist as they walked across the parking lot. When they reached her car he backed her up against it and dropped the bag. Taking her face between his hands, he kissed her. Her arms came up around his neck and he felt her relax, her body melting, yielding to his own in what felt like an invitation. Eventually he lifted his head and looked into her eyes. They were full of a longing that pulled at him. Touching something deep inside him, something that felt like it might be his heart.

He rested his forehead against hers. "I can't make myself walk away, Laura."

"Then don't," she whispered. "Stay with me."

He couldn't help the smile that spread across his face.

Chapter Eleven

Laura pulled up outside her apartment. "Here we are." She looked nervous now. Smoke felt it too. This was weird. He'd felt weird going back into the airport, getting the overnight bag that he kept in the plane, telling the guys at the FBO that he did need a tie down for the night after all. Suffering the knowing looks—he and Laura had put on quite a show, kissing in the parking lot like that. But weird or not, nervous or not, he was still glad he was here. He needed to know that she was.

"Are you sure about this?"

She nodded, then seemed to relax a little as she smiled. "It's just that I don't know what game we're playing any more, Smoke. But I don't want to stop."

They really were on the same page then. He touched her cheek. "I'm right there with you, lady."

He looked around the apartment. It was very Laura. It was classy, stylish, with touches of humor here and there. The artwork was eclectic to say the least. There was a bright, oriental rug thrown over the back of the sofa, an ornate chandelier hung over a super modern dining table. Smoke loved it. "Nice place," he said as he followed her through to the kitchen.

"Thank you. It's not much, but it's mine. I've only been here a year, but it's all me. It's like my little sanctuary, you know?"

He nodded, "I feel honored to be invited in, then."

The pink stains appeared on her cheeks. "Yeah." She looked away. "Would you like a glass of wine?"

"I'd love one."

"Why don't you choose?" She pointed to the wine rack. "I just need to check for messages." She went through the door to what looked like an office.

Smoke checked out the bottles. Jesus! Every single one of them was from the same winery. Well it was hardly a winery any more. It was a huge commercial operation that mass-produced for the national and international markets. He rolled his eyes—no matter how hard he tried, it seemed he could never get away. He decided on a red blend. It wasn't bad—he should know. He uncorked the bottle and found the glasses. As he poured, she came back into the kitchen with a delighted smile on her face.

"They want me in London a week from tomorrow!"

He couldn't help but smile at her excitement. "That's great." He handed her a glass. "We should drink to your new ventures."

"And to yours." She raised her glass. "It seems we've both got some new adventures on the horizon."

He was unsettled by the thought that her adventures would be taking her overseas while his would potentially be making his world smaller. He was even more unsettled by the realization that he wouldn't mind a smaller world, if she was going to be a part of it. "Would you really consider buying that first place we saw today?" Where the hell had that question come from?

She seemed as surprised by it as he was himself. "I...I don't know. I mean, if you don't want it, then...maybe. If I sell the store here, I could. I'll have a store at Four Mile when it's built.

And by the looks of it I'll be able to travel some, soon. I already told you, I've had enough of San Francisco. It would be kind of cool to live in Summer Lake, be in a small town with friends and family around, but still be able to escape for work. And it is such a darling little house."

He could see her enthusiasm building as she spoke, but then she stopped. "But you loved it too. And, honestly? I'm scared that you are part of the appeal of moving there, and that's not right."

Damn! She really was laying it out there, and even stranger was that he didn't want to run. He wanted to persuade her that it was a good idea!

"Why is it not right?"

She gave a short laugh. "Because given both of our track records, it probably won't seem so appealing in a few weeks, will it?"

"It might." Had he really just said that?

"Smoke, look at us. Neither of us is exactly a good long term prospect, are we?"

"Okay, so we've both been shaped by our past." He smiled. "We've both learned to avoid anything heavy. But there's no denying we've got something going on between us. Something that feels really, really good. So good I don't know how it could ever be a bad idea."

He put his glass down and pulled her to him. She looked stunned. Smoke felt stunned, but the words were out and he didn't regret them. As her arms came up around his neck and he tasted her sweet lips, slid his tongue into her mouth and crushed her to his chest, he knew he wouldn't take those words back even if he could. They were too true.

When that kiss finally ended, she still looked stunned. "Do you really mean that?" she asked, her voice barely a whisper.

He ran his fingers down her cheek. "I do. I have no idea what we're going to do about it, but I know I'd like for us to try to do something." He held her closer. "If you feel the same?" She nodded. "I do."

He felt himself relax. "Then that'll do for starters." He slid a hand down her back 'til it closed around her ass as he pushed his hips against her. He smiled at the moan that escaped her lips. "We should probably start with the one thing we already know we're seriously good at.

She smiled and, taking his hand, led him through to the bedroom. He watched her lift her T-shirt over her head and hurried to remove his own shirt in time to see her bra come off and those great little breasts peek out at him. Her nipples seemed to be begging for his hands on them. Not wanting to keep them waiting, he got rid of the rest of his clothes. She was still unfastening her jeans, so he gladly helped her. He had her out of them and naked underneath him in seconds.

He dropped his head and teased her nipples with his tongue and teeth until they stood erect and she was moaning. His hand slid its way down over her smooth skin until he found her heat. She was soaking already. To his surprise, she caught his hand and brought it up over her head, holding it to the pillow. He smiled, understanding what she wanted. He brought her other hand up and laced his fingers through hers, pinning one hand on either side of her face.

"Take me, Smoke. Make me yours."

Jesus! The effect those words had on him! As he spread her legs, she arched up to him, her body begging him, the same as her words and with the same effect. He filled her with one deep thrust. Damn, she felt so good, so hot and tight—and so damned wet for him. He slowly circled his hips. This time was different. She wanted to be his? He'd make her his alright. This

time there would be no doubt whose she was—or whose he
was either.

He brought her hands up so he could trap them both in one of
his and brought his free hand down between their bodies.
Matching the movement of his hips, he worked the little nub
that could give her so much pleasure. Once he had her
moaning and writhing, about to lose it, he took his hand away.
He moved slowly inside her now. Keeping her right at the
edge, but not allowing her to slip over and come.

"Smoke, please?" her voice was so full of need, he almost lost
it himself.

He focused on her breast, tormenting her, rolling and twisting
her nipple hard enough that he could feel her response
tightening around him. He was so close to the edge himself
that one deep thrust would have them both screaming. But not
yet. He watched the ecstasy and the anguish on her face. She
thrust her hips desperately, her head thrashing from side to
side as she moaned.

"Do I feel good, Laura?" he breathed.

She met his eyes and nodded rapidly.

"Good enough that you want to be mine?"

She nodded again as he kept the torment going, moving in and
out of her so slowly.

"Good enough that you'll believe me this time? Last time you
thought it was just words, didn't you?"

Her eyes widened. "Yes!" Her body arched up, begging him to
finish her, finally giving it up to him. He couldn't hold back
anymore if he'd wanted to. He thrust deep inside her body.

"You. Are. Mine." He gave it up to her, letting himself soar
away, taking her with him. As she screamed his name, he
gasped hers on a ragged breath. He released her hands. Her
arms and legs came up around him, clinging to him tightly as
her orgasm shook her and intensified his own. She was so

damned responsive. Drawing him deeper as his need pumped inside her, their bodies straining as one.

He finally lay still, loving the feel of her body still quivering underneath him. Right where she belonged. His lips curved up into a smile. The thought didn't even scare him; she did belong right there, her arms and legs open for him, because she was his. He buried his face in her neck and grazed his teeth over her delicate skin. She shivered, sending an aftershock through him as she tightened in response. Damn! He would never get enough of this woman. He brought his lips up to her ear and brushed them over it as he whispered. "Mine."

Her body signaled its agreement, trembling as her arms, her legs, and everything else tightened around him.

~ ~ ~

Laura gasped. His lips on her ear sent shock waves through her, drawing out the last ripples of what felt like 'the orgasm that refused to end'. She still had her arms and legs wrapped tightly around him.

"What are you, lady?" he whispered.

"Screwed, well and truly screwed," she mumbled. Even her voice was weak after that.

He chuckled, the sound rumbling through his chest and into hers before he propped himself up on his elbows to smile down at her.

"Okay, so I'll rephrase. Whose are you?" His eyes were serious. He really meant it then?

She stared at him, not sure what to do with this. She wasn't exactly running scared, or even feeling trapped. But still, she didn't know what to do with it.

He rocked his hips. God! He couldn't be ready to go again just yet?

His smile told her he wasn't. "If you don't know the answer, we'll have to start again at the beginning until you do. You're mine, Laura. All mine. Only mine."

Part of her loved the idea, part of her felt queasy. "What does that even mean, Smoke?"

His face darkened, surprising her. "I think it probably means I'm just a jealous, possessive jerk." He rolled off her and lay on his back, staring at the ceiling. "It means I don't want to let you go." He turned his head to look at her. "But I don't know how to let you in." The bed bounced, he stood up so quickly. "I should just go."

Laura's stomach tied itself in a knot. She scrambled to the edge of the bed and grabbed his hand. "Don't! Don't you dare!"

He looked down at her, face set and angry.

She pressed on. "No way are you leaving. That's the coward's way out. You just laid yourself open to me, and now you're scared. Well, guess what, Smoke. I'm scared too. I'm scared of the way you make me feel. I'm scared of what your body does to mine. I'm scared to be yours when I've never allowed anyone to get that close. But what scares me the most is the thought of you walking out that door. Because we both know that if you do, that's it. We'll both run scared. We'll put our walls back up, and there will be no letting them down again."

He stared at her for a long moment, his whole body rigid with tension, fighting with himself. Stay or go? She held her breath as she watched the struggle on his face. After what felt like forever his face relaxed. The corner of his mouth lifted in the tiniest smile and he dropped back down on the bed. He closed both arms around her. She could feel his heart thundering in his chest.

"You're right. I admit it. I am scared. I'm scared shitless. I feel like I'm exposing my soul to you, and giving you everything you need to destroy me. That scares me more than you can know. But the thought of this...." He squeezed her tight. "Of you and me, ending now. That scares me a whole lot more." His face looked pained. "I want to keep seeing you. See where this goes, but part of me knows...I can't give you what you want. Be what you need. You're right, if I walk away I am being a coward. But if I stay, maybe I'm being a selfish bastard and you just don't know it yet."

Laura held him tight, relieved he was still here, but afraid of what he might mean. "Smoke, I don't think I can give you what you want, be what you need either. I don't know where we can even go with this. It would be easier, safer for me to run and never look back." She looked deep into his troubled gray eyes. "But a part of me knows that if I did, I would spend the rest of my life looking back, always wondering, never knowing. I don't want to do that. I am scared, but I trust you, I believe you trust me. As long as we have that we'll do okay. So, let's just see where this goes, can we?"

He nodded. Then his hands were in her hair, his mouth was on hers, and she was lost. She couldn't know where they were going, but his kiss told her they were going somewhere. Together.

Chapter Twelve

Smoke sat in the lobby bar waiting for Pete. It had been a while since they'd done this. It seemed whenever he flew Pete these days, Holly was along with him. This was like old times, getting together for dinner after Pete's meetings. Except it wasn't like old times at all. Dinner used to be followed by hitting the bars, checking out the ladies. In his case, going home with one more often than not. Now he had no interest. There was a blonde in a suit at the end of the bar who'd been trying to catch his eye since he came in. Not so long ago he'd have been over there by now, setting up the rest of his night. Tonight though, she barely registered. His radar for hot, available women was too finely tuned to not notice her—or the signals she was sending loud and clear—but that was it. He didn't want a blonde in Seattle, he wanted a dark-haired, blue-eyed beauty in San Francisco.

She'd taken him back to the airport early this morning. Even then he hadn't wanted to leave her. For the first time in his life he'd considered canceling a flight to be with a woman. Pete would have been pissed, but he'd almost done it. She'd insisted she had to get to work though. That they'd see each other soon, even though they hadn't figured out when 'soon' would be. As he'd kissed her up against her car in the parking lot, she'd clung to him. He'd clung to her, not letting her go until their kisses had left him with only two choices: leave, or get her into the back seat of her car and out of her dress. It had taken every last shred of self-discipline, but he'd left. All he could think about now was when he could see her again. He dug his phone out of his pocket and tapped out a text.

Come stay with me this weekend?

She wouldn't say no to that, would she?

I can't. :(By the time I get there I'd have to leave.

Flying to London Sun night.

He shook his head. He hadn't meant for her to drive.

I'll come get you in Papa Charlie.

Have you back to SFO in time for your flight.

He stared at his phone, waiting.

I'm not Dan! I can't afford jet fuel!

Oh. Yeah. He hadn't thought of that. Well, if they were going to do this, she needed to know.

I've got it. My plane. My fuel :0)

This should be interesting. It took her longer to reply this time.

YOUR plane??? WTF?

He laughed out loud.

I told you the guys just lease him. No more excuses.

Be at the airport 5pm Fri, lady. If you're not there I'll have

to come find you!

This time she was quicker.

I think I like the come find me option – sounds like fun :)

Good. No interrogation about Papa Charlie.

Either way. I'll have you Friday.

He hit send and waited a couple of seconds.

SEE you – I meant I'll see you Friday – honest :0)

She came right back.

I'll look fwd to it – and to SEEing you too.

Smoke spotted Pete through the window. He was handing his keys to the valet. He'd be here in a second, but Smoke couldn't resist sending one last one.

> *I'll come find you. I'll need to SEE you before we can go anywhere!*

He stared at the screen a few more seconds as Pete came sauntering into the bar and pulled up a stool beside him.

"S'up partner. How's it going?"

Smoke grinned. "Just great. How was your day, dear?"

Pete laughed. "You're not going to let me off the hook for saying I don't want to lose you, right?"

Smoke laughed. "Too right. It gave me the warm and fuzzies to know how much you love me."

Pete rolled his eyes. "Well it's true! I need you. I can't live my life without you."

Smoke's phone beeped.

> *Can't wait to SEE you too xx*

He laughed and put it back in his pocket.

Pete was smirking at him. "It's not like you to give 'em your number."

Smoke scowled at him. "What makes you think that was a woman?"

Pete laughed. "The goofy grin! Though I must admit I'm more used to seeing it on Jack's face than yours. In fact.... Who the hell was that? I've never seen that look on your face, Hamilton! What's going on?"

Smoke shrugged. "Nothing."

Pete's lips quirked up in that weird little smile of his. Damn! He wasn't going to let it go. "It was Laura, wasn't it?"

Smoke shrugged again.

"Man! We're dropping like flies since we started moving to Summer Lake! Jack and Em, me and Holly, Dan and Missy.

And now you? I never thought I'd see the day that Captain Cole Hamilton got over his shit and fell for a woman again." Smoke scowled at him. There was no point denying it, but he wasn't sure he wanted to talk about it either. "I think I am falling for a woman, Pete. But I'm a long way from being over my shit."

Pete nodded. "Well if the woman you're falling for is Laura, you'd better get over it in a hurry. I've heard Jack go on about her for years, and I'll tell you two things. First, she's as much of a flight risk as you are—and I don't say that lightly. Second, Jack sees her as his little sister, and you know what he's like."

Smoke nodded. "I've already talked to Jack."

Pete looked taken aback. "Damn. You must have it bad."

"I do." He was puzzled though, he had to ask what Pete knew, to call her a flight risk. "What do you know of her story?"

"Only what Jack's said over the last couple of years."

Smoke raised his eyebrows, waiting for more.

"Don't you think you should be asking her?"

"Yeah, I do. But unfortunately I'm having dinner with you, not her. So tell me what you know."

"You might want to work on your charm and persuasion skills?"

"I've got charm and persuasion down to a fine art. I just know I don't need 'em on you, Hemming. I already know you don't want to lose me, so you'll give me what I want, however I ask for it!"

"Wow! I'm glad I'm not a woman," said Pete with a laugh. "I think they'd either be slapping your face or dropping their panties at that one."

Smoke smiled though pursed lips. "It's usually the latter, but that's beside the point. Get back on track and tell me what you know about Laura."

"She needed to get out of Texas a few years back, and Jack set her up in San Francisco. She was making her jewelry already. She's done pretty well for herself, opened a store, is building quite a reputation as one of the names to go to when the money crowd want something special made."

Smoke nodded. "I know that much. None of it makes her a flight risk, though. What else?"

Pete shrugged. "She was engaged to a guy in San Francisco. Nice guy. I met him a couple of times."

Smoke hated the way his heart pounded in his chest at the thought of her with another guy. He needed to think of him as an asshole, not a nice guy. Besides, he must be an asshole if he'd let Laura get away.

"For fuck's sake, Smoke! I said she was engaged. She's not anymore, so can you drop the murderous look?"

Smoke ran a hand over his eyes. "Sorry. Go on."

"Like I say, he is a nice guy. It was a big shock when she called it off. His family is old money, their engagement had made the society pages. You of all people know how that goes, right? She went into hiding for a while. Jack went and spent some time with her. Apparently she cracked under the pressure, the expectations. The guy, Dale, wanted her home, there for him. He's a rising star in city politics. His family had tried to draw her in, make her one of the 'ladies-who-lunch,' all that shit, you know? According to Jack she tried to roll with it for as long as she could, but in the end she freaked and ran."

Smoke stared out the window. He and Laura really were the same kind of animal. She'd run from being tied down just the same way he had. He should be glad to hear it. So why wasn't he?

"Earth to Smoke. You still with me?" Pete gave him a worried look.

"What?"

"Well, I'm thinking I probably just screwed up. All of that is for her to tell you, not me. But since I have told you, I'm wondering if you're going to talk to me."

Smoke shook his head. "Not tonight, I'm not. Do you want to go eat?"

Pete nodded. "But do you want to eat here? I'd just as soon have a burger and a beer at the bar than go sit in the restaurant. Much as I don't want to lose you, I don't think we need a romantic table for two overlooking the water, do we?"

Smoke smiled. "Nope. I'm a cheap date when it comes to you. Buy me a beer and tell me about Laura and I'm all yours."

"Come on," said Pete. "Talk to me. Spit it out. I haven't seen you look like this since...."

Smoke cut him off. "Don't even say it!"

Pete held up a hand. "Okay. Don't bite my head off. You just look like you need to talk."

"I do."

"So talk?"

Smoke stared into space again, until he realized he was staring in the direction of the woman at the end of the bar and she was smiling at him. He shook his head looked back at Pete. "I'll tell you one thing."

"About Laura or about Anabel?"

Smoke pressed his lips together to hold in the anger that still rose up every time he heard that name.

Pete raised his eyebrows. "Sorry partner, but you've not moved on 'til you can hear her name without wanting to punch someone. And there's no point talking about Laura until you have moved on."

Smoke fumed silently for a few moments. "What I was going to say is that I almost canceled our flight today."

"Why?"

"Because last night, when I took Laura back to San Francisco, I stayed with her. And this morning, I didn't want to leave."

"So much that you considered canceling our flight?"

"Yup. That much."

"Wow! Isn't that a good thing? You've never, ever done that, so what's the problem?"

"The problem is...Anabel—there I said her name out loud, happy now? And just so you know I am well and truly over it, I'll say it again. Anabel, for everything else she did to me, did me one big favor. She taught me that I am no freaking good for a woman. That in order to be what a woman wants, I'd have to give up on everything I want. You remember what she was like, all the times she wanted me to cancel flights, to give up the long haul, to put her first. Since her, I've done a good job of avoiding the whole issue. I refuse to give up who I am. But I like women, so I trade with them short term. I give them what they want, they give me what I want, physically, and I stay the hell away from anything more than that."

"But with Laura you want more than that?"

Smoke nodded. "I do."

"And what makes you think she wants you to be anything other than what you are? What makes you think she would want everything from you that Annabel wanted? Anabel didn't teach you what women want. She only taught you what one crazy-ass bitch wanted. The sooner you stop judging all women by her example, the better off you'll be. From what I know of her, Laura would run a mile from everything Anabel told you a woman needs. Hell, she did run from it. Think on that."

Smoke did think on it as he sipped his beer.

"You know it's her you should be talking to, right."

He rolled his eyes at Pete. "You were the one that wanted me to talk! And like I said, she's not here and you are."

"So when are you seeing her again?"

"Weekend. Which reminds me. I'm taking the weekend off. If anyone needs to fly...tough."

Pete laughed. "Fair enough. I don't think anyone does, and if anything comes up we'll make other plans. I've wondered for a long time if you were going to end up the creepy old guy at the end of the bar, still hoping the uniform will be enough to attract the ladies. This is making me think you might not."

Smoke laughed out loud. "Thanks, Pete, and I thought you loved me!"

"I do. That's why I'm happy to see that you're finally ready to get over the past and build something healthy with a good woman. Now, if you'll just mend the bridges with your family, I'll know that you're really getting over it."

Smoke scowled at him. "I have started mending those bridges. I've been out there twice in the last couple of months and I'm going again soon."

"Good. Glad to hear it, and maybe soon you can take Laura to meet them, too."

"Fuck off, Hemming!"

"Okay. I think that is enough for one night." Pete raised his hand to the bartender. "Could we get a couple of menus? We're going to eat here."

Smoke blew out a big sigh and slapped Pete on the back. "Thanks, Pete."

Pete nodded. "Not a problem, old friend. When you meet the right one, she can prove that everything you think you know about women and relationships is completely wrong. That's what Holly did to me. It just took me way too long to see it. I think it's what Laura is about to do to you. If I can help you get there any quicker than I did, then I'm all in."

~ ~ ~

Laura looked up when Maria popped her head around the door to her workroom. "Sorry to disturb you, but there's someone out front to see you."

"Who is it?"

"She said she wanted to surprise you."

Laura frowned. She'd been really getting into these designs and had hoped to have a good run at it this afternoon. She wanted to have something good to show Colin next week. "Okay. I'll be right out." She checked herself in the mirror, yep she looked good. It bothered her that she still worried about Dale's family catching her unawares, finding her looking like the untamed Texas girl she really was, instead of the demure, well groomed fiancée they'd wanted for their boy. It could only be one of them. Who else would stop by for a surprise visit?

"Leanne!"

"Hey, Laura! I hope you don't mind a little surprise?"

"Mind? This is wonderful! How are you? What are you doing here?"

"I had to come over to see some clients and I realized I was only a couple of blocks from you, so I thought I'd come say hi. I haven't seen you for ages, and since Dan moved out to the boonies it's going to be down to us to keep in touch all by ourselves."

Laura smiled. Leanne had gone to college with Dan, and Laura adored her. In the beginning she'd hoped that Leanne and Dan would get together, but with time she'd realized that the two of them really were just good friends. "I'm so glad you made the first move. I've been meaning to call you ever since the party. I wish you'd been there, Lee. You would have been so proud of him! He made this whole big speech in front of everyone about how he knows what love is, and how much he loves Missy. How he's found his family, and his home, and she's his perfect. There wasn't a dry eye in the place! He totally shot

Olivia down in flames! And then he went down on one knee! Our Danny! With a whole crowd watching him!"

"Aww, bless him!" Leanne grinned. "I do wish I'd been there to see that. It was so cool to see him all starry-eyed, even while the bitch was trying to sell his business out from under him. He was too head-over-heels to even care. I swear he would have sold to Steven for peanuts if I hadn't ridden his ass so hard. The only way I got him to accept Corey's bid instead was to tell him to think what it could mean for the kid's future. What's his name? Scot?"

Laura laughed. "Yes, Scot. And you want to see them together. It's like he's got a little mini-me!"

Leanne laughed with her. "Now that I really do need to see. I can't imagine him even knowing what to say to a kid."

"Oh, you have to see them. They're so cute. They chatter away together, though of course no-one else has a clue what they're talking about, because it's all geek-speak."

"I really should get up there to visit them. I haven't even met Missy yet."

"Well, are you going to the Phoenix fundraiser?"

"I am. So I will meet her then. Oh, and...Dan is supposed to be setting me up with a guy from Summer Lake as a date too."

"Oh, my God! Who?"

"The good looking one, of course!"

Laura laughed. "You really do need to visit Summer Lake, Lee. The place is overrun with good looking men. It's like there's a magnet that draws hot men to the place and once they get there, they stay. So you'll have to be more specific. What's his name?"

"Ben."

"Yay!" Laura clasped her hands together. "Ben is gorgeous! Inside and out, he is such a good guy. Oh, Lee! You'll love him! I can't wait, now!"

Leanne grinned, "So you're going this year? Who's your date?"

Laura bit her lip. "Have you got time for a cup of coffee?"

"I do now. Come on. Save it 'til we get there. The look on your face says this may be a sit down story. Am I right, or am I right?"

Laura grinned and waved at Maria, who was with a customer on the other side of the store. Her designs could wait. Talking to Leanne would no doubt be much more productive.

~ ~ ~

They settled in to a booth in a coffee shop just around the corner from the store. "Okay, out with it." Leanne grinned at her. "Who are you going with? Your face was the perfect mix of fear and lust when I asked. And your description of the men in Summer Lake makes me think he's someone you met up there. So which one is he? Have I even heard of him?"

"Oh, Lee. You've seen him. You remember that time you picked me up at the airport after Jack's wedding?"

Leanne's eyes were wide. "Not the pilot?'

"Yes, the pilot!"

"Oh. My. God. Laura! He is smoking hot!"

Laura had to laugh. "Yes, he is. So much so, that's his name. Smoke!"

"I can see why! Damn girl!" Leanne's raunchy grin turned serious. "Be careful, he struck me as a predator."

Laura nodded. "He is."

"As long as you know. So, you're just taking him as arm candy and for the sex afterwards, right?"

Laura bit her lip.

"Don't look at me like that! He just wants into your panties! If you hadn't seen me pull up, he would have made a move on you right there in the airport that night. I could tell. But you ran out when you saw me. The way he watched you walk away? It was like watching a starving man have a feast snatched away from him before he got chance to stick his fork in!"

Laura started to giggle, remembering why she enjoyed Leanne's company so much. She had thought Smoke was going to kiss her that night, but she'd pulled her usual stunt and run as soon as she'd spotted Leanne's car.

Leanne wasn't laughing. "Do. Not. Fall for him! You know that type. You're smarter than that."

"I think I already am, Lee, and I think he's falling for me too."

"Laura! Don't give me that shit! That's what guys like that say to get you into bed, you know that!"

"It's not like that, Lee. Honestly."

"Jesus, Laura! Is that what he told you? That he's falling for you and his days of screwing around are over now he's met you?"

"No."

"Then what? What's he said that's gotten to you? Because you, my friend are smarter than this."

"Honestly, it's not like that. We've seen each other a couple of times now...."

"And how many of those times have you not had sex?"

Laura thought about it.

Leanne shook her head. "None of them, right? Every time you're with him, you screw like bunnies, don't you?"

Laura laughed. It was true. She hadn't ever seen him and not had sex with him. Well, apart from the time she'd seen him in town—and then he'd been walking arm in arm with another woman. A happily married woman, who was just a friend, she reminded herself quickly.

"Listen, I'm not judging, you know that. Damn, with his looks and that body? I'd be all over him myself given half a chance. All I'm saying is that he would probably be all over me too, and any other woman he sets his charm to. Enjoy the sex, but don't turn it into something it's not, okay?"

Laura nodded. Maybe Leanne was right? No. He couldn't have faked his struggle over whether to stay or go on Sunday night. Or so many other things. He'd no doubt been what Leanne thought he was, but he was genuine about whatever was going on between the two of them. She was convinced of it. But she knew she wouldn't be able to convince Leanne.

"Just don't get your heart broken. I'd hate that."

"So would I, but Lee I have to see where it goes. I can always run."

"Well, don't say I didn't warn you, and don't let this conversation stop you from coming to me for a shoulder to cry on when it all blows up in your face. I hope for your sake I'm wrong, but I don't think I am."

Laura smiled. "Thank you, I'll remember that." She just hoped she wouldn't need to.

Chapter Thirteen

As she checked her apartment one last time, Laura wondered again whether she should just wait here for Smoke to show up. She hadn't heard from him since their texts on Monday night. He'd said he would come get her. But that was just so they could have sex before they left, wasn't it? Not that she didn't want that, in fact she couldn't wait, but Leanne's certainty that that was all he was in it for had stuck with her all week. And as each day ended with no word from him, her own conviction had gotten a little shaky. The little seeds of doubt Leanne had planted in her mind were starting to take root. If she wanted to weed out those doubts, she could hardly do it by sitting around here waiting for him to come and take her to bed. She had everything packed and ready to go, everything for the weekend and everything for London next week, too. He'd said in his text that he'd have her back to the San Francisco airport in time for her flight on Sunday, so she was ready to go straight there.

She picked up her phone.

I'll be at the airport at 5.

Hopefully he'd see her text when he landed.

He must have landed already because by the time she'd put her bags in the back of the car her phone buzzed.

I thought I was coming to SEE you before we go?

Her heart sank a little at that. Was that really all this was
about? She needed to know.

I want to 'see' you. You can SEE any woman you want.

Do you want to 'see' me – or just SEE me?

She stood next to the car, waiting for his response to tell her
whether there was any point getting in.

I missed you. I want to 'see' you.

We can stop SEEING each other if u want?

But you are the only one I want to SEE.

She stared at her phone, wondering how, or if she should
respond. It buzzed again.

Come to the airport? Let's talk about it? Please?

That made her smile.

On my way.

~ ~ ~

Smoke sat on one of the benches outside the FBO, wondering
what was bothering her. He had been in a cab, on his way to
her place when he'd got her text. Twenty minutes ago he'd
been on his way to SEE her, he'd had a major hard-on, and
had thought he was about to put it to very good use. Now he
was sitting out here. He wasn't angry, he had no desire to turn
around and fly away. What he was feeling was concern. He was
concerned that something must have rattled her, and
concerned that she might have decided to run. Now that he
understood she was just as likely to do that as he had always
been, it made him nervous. He didn't want to do or say
anything that would make her feel trapped—make her feel the
need to escape from him. What Pete had told him had helped
him understand some of her reactions—and left him mystified
about others. He hadn't called her all week, even though he'd
had his phone in his hand ready to—several times a day, every
day. He'd thought it best to give her space; she'd call him if she

wanted to, but she hadn't. And now this. He shrugged, he'd find out soon enough.

He watched her Audi pull into the parking lot and his throat went dry. Such a strange reaction, but he was getting used to it. It couldn't be purely physical. He already knew she didn't want to have sex with him. The pressure was back in his pants, begging to differ with him on that one. He pursed his lips as he stood to go meet her. For once he was prepared to do some serious thinking about a woman—using the head on his shoulders.

She was getting her bag out of the back of the car by the time he reached her. Damn, did she really have to present him with that ass, and those legs, and yet another pair of sexy heels? He adjusted his pants, unable to tear his eyes away. She turned around and smiled at him. Now it was her face he couldn't tear his eyes away from. She was even more beautiful than he remembered.

"Hey, gorgeous."

"Hey."

Hmm. This could be serious. There was none of the fun or laughter in her eyes that he'd grown to love. Grown to what? Not going anywhere near that thought. He may as well dive in and find out what the score was. She might not even be coming back with him. No. He wasn't prepared to accept that as an option.

"Can I least get a hug?" he asked cautiously. All he wanted to do was pull her into his arms and kiss her, pick up right where they'd left off on Monday morning. But for the first time he felt uncertain about whether she would want him to.

She nodded and stepped into his outstretched arms. He felt her relax as he closed them around her. He relaxed a little himself. Whatever was going on in her mind, her body felt happy to be next his again. He rested his forehead against hers and looked into her eyes. Some of the light was coming back. He smiled; it was going to be okay. Her arms came up around his neck, her hands on the back of his head, pulling him to her. She nipped his bottom lip, then laughed, the sound of it chasing away the last of his caution. Backing her up against the car, he took her face between his hands and bit her lips before tilting her head back, slanting his mouth over hers to give him full access. Their tongues danced together, asking questions, giving answers, challenging and conceding. Her body melted against him when he stepped it up, demanding, possessing, because there was something about her that did that to him. He had to know she was his and only his, and her kiss gave him the answer he needed, surrendering to him. The last of his tension ebbed away as he kissed her. This was what had had him concerned; now he had his answer. Whatever was in her head, she was still his and, on some instinctive level, they both knew it.

He chose when that kiss ended, and it wasn't until he was sure that they'd told each other everything they needed to that way. The conversation would happen, he had no doubt, but words tended to get complicated, the heavy stuff made him shut down. This kiss, however, would see him through that, because whatever words might be exchanged, he already had his answers. She was confused, but she wanted him. She was scared, but she wasn't ready, or able, to walk away. They were still on the same page.

She looked dazed when he smiled down at her.

"Was there something you wanted to talk about?" he asked,

"I think we just did."

He smiled. "I got almost all the answers I need."

The laughter was back in her eyes. "What do you still need to know, Smoke?"

"I need to know what happens now. Do you still want to come with me? Would you rather I take you for dinner here and then go home and leave you to your weekend? Or...."

"I still want to go with you, if you still want to take me?" He couldn't resist teasing her. "Oh, I want to take you, lady. I'll always want to do that. But apparently you're not up for it anymore. So instead I shall simply invite you to come spend the weekend with me. No sex, no obligation." He pressed his lips together to keep the smile away. The look of disappointment on her face was the perfect confirmation of everything her kiss had told him. Maybe not having sex could be fun too.

~ ~ ~

As Smoke taxied off the runway and towards the hangars at Summer Lake, Laura watched the mountains grow dark. She was starting to love this place. She already loved flying in here, looking out for the lake as they flew over the mountains. Seeing it appear, shining like a fragment of broken mirror way, way below them, then watching it grow bigger and bigger as they descended. The way the mountains that looked so small rose up to meet them, and then huddled around them like protective giants once they were on the ground. Her mind strayed back to the house they'd looked at last weekend. That would be something—to buy that place and work from there. She'd have the little store at Four Mile whenever they got done building it. Smoke's voice filled her head through her headset. "Would you like to have dinner at the resort with everyone?" She turned to look at him. She'd assumed they'd be going to the cabin, by themselves.

He was giving her that wicked grin of his. "No sex, remember?"

She narrowed her eyes at him, but said nothing. He was enjoying this way too much. They'd agreed that they needed to talk, but that it was better to wait until they got up here to do so. She was hardly going to say anything while he was flying and he'd said if they were going to leave they'd have to be quick about it. There was a weather front coming through and they'd have to get out ahead of it.

Now she had a feeling he was going to play this for all it was worth and make her regret ever having implied that he only wanted her for sex. Just being around him again reassured her that wasn't true. And the way he'd kissed her in the parking lot? That had told her so much more than words ever could!

"I think we probably should, don't you?"

He shrugged innocently. "I said we might stop in, but I'm sure no-one really expects us to join them. We could go home and...just talk."

"You know damned well that's not what I mean, you wicked man," she said with a laugh. "I think we should go out for dinner with the gang, because the minute we are alone you are going to torment me and make me pay for doubting your intentions. Aren't you?"

Smoke shut down the engines and took his headset off. He waited until she'd taken hers off then put his hand on her thigh as he unfastened her belt for her. "You still have such a low opinion of me don't you, lady? It's just that I understand your concerns and would like to do my best to prove you wrong."

Just the feel of his hand had her wanting him. And he knew it. This was going to be torture!

She followed him out of the cockpit and waited as he let down the steps. "Dinner at the resort it is then. I hope the band is playing 'til really, really late."

He grinned at her. "Me too. Dancing will be fun."

She tried to glower at him, but she couldn't help laughing.

~ ~ ~

The band was playing when they got there, and the place was packed. Laura had thought it might be quieter since the summer season was definitely over, but it seemed that Ben had managed to build a regular base of weekend visitors that came year round. Of course there were plenty of locals, too. She spotted the gang. They were sitting inside tonight, having pushed a couple of the high top tables together to make room for everyone.

"Hey you two!" shouted Pete. "Glad you decided to come, we saved you a couple of seats." His lips quirked up in a knowing smile as he shook Smoke's hand. Laura had to wonder what that was about.

"I thought you were going to London this weekend?" Missy was looking at her, puzzled.

"Not 'til Sunday night. I wanted to come up here first."

Smoke caught her eye and shook his head with the briefest flash of that evil smile. Oh, God. She hoped he wasn't saying he wasn't going to make her come up here. She was so over her doubts and all she really wanted was to get back to the cabin with him.

He pulled out a stool for her to sit, then leaned against the back of it, standing close enough that she could feel the heat of his body. He really was planning on tormenting her. He rested his arms against the back, and leaned his head over her shoulder, making her body heat up with need. At the same time he was making it clear to everyone that the two of them were together.

Emma smiled at her. "You will be back in time for the fundraiser won't you? I'm so excited that we're all going!"

Laura nodded. "I will. I'm looking forward to it too." She felt Smoke lean a little closer—apparently so was he. She looked around for Ben, wanting to ask him about Leanne. She hoped they would have a good time together, but was concerned that

Leanne might be a bit much for him—she was such a strong personality. She couldn't see him anywhere.

"Hey, Dan. Leanne sends her best. She came into the store the other day and we had coffee."

Dan grinned. "I must call her. Did she tell you she's coming to the fundraiser, too?"

"Yep, she's excited." Laura didn't know if the others knew about the plan with Ben, so she didn't mention it.

Jack looked at Smoke. "And you're really not flying that night?"

Laura turned to look up at him. She was surprised when he rested a hand on her shoulder. "No. I'm not working it. I'm bringing my lady."

He certainly knew how to go for effect! Her three girlfriends grinned happily at her while Jack and Pete both looked at Smoke in shock.

Michael stepped in to fill the silence. "Blimey, guys. Don't look at him like that. So, he wants the night off to focus on his girl instead of playing air taxi for you." He winked at Laura. "It's hardly surprising!"

Laura was liking him more all the time. "What about you?" she asked. "Are you coming?"

He hung his head and looked out at them sideways. "Nah. Nobody loves me, darl'. Just call me Cinders. I'll stay home, all alone, while you all go to the ball."

Missy gave him a push. "Michael Morgan! Stop going for the sympathy vote. If you'd stop putting moves on women that are already spoken for and try finding one of your own then you could come too! There's still time."

Michael laughed. "Not for me there's not. I'm destined to remain forever alone. I never get the girl. I just act as a catalyst to help other guys get it together." He grinned at Dan, then looked up at Smoke. "Isn't that right, mates?"

Ben appeared at that moment and sat down next to Michael. "Sorry guys. Seems that everything that can go wrong is going wrong tonight. How's everyone doing? What am I missing out on?"

Michael looked at him. "We're missing out on this big party they're all going to, mate. Unless we can find a couple of hot chicks to invite."

Missy laughed. "Ben's not missing out, it's just you."

Ben grinned. "Yeah, Dan already set me up, with a stunner apparently."

Michael shook his head and gave an exaggerated sigh. "What did I tell you? Just call me Cinders." He looked at Dan, "And with all I've done for you, you didn't find me one?"

Dan laughed. Laura loved seeing the way he'd come out of his shell so much since he'd started coming up here. "Sorry, Michael. Bad timing I guess. Although," he looked at Missy, "isn't that when your friend is going to be in LA? We could invite her as Michael's guest?"

Laura was surprised at the look Missy gave Dan. It seemed she didn't like the idea one bit.

"Which friend?" asked Emma.

It was obvious Missy really was not happy about this. Instead of looking at Emma when she spoke, she looked directly at Ben. "Charlotte is coming over from England. We're planning to meet up."

Talk about a bombshell! Laura had no idea what it was all about, but all the color drained from Ben's face. Emma and Pete were both looking at him with a mixture of panic and sympathy and Missy looked like she might cry. "I'm sorry, hon. I was going to tell you."

Michael looked at Ben, apparently trying to make him smile. "No need to look like that, mate. I'll trade you. I'll take your stunner and you can take Charlotte."

Ben stood up. "You know," he looked at Dan. "That's a better idea. Let Michael take Leanne. I'll probably end up getting stuck here with something anyway and not be able to make it. I'd better go check on the kitchen." He turned and disappeared into the crowd, leaving them all staring after him.

Pete looked at Missy. "Are you going after him, or should I?" Missy was already on her feet. "I'll go. I was going to get him on his own and tell him, I just haven't had a chance yet."

Dan looked miserable. "I'm sorry, Miss, I had no idea."

Laura's heart melted a little, seeing the way Missy reassured him with a hug. "It's not your fault, Danny. You couldn't have known. I'll be back." She went after Ben. She may only be tiny, but she parted the crowd like Moses in her determination.

"Is he okay?" Holly asked Pete.

"He will be."

Pete looked at Emma. "Did you know she was coming?"

"Miss had mentioned a while ago that she might be over this fall. We'd talked about maybe getting together in the city. She was hardly going to come up here."

Pete nodded.

Michael looked around. "So I guess I screwed up there! I thought he'd be glad to take Charlotte."

Emma shook her head. "You missed a lot after you left for Australia."

"Yeah, I gathered! What's the deal? "

"She's married," said Pete.

"Ah!"

"Are you sure?" asked Dan. "Missy didn't mention a husband coming. Just that Charlotte was."

Emma nodded sadly. "Oh, he'll be coming."

"So what's the story?" asked Jack "Is anyone going to explain it to those of us who didn't grow up here?"

Pete shook his head. "Not me. It's Ben's story. It's up to him if and when it gets told."

Laura listened to the exchange, hoping that Ben was okay, and that Missy would talk him into coming to the fundraiser anyway.

Chapter Fourteen

They left the pickup in the square and took the waterfront path back to the cabin. Smoke slung an arm around her shoulders as they walked. She smiled up at him.

"I feel so bad for Ben. I don't know what the story is, but he looked devastated."

Smoke nodded. "Poor guy. It sucks when the past sneaks up on you out of the blue like that."

"That sounds like the voice of experience?"

"It is." He really did not want to go there right now, even though he knew that if he was going to keep seeing Laura, he'd have to someday.

"But you don't want to talk about it, right?"

"Right." They walked on in silence. His arm tightened around her shoulders. "We'll get around to it, gorgeous, but not tonight, huh?"

She nodded. "You're right, not tonight. Seeing the way Ben looked, I don't feel like opening up old wounds either."

"So, are you going to tell me your story someday, too?"

She nodded. "It looks like that's where we're headed, doesn't it? But we can do it when we're ready."

Smoke stopped walking and took her face between his hands, kissing her deeply. When they came up for air she was breathless, but looked puzzled. "What was that for?"

He planted a kiss on her forehead and took her hand as he started walking again. "Just for being you."

The smile on her face had his chest buzzing with that happy feeling again. She wasn't like any other woman he'd ever known. Well, he hadn't really known many, other than physically. In fact he'd only really known one. And Laura was sure as hell turning out to be nothing like her. He was starting to think that maybe Pete was right. That everything he had thought a woman wanted and needed was based on Anabel's twisted ideas, and not on reality.

When they got to the cabin, he unlocked his door and let Laura step in ahead of him. He couldn't help but watch her ass sway as she walked down the hallway in those heels. He took a deep breath and adjusted his pants before following her. He wasn't going to have sex with her again until she begged him. He knew she would. Part of it was about making her pay. He'd already done so much for her that he'd never done for a woman before. Part of him resented that she couldn't see that, and was hurt that she could doubt his motives. Another part of him understood completely and wanted to reassure her. He could satisfy both those parts by making her want him so badly she would beg for it. Then he would thoroughly satisfy her—and himself—and the issue would be settled.

She stood in the kitchen, leaning back against the counter, smiling her sexy smile. "So, Captain Hamilton, you've got me here, and we've already established that we don't want to talk, so what do you suggest we do?"

Jesus, he was going to need some will power if he was going to be able to see this through. He stepped towards her, caging her there with his arms, just like he had that first night. He felt her body respond, going soft, yielding to him as he leaned his weight against her. He brushed his lips over hers and then stood back.

"I thought perhaps a glass of wine on the deck?"

She narrowed her eyes at him. "If that's what you want."

This would be fun—if he could keep it up. He brought the bottle and a small box outside, then poured just one glass. It was much chillier now; the seasons were changing. "I'll go get us a blanket."

When he returned she was sitting huddled on the sofa hugging herself against the cold. "Come here, that's my job." He sat down next to her and wrapped the blanket around them. "Better?"

She snuggled against him and nodded. "A little. I think shared body heat is supposed to help, isn't it?"

He laughed and hugged her to him, rubbing her arms briskly. "How's that."

She looked up into his eyes and pouted. "It's not quite what I was hoping for."

So she admitted she was hoping? This was going well. Her tongue came out to moisten her lips. He watched, mesmerized. He didn't miss the little smile before she bit her bottom lip— she knew full well the effect that had on him. He shook his head at her with a rueful smile. He wasn't going to fall for that so easily. He dragged his eyes away from her face before he changed his mind.

"Do you like chocolates?"

She frowned, disappointed that he'd been able to resist. "Of course I do. Who doesn't love chocolate?"

"Try this then." He reached an arm out of the blanket and opened the little box. He brought a chocolate toward her mouth, holding her gaze as he did. "Open up for me, Laura," he said, his words another echo of their first night together.

Her eyes narrowed again. "I would love to."

He laughed and teased her, pulling the chocolate away just as she opened her mouth. "You'd love to, but what?"

"But you're not going to give it to me, are you?" she laughed.

"I might, or you might have to take it." He brought the chocolate up to his own mouth and held it between his lips. Lowering his mouth to her, he raised his eyebrows, inviting her to take it.

She put her hands on his shoulders and brought her mouth up to his, her eyes sparkling with a mixture of lust and mischief. She closed her lips over the chocolate and pushed it into his mouth with her tongue, tangling with his in a deep, chocolatey kiss. He crushed her to his chest, holding her against him, letting her feel how much he needed her now.

She broke away. "If you don't want to give it to me, I don't think I should take it, Captain Hamilton."

He laughed. So competitive. She wasn't going to give in or admit defeat easily. "Fair enough." he reached for the glass of wine and brought it to his lips.

She pouted. "You didn't pour me one?"

He smiled at her over the rim. "I thought we could share."

He handed it to her and caught her free hand, bringing it down to cover the bulge in his pants. Her eyes closed as her fingers kneaded at him. "This is how badly I want you, Laura."

"I want you, Smoke," she breathed.

It took him everything he had, but he removed her hand, and took the glass from her. "But I can't have you thinking that's all I want."

She stared at him wide eyed. "But Smoke...."

"But, what lady?"

"I don't want to play this game anymore."

She looked and sounded as petulant as a toddler. He laughed, which probably wasn't the wisest move he'd ever made.

She looked hurt. "Is this just another small victory to you?"

"No!" Damn! He didn't want her to think that! "Yes, it's a game, but I'm only playing it to make a very important point—

to you, and to myself. You already know how badly I want to lay you down right here, right now. I need to feel you naked under me. I need to be inside you so badly. But you need to know that this...." He tapped his forefinger on her chest, then tapped his own. "Us. That we're about more than that. It's killing me not to pin you down and make you scream my name as you come. So, yes, I'm making it a game. Because that's the only way I can survive this. If I give in, take you now, you'll still be wondering, won't you?"

She shook her head rapidly. "I already know, Smoke. I had a moment of doubt, but you've reassured me in every way possible that this is about so much more than sex. You told me with your text. You made the point crystal clear when you kissed me at the airport. And you've shown me all evening long, by the way you took me out with everyone, made it perfectly clear to them, and to me, that we were together. Smoke, I need you to know that deep down I already knew it. You keep breaking your rules for me. I keep breaking my rules for you. Neither of us would do that just for sex. It's just that this is scary, for both of us, and I don't think either of us knows what to do with it."

She reached up and closed her hands around the back of his head, drawing him down into a kiss. A kiss that tasted of wine and chocolate and the sweetness that was just Laura. It wasn't any kind of game anymore. That kiss was raw and honest, it reached deep inside him and touched that part of him that he'd thought was untouchable. It did touch his heart.

When he finally lifted his head, he took her hand. He knew what he needed to do. What they both needed to do. He stood up and pulled her to her feet. Her eyes were full of questions, but he shook his head and led her inside, into his bedroom. He brought her to face him and took hold of both of her hands. "I don't want to have sex with you, Laura." Looking into her

eyes he raised his eyebrows slightly in question. She searched
his face, then gave the tiniest nod.

~ ~ ~

Laura could feel her heartbeat in her chest. She knew exactly
what he meant. And she'd said yes. She felt so safe here in his
arms. She should feel scared, they were about to do something
they'd never done before. She didn't think she ever had. He
was kissing her now, holding her close. Their mouths
communicated so much better without words, their tongues
seeking and giving reassurance, making promises, in a way
their words hadn't been able to express.

There was nothing rushed about this. His hands moved over
her slowly, tracing lines, leaving burning trails on her skin in
their wake. Her top was gone, her bra soon followed. This
time he let her unbutton him. She ran her hands over his
smooth chest, up to his shoulders so she could push his shirt
off. His hands were on her zipper. She mirrored his
movements, pushing his pants down as he pushed hers. Once
they stood naked, he put his hands around her waist. He
looked down and shook his head. Her waist was small, she
knew that, but his hands were so big they weren't so far from
being able to close around her. It brought back his words. I'm
bigger than you. I'm stronger than you. And I will never, ever
push you around. She knew how true it was. She brought her
hands up to cup the back of his neck as she looked into his
eyes. He looked pained.

"What is it, Smoke?"

He shook his head.

"Please tell me?"

Keeping his hands around her waist he pulled her closer. He
leaned his head back into her hands as he looked down at her.
"This is the one rule I swore I would never break. You already
know I'm no saint. You already know I've screwed a lot of

women. But this? I swore I would never let a woman do this to me. I told you, you were trouble."

"Smoke, we don't have to."

"Yes we do. It's what we both want...what we need. We have to do this just like the sun has to rise tomorrow."

His erection was pressing into her belly, his fingertips stroking her back as he held on to her waist. "But I need you to know something, Laura."

She nodded, she felt completely overwhelmed by the way he was surrounding her—and more so by the honesty in his eyes. "What, Smoke?"

He took a deep breath then let it out slowly. "That's not my name. That's what I need you to know. My name is Cole Alexander Hamilton."

"Cole?" She tried out the sound of it. It sounded good. It felt good on her lips.

From the look on his face, he liked it too.

She smiled up at him. She understood that telling her his real name was something very important to him, but she didn't understand why. Hopefully he would explain to her— afterwards. For right now...she planted a kiss on his lips. "So, Mr. Cole Alexander Hamilton, are you going to make love to me?"

His eyes were so gentle as he backed her up to the bed. "I am. And you, Miss Laura Benson are going to make love to me."

And they did.

Their bodies already knew each other so well. They fit together like they were made to. This time when he thrust his hips and filled her, she was really letting him in. He gazed into her eyes as they moved together, telling her so much with that look. They rolled over and she took the top, but this was about sharing, not winning. His hands circled her waist, moving her in his time and she gave herself to him, letting him direct her as she sat up to take him deeper. Every inch of her came alive as she moved above him, eyes locked with his in an exchange as intense as the one between their bodies. She was close, so close, he was too, but she didn't want this to end. She lay forward against his chest. "I want to be underneath you...Cole."

He closed his eyes and bit the inside of his lip, deep furrows creasing his brow. Oh, how she hoped she hadn't done wrong. He was still rocking his hips underneath her, slowly now, his eyes still closed. When he opened them he flipped her onto her back and was back inside her in one smooth move. "Now you really are mine, Laura. And you're where you belong."

She clung to him, giving herself up to him as she moved with him. He took a handful of her hair and drew her head back, holding her gaze as the heat built and built. She felt herself tense in the moment he threw his back and gasped, "Mine, Laura."

His climax ignited hers, sweeping through her, taking her soaring away with him. "C-o-l-e!" She screamed his name, finally understanding the difference as they flew together. She wasn't having sex with the guy she knew—she was making love to the man she wanted to know.

Chapter Fifteen

Smoke came around to open the door of the pickup. She sat there smiling at him, looking abso-fucking-lutely gorgeous, that was the only word to describe her. He reached in and wrapped his hands around her waist, lifting her out and holding her up. She laughed as she looked down at him.

"You like throwing me around don't you...Cole?"

The sun was shining behind her, turning her into a beautiful silhouette. He loosened his grip and let her slide down his front—that was a big part of why he liked picking her up, feeling her slender body moving against his, until her feet hit the floor.

"I do. Apparently I'm just a big Neanderthal, or at least that's what someone told me."

She laughed. "I think that someone was, right." She reached up and planted a kiss on the tip of his nose. "But I like it."

"It's a good thing you do, because I'm not going to stop doing it any time soon." He took her hand and led her around the back of the house. "But for now, let's go see inside again."

He'd brought her back up to the house. He'd talked to the realtor and was getting ready to put in an offer, but he'd wanted to bring her back here before he did. Especially after last night. He was trying not to think about last night. He needed to, but thinking about it would mean taking a long hike, by himself, to work it through. For now, he was happy to just ride with it. More than happy. It felt good. It was crazy, dangerous, but it felt good. As he unlocked the door she tugged at his hand, since he hadn't yet let go of her. For some reason he always needed to be touching her—lifting her up, holding her hand, just resting a hand on her shoulder, or raking his fingers through her hair.

"What?" He turned to her as she tugged again, laughing now.

"Can we go see the workroom first?"

He laughed. "I told you, it's not a workroom!"

"It would be if I bought the place!"

"But you're not buying it, lady. I am."

She pretended to pout at him. "That's just plain mean! I want it!"

"Well you can't have it! It's mine!" He laughed. "Tell you what though...." He was leading her past the orchard now. "If you did move up here you could use it as your workroom, I wouldn't even charge you rent on it."

She stopped and looked at him. "Are you serious?"

He nodded. Apparently he was, even though he hadn't considered the idea until it came out of his mouth. "Sure, why not? I'm not going to use it for anything." He pulled her to him. "It could work, don't you think?" He was talking about so much more than the little outbuilding. Her face told him she understood that.

"It could. It might work out well, but there are a lot of steps between here and there, aren't there?"

She was right, of course. A hell of a lot of steps between here and the place they weren't talking about. He shrugged. "There are. Hell, I haven't even put in an offer yet." He opened the door and let her enter ahead of him.

She looked around then came back to where he stood in the doorway. She put a hand on his shoulder and planted a kiss on his lips. "A lot of steps, but I hope it works out."

So did Smoke.

"This view is amazing!" They were sitting out on the porch swing.

Smoke nodded. "It is. And you know when I stand in the living room and look out those windows it's almost like being in the cockpit, coming in to land here. This place is on the approach to the airport."

She laughed. "Well, that seals it then. I wouldn't want to buy the place out from under you if it reminds you of being in your plane." She looked at him now. "Which reminds me, Cole. Man of mystery that you are turning out to be. What's the deal with your plane?"

Smoke took a deep breath. He'd known this conversation would have to happen. He even wanted to have parts of it now. He still wasn't ready to go near other parts, but he didn't know how to untangle his story, to tell only as much as he was comfortable with. He looked at her, wondering where he could start.

"Sorry, we don't need to go there. I didn't mean to get heavy on you." She smiled, willing as always to let him off the hook.

He took hold of her hand—there he went again! Why did he keep doing that? "The thing is, Laura, we are starting to get heavy, aren't we? And I'm up for that. It's just, like I told you, I don't know how to you let you in. There's so much I need to tell you, and so much I'm not ready to tell you."

She nodded. "I know. But we don't need to rush. It'll all come out over time, won't it?"

"It might, but then I've never been the kind of open I'd need to be for that to happen. I'm going to have to make a conscious effort. If we just wait for it to happen naturally—it won't. Because it doesn't come naturally to me to let anyone in. And some of it I need to tell you sooner rather than later, because it'll only sound wrong if you hear it somewhere else first."

She wrapped her arms around his neck. "So how about we tell each other one or two things and then leave it. Do another one tomorrow?"

He pecked her lips as he hugged her to him. "You are something else, lady."

She snuggled in his arms. "Why thank you...I think!"

"It was a compliment. So, do you want me to go first? What do you want to know?"

She looked at him for a long moment. "I want to know everything there is to know about you. So maybe you should decide what you want to tell me first?"

He nodded, grateful that she understood. "Okay, the plane. I own two of them. Papa Charlie and another one just like it that's leased to a company in New York." He paused. He'd told her the facts, but knew he should still give her an explanation. "I come from money. I...." How could he say it without getting into his whole life story? "I was supposed to go into the family business. There was a falling out. I sold a part of my interest and moved on to doing what I love." That was the bare bones at least. He stared out into the distance, bracing himself for the barrage of questions.

"Wow!"

He waited. No questions came. He turned to look at her. She was smiling. She touched his cheek. "Thanks, Smoke. Want to hear one of mine?"

He stared at her. She really wasn't going to interrogate him?

"Sorry, you go on, if you want to. I thought you were done."

He framed her face in his hands and pecked her lips. "I am. For now. Thank you." He wrapped an arm around her and

held her hand, needing her to feel how grateful he was, since
he didn't know how to say it.

Her smile told him she understood. "So what do you want to
ask me?"

"Why you don't wear an engagement ring anymore?" Pete had
told him some of her story, and he felt bad about that. He'd
feel better if she told him herself, and he hoped she'd tell him
more than he already knew.

She leaned her head against his shoulder. "I don't think I can
be as concise as you were, but I'll try." She stared out at the
lake. "Dale was...is, a nice guy. He just wanted more from me
than I could give him."

Smoke nodded. He understood how that went.

"He's in politics. His family is quite influential. He—and
they—wanted me to be the supportive wife. You know how
some women make a career out of supporting their husband's
career? That was what he wanted, what he needs. And
Smoke...." She turned to look up at him, her eyes begging him
to understand. "That is so not me! I felt bad, I thought maybe
I just didn't love him enough and it would be alright if I could
figure out how to love him more. But I couldn't. I'm not even
sure I loved him at all. He's just a good guy. He was kind to
me. When we met, I...was in a bad place. He helped me when I
needed it. I wanted to help him, but I couldn't. Even if I had
loved him, or loved him enough. I'm not the kind of woman
who can give up on everything she wants, everything she is, to
give someone else what they need. That's what I meant when
we talked about it. I don't know that I can give you what you
want, or be what you need."

Smoke hugged her close, wanting to reassure her. "It's okay,
lady. I get it. Believe me, I get it." She'd just described how he
felt, the way he justified never getting involved with a woman

outside of her bed. He wasn't prepared to give up who he was or what he wanted for someone else either.

They sat in silence for a while. Each lost in their own thoughts, fingers still entwined.

"I do get it, Laura, because for the longest time I've felt the same way. I don't want to be with someone if it means I have to stop being who I am in order to do so. Like I told you, I've always thought that there had to be a loser. Do you want to know what I've been wondering lately, though?"

"What?" she didn't look at him, just kept her eyes fixed straight ahead.

"I've been wondering if maybe it's not true. Maybe two people can get together and both keep being who they are, and doing what they do. Maybe that can work...and work well."

She shook her head. "Maybe in sappy romance novels, but not in my experience."

He laughed. "Not in mine either, and I don't read sappy romance novels. But just look around this place. Take last night, for example. Look at the people we were with. Jack and Emma. They're both still doing what they want to. She's still writing, he's still running Phoenix. They've made a few adjustments, but only in ways that suit them as individuals. She wanted out of the city, he wanted to slow his schedule down. They both got what they wanted, and so much more, by being together."

Laura nodded. "I guess so."

"Then there's Pete and Holly. Same thing. She still has her store, goes to her fashion shows. Pete's still running Phoenix, traveling as much as he needs to. Spending more time with his folks. And now they get a life up here and each other too. And Dan and Missy? He got the family he didn't know he needed and escaped the golden handcuffs he'd locked himself into. Missy got a whole new life and didn't have to give up anything of herself, because Dan just loves who she is. In fact she gets to be more of herself because Dan needs who she is. Even little Scot got a dad out of that deal. And Dan gets to be more of himself because of it."

"So what are you saying?" She still wasn't looking at him.

"I'm saying that maybe there doesn't have to be such a compromise of self. Doesn't have to be a winner and a loser. If you're with the right person."

She was quiet as she leaned against him, nestling closer under his arm. When she finally met his gaze, her eyes were big, serious and scared, too. "I'd like to believe that, Smoke."

He nodded. So would he. But he still wasn't sure he did.

~ ~ ~

Smoke held her hand tight as they walked through the terminal. Considering he was supposed to be the guy who flew away at the first sign of anything heavy, he was doing a lot of hand-holding. She smiled to herself. And considering she was supposed to be the girl who couldn't stand men holding on to her, she was doing a lot of smiling about how hands on he was being. They'd had such a wonderful weekend. They'd had dinner and hung out at the cabin last night. Made love and slept in each other's arms. Made love some more before going for breakfast with the gang this morning. Well, most of the gang, no one had seen Ben since Friday night. Laura hoped he was okay.

Smoke had flown her back to San Francisco and left the plane at General Aviation. He booked them a cab to take them to the commercial terminal and now here they were. He was pulling her case and holding her hand. She smiled again, wishing Leanne could see him now. This would shut her up!

"You are going to call me to let me know you got to your hotel, right?" he asked.

She had to laugh. "I'll send you an email. It'll be four o'clock in the morning here when I land."

He stopped walking, causing people to have to swerve around them in all directions. He didn't seem to notice, he was too busy fixing her with a dark look. "I don't care. I'm not going to sleep 'til I know you're there safe. So call me when you get checked in, okay?"

She pursed her lips. "Seriously?"

He nodded. She could see the smile lurking behind the scowl. "I'll track your flight, I'll know when you've landed safe, but until you call me I won't know that you're okay. And that you haven't picked up some Englishman on the plane."

Wow! He was only half joking. "Do you want to just come with me to make sure I don't?"

"If I didn't have to fly, I would!"

She laughed and planted a kiss on his lips. "You know I'm not going to be picking anyone up, let alone an Englishman on a plane."

"You'd better not, lady!" He hugged her to him. "You are all mine and you'd better remember it, okay?"

She smiled into his neck as she hugged him back. He meant it! She felt like she should be freaked by it, but she loved it. "I'll remember, but you do surprise me. I thought I'd be in for a more Smoke-like send off? You know, waving me off then on to find the next one?"

"That was the old Smoke. The new Smoke doesn't want a next one. He wants you. And Cole wants you too. And I did warn you," He shrugged his shoulders and smiled, but it didn't quite reach his eyes. "I'm a jealous, possessive jerk!"

She laughed. "So how many guys am I dealing with here? There's Smoke, who's no saint, Cole who is a rather elusive mystery, then there's the jealous possessive jerk. Is there anyone else I need to know about?"

He shook his head. "Nope. That's all of me. And you are getting to know Cole, you already know him better than most people do. Give him time, he's a good guy."

That made her smile.

He cupped her face between his hands and nipped her lips. He didn't care that people continued to mill around where they stood in the middle of the concourse. "The one you need to worry about for now is the jealous possessive jerk. Even he wishes you a great a trip, but he needs to know you'll still be his when you get back."

She nodded.

"Good. Then let's get you checked in and on your way."

Once her bag was checked and she had her ticket in hand he walked her to the security line. "Okay, lady. This is me gone." He wrapped his arms around her waist. Enjoy yourself. Knock 'em dead with your designs. I know you will."

"Thanks, Smoke. And I will call you when I get to the hotel."

"Thanks. I'll be here waiting to meet you when you land."

"You will?"

"Yeah." He grinned at her now. "I want to."

She grinned back. "Then I'll look forward to it."

He brushed his lips over hers and she clung to him for just a moment.

"See you Saturday then. I'm going to go through now. I'm not good at long goodbyes."

There was no mistaking the relief on his face. "Me neither. See you soon." He gave her one last brief kiss and disappeared into the crowd.

She joined the long line to pass through security with a big smile on her face.

Chapter Sixteen

"I'll go ahead and send all three offers when I get back to the office, then."

Smoke shook the realtor's hand. "Thanks. And see what you can do to move it along? I'd like to close as soon as you can pull it together. What I don't want to do is close on the house if I don't get the others."

The realtor nodded. "I understand where you're coming from, Mr. Hamilton, but I'm not sure you need to worry. There's no way to build anything that could obstruct your views and the parcel to the south has been in the same family for decades. I doubt they would sell to a developer."

Smoke looked at the man and shook his head. "I want all three properties together, or none of them. You could be right, but I don't do well with uncertainties. You doubt that family would sell to a developer. I prefer to guarantee it and the only way to do that is to buy it myself. That parcel is the only buffer between this house and the new development at Four Mile Creek. It's not unusual for further construction to happen around a Phoenix development to serve the new residents. I don't want any of that on my doorstep." He smiled now. "So go make the offers. You'll be looking at three commissions instead of one."

The realtor smiled. "Don't worry, I'm aware of that! I was trying to look out for your interests instead of my own."

"Thanks, Austin." He shook the guy's hand. "I appreciate it. But I'm more interested in having a peaceful spread of land than how much I'll need to spend to get it. So, make it happen."

Austin grinned. "Will do, Mr. Hamilton. I'll get back down to town and get straight on it. Are you ready to leave, or do you want to look around some more?"

"I think I'll stay a while. I want to check a few things out, if that's okay?"

"Of course. You know what to do with the key. I'll be in touch as soon as I have anything to report."

"Sounds good."

Smoke watched the car to the end of the driveway until it turned the corner and disappeared from sight. He grinned and turned back to the house. He liked the place. It felt good, right somehow. Which was really weird. He was the guy who was always 'just passing through.' He never stuck around a place long enough to get attached to it, let alone put down roots. But there was something about Summer Lake. It was a good place. He had good friends here. For the first time he felt like he could stop running, be still for a while and maybe even build a life here. He shook his head. It was so out of character for him it should be worrying, but instead it made him smile.

He knew one person who would smile if she knew what he was thinking. At least she'd smile after the shock had worn off. It had been too long, he should call her anyway. For everything that had happened, he still loved her, still missed her. And things had been getting better between them for a while now. Calling her with this kind of news could only help that along. He went to sit on the swing on the front porch to look out at what he hoped would soon be his view.

He pulled his phone out and hit the speed dial. Even that was progress. For a few years he'd had this number blocked. He listened to it ring, hoping she would pick up.

"Cole? Is that you?"

He laughed. "Who else would be calling you from my phone?"

"Oh, darling it's just such a lovely surprise! How are you?"

"I'm good, Mom. How are you?"

"Everything is the same here. Everyone's fine. What's going on with you? We'd love to see you sometime."

He smiled. He wanted to see her too. He was glad that they were getting closer again. It had been tough in the beginning, after all those years of hardly speaking. But the last few months things were getting better, more natural.

"I thought you'd like to know that I'm about to put in an offer on a house."

"Oh, my goodness! Where? Why? How? You mean a house to actually live in, or an investment?"

He smiled to himself. She sounded shocked and thrilled at the same time. "Let's see, I'll try to answer one at a time. The 'where' is Summer Lake, where Jack and Pete and are based. The why I'm still trying to figure out, Mom. I'm not sure I know myself. Just that, it's a good place. The guys are here, and I don't know it...it just feels right. From which you probably gathered that I mean a house to actually live in. To make a home."

"Darling, that's wonderful! And you'll be so close, perhaps we'll see more of you if you move there? You know we'd love that."

She tried so hard to never ask him outright to come visit, but he knew she was hoping to see him. "That's why I called. I thought I might stop by on Friday, stay the night if you don't mind. I have to pick up a passenger in San Francisco on Saturday morning."

"That would be wonderful! And don't worry, I'll tell your father that I want you all to ourselves. I won't let him invite the hordes."

"Thanks, Mom. I'll call you before I leave. There shouldn't be any hitches, but I'll call you if I need to fly, okay?"

"Of course. I'll just keep my fingers crossed."

"Well, I'll see you Friday then."

"I hope so. Love you, darling."

"Love you too, Mom."

As he hung up he stared out at the lake. They really had come a long way. It seemed like everything was changing for the better. The scars of the past were healing. Now he had to decide what he wanted the future to look like. He looked around. With any luck, this house would become his home. That would do for starters. He was reshaping his career, too. Bringing Jason on board to take over some of the Phoenix schedule would be a big change. Not as big as going back to instructing, though. He was pretty sure now that he wasn't going to get involved in any of the long haul gigs that the New York plane was scheduled for. Not so long ago he'd loved that life. Traveling the world, living out of a suitcase. He'd thought he might give it another go, but when it came down to it, he'd been there, done that. It was a young man's game.

He pressed his lips together. When it came down to it, he wanted to build a home. As long as it could be a base and not a burden, he might just be happy here. Especially if Laura was going to move up here. He liked that idea. He liked it a lot. He didn't think he was turning his back on the long haul because of her, was he? He shrugged. Even if he was, it was because he wanted to. Not because she'd asked him to. Or would ever ask him to. He understood that about her. She would never ask him to give anything up in order to be with her. Just as he would never ask her to give anything up to be with him. He wouldn't ask her, but he selfishly hoped that her plans would involve moving up here. He looked at his phone. He couldn't call her. It would be midnight over there by now. She had called him when she arrived, just like she said she would. She'd sounded tired. She'd be fast asleep by now. He hoped. He hated to think of her out, in London with who knew who?

He stood up. Time to take another look around. He didn't need to be thinking like that. He'd only drive himself nuts. She was just as into him as he was into her, he knew that. He frowned, though. She was just as scared and confused about where they could go with it, too. He'd text her tomorrow. Wish her luck with her meetings.

~ ~ ~

Laura looked around as they stepped out of the Levy store. So this was the famed Jewelry Quarter. It was like stepping backing in time. Of course she knew about Hatton Garden, but actually being here was something else. This had been the diamond district of the UK since medieval times. This place was known worldwide. Some of the world's wealthiest people came here to have bespoke pieces made by some of the world's greatest jewelers. She smiled: and now she was here.

So far London had not lived up to its gray and dreary reputation; the weather was beautiful. Colin took her arm as they stepped out into the sunshine. Laura wanted to shrug him off, but forced herself to smile. He was a nice enough guy, good looking in a quiet, British kind of way. Bookish, that's what he was. Actually he was very much her type, or would have been before she met Smoke.

"We're so glad you're here, Laura. I hope you found today informative."

Had she ever! Colin had taken her through how they operated and what they hoped she would contribute. Apparently they did this every couple of years, found a new designer they liked

and showcased their work with a new line that they marketed
the heck out of. The idea was that the designer, and of course
Levy, would build a new following. The hope was that
amongst that following would be some wealthy clients who
liked the new line, but wanted bespoke pieces made. It was a
great strategy. Laura could see how it worked so well.

"Very informative. And very pleasant. Thank you."

Colin had been a real sweetheart, showing her around,
explaining how they liked to run things and why. He'd talked
her through the history of the business...well it was his family
history. His father, Mr. Levy Sr. was still the head honcho, but
Colin was being groomed to take over in the next year or two.

He smiled at her. "You are very welcome. I hope you will do
me the honor of having a drink with me? Since it's your first
evening here, we left your schedule clear in case you're feeling
jet-lagged and would prefer to rest. However, I do hope you'll
at least feel up to a quickie before you need to sleep."

Laura had to bite back a giggle. She'd love a quickie before she
went to sleep, but it would be with a big American pilot, not a
bookish British jeweler. She must be jet-lagged. She was six
thousand miles away from that pilot and she still couldn't get
him out of her head. She realized Colin was looking at her
hopefully. It would be rude not to go.

"Thank you. I'd love to."

Colin smiled. "Great. There's a place just around the corner.
Another Hatton Garden landmark, it's called the Bleeding
Heart."

Laura bit back another giggle. What was it with these Brits?
They liked to call their pubs such weird names!

Once they were settled at a little table in the corner, Colin
raised his glass to her. "Here's to our new ventures. To the
beginning of a very long, and mutually beneficial, partnership."

She raised her glass. "Cheers." She certainly hoped so.

"I talked to Father again before you arrived. We've decided that we would very much like to buy your San Francisco store. It would be perfect for us."

Laura swallowed, hard. She'd been hoping for this, but there had been no mention of it in any of their meetings today. Strange that he should wait to bring it up now. But hey, it was what she wanted.

Apparently he sensed her hesitation. "I believe it would be beneficial for you too. To not have the retail responsibilities? It will free you to travel more. In fact...." He smiled at her over his pint glass before taking a drink.

Laura wished he'd hurry up. He was obviously going for effect, building up to something. She raised an eyebrow as she waited for him to put his glass down and continue.

"You could establish a base here. Avail yourself of our facilities and be more central to our client base."

She stared at him. Now that was something she'd never even considered. "You mean, live in London?"

"Yes. It is a wonderful city. New York is still only a short hop and you'd be much closer to our European and Middle Eastern clients."

Laura thought about it. Her idea had been to travel to the East Coast and Europe, or to fly out of San Francisco to Australia and Hong Kong. This would take some thought.

Colin seemed a little deflated by her reaction. "We would love to have you. Make you one of the team?"

"Thank you." She tried to pull herself together. "I'm just a little surprised. I hadn't even considered it as a possibility."

He smiled now. "I'm sorry. There's no need to give me an answer right away. But think it over. Keep it in mind this week. It might make you look at things a little differently if you bear in mind that you could be here permanently."

What did that mean? "I will, thank you."

Back in her hotel room Laura did think it over. It could be a great career move. So why did she feel so flat? She loved London. Why wasn't she excited at the thought of living here? Was it because she'd been thinking about moving to Summer Lake? She looked out of the window. The street far below was packed with tiny cars, black cabs, and red buses. She shook her head. She'd much rather be swinging on a front porch looking down at tiny boats on a blue lake, backed by green mountains. And sitting next to a certain pilot—but how realistic was that? And what exactly would it do for her career?

Chapter Seventeen

Smoke pulled in to the square at the resort. He'd been surprised that Austin had called him back so quickly. Seemed like this might be a much quicker and easier purchase than he'd thought. The most interesting part of the conversation had been that the family who owned the parcel to the south was named Walton. That was Ben's name. Smoke had kept thinking about Ben since Friday night. He'd wanted to check in with him, see how he was doing, but they weren't exactly best buds or anything. Wanting to buy the land gave him the perfect excuse to seek Ben out.

He wandered into the bar, but there was no sign of him there. "Hi. What can I do for you?" The girl behind the bar was smiling, batting unnaturally long lashes at him.

As he looked her over, Smoke registered that not so long ago he would have been settling at the bar for some serious flirting—'til her shift was over. He smiled at her, grateful that she was reminding him how empty and meaningless that all seemed since he'd met Laura. "You can tell me where Ben is."

"Sorry, he's not working tonight. You'll have to make do with me." There went the eyelashes again, the classic flick of the shoulder length hair. All the standard come-ons.

"No thanks. Can you tell me where I'll find him?"

Her face fell. "Probably in his apartment."

"Thanks." Smoke turned around and left.

"Ben! You home?" He'd been knocking on the door for a couple of minutes now. Maybe he wasn't here. No, he definitely heard movement in there. "Open up, bud." He heard footsteps and then the door opened.

"Jesus! You look like shit!"

Ben shrugged. "Nice to see you too. What do you want, or did you just come to insult me?"

Smoke held up a six pack with a grin. "Thought I'd stop by to see if you want a beer."

Ben looked at the beer, then back at Smoke. He thought it over then brought both hands up and rubbed them over his face. "Sure. Come on in."

Smoke followed him inside. The place was immaculate. He'd been half expecting to find a drunk Ben sprawled in the middle of leftover takeout boxes and empty beer bottles. That wasn't the case at all.

"Want to take it outside?" asked Ben.

Smoke nodded and followed him out onto a balcony right above the water. "It's a great apartment."

"Thanks. It's useful. It keeps me in the middle of things. I'm always right here when I'm needed."

"Yeah, wouldn't that be a good reason to live somewhere else, though?"

"Maybe. If I had any sense...or a life! Are they cold?" He jerked his chin towards the beers Smoke was still carrying.

"Not stinging, I just picked 'em up at the store. We can maybe stand one, if you stick the rest in the freezer while we do."

Ben smiled. "Great minds!" He took two bottles out and went inside with the rest. "I would say don't let me forget about them, but I don't think they'll be in there long enough to freeze."

"I doubt it."

Ben came back out, sat down, and popped the top off his beer. "This is a first. I mean it's good to see you and everything, but what are you doing here, Smoke?"

Smoke wondered himself. He wasn't normally the type for social visits. "Whatever the other night was about, it obviously got to you. I haven't seen you around since. I wanted to make sure you're okay. I kept putting it off. I didn't want to barge in where I'm not wanted. Like you say, I've never come knocking before, but today I got the excuse to come talk to you about buying some land. So, if you want me to butt out, we can just talk about that and have a beer. If you do want to talk about anything else..." He shrugged. "I'm here."

Ben looked him over. "You know, I wasn't sure about you at first."

Smoke laughed. "I could tell."

Ben nodded. "But you're alright, Smoke."

Smoke was surprised how much that meant to him. He nodded back, but said nothing.

"Thanks for making the offer, but I really don't want to talk about it. There's nothing to talk about. It just brought up memories of something, someone, a long time ago. It threw me because it was so unexpected. I've spent the last couple of days trying to put it all back in the box. Talking about it would only keep it alive and...." Ben rubbed his hands over his face again before looking out at the lake, then looking back at Smoke. "All I want to do is forget."

Smoke nodded again.

"So. That leaves you wanting to talk about buying land, right?"

"Yeah. You know I've been looking at the house up on Cottonwood Creek? I want to buy the place, but I want to be sure that any new development around Four Mile doesn't end up spreading as far as my doorstep."

"Wow! So you want to buy the strip in between?"

"Yep."

"Joe and I had decided we wouldn't sell it for exactly that reason—so that it can't be built on. That's why it wasn't part of the Four Mile deal. The guys will stay within reasonable limits, but there are bound to be folk with their eye on the ball who want to capitalize on a new community. Someone would build stores, a gas station or even second tier housing for those who want to be out there, but can't afford what Phoenix builds."

"I know. That's why I can't risk buying the house without buying that land as well."

Ben looked at him. "I just told you, we agreed not to sell it in order to make sure it doesn't get built on."

"Which would mean you had an unusable piece of land sitting on your hands doing nothing but cost you taxes every year. Whereas if you sell it to me, you'll have some cash in hand and be done. I'll be happy to work out covenants as part of the sale if you want. Don't worry, I'm not trying to pull a fast one and start building a gas station out there myself. I just prefer to control my own environment. While it's nice to know you would keep the place as it is, it doesn't seem fair to ask that. I should pay you for it. I'll give you my guarantee, in the form of covenants or whatever, that I will keep it the way it is."

"Fair enough. Let me talk to Joe."

"Thanks, Ben."

Ben looked puzzled. "Can I ask you something?"

"Go ahead."

"How can you afford to even think about buying the house on Cottonwood and our acreage? And more to the point, why would you want to? Last time we talked you were asking about renting it out if you changed your mind about living here. You hardly need—what will it be, six hundred acres total?—to make it rentable."

Smoke blew out a big sigh, wondering now whether he'd come here because he thought Ben needed to talk, or because he needed to himself. "No, I don't need all that land, but if I'm going to live there, I want it. I don't know, Ben. Maybe I'm just getting old or something, but the idea of living here...of settling here, appeals to me. But if I do it, it's partly because I love the country and the open space. And let's just say I can afford it. In fact it'll be a cash deal."

Ben raised his eyebrows. "You do realize that raises more questions than it answers?"

Smoke laughed. "I do and this way I make you ask instead of getting into a major info dump!"

Ben laughed with him. "Okay, so first off, back to my original question. How can you afford it?"

Smoke had already decided that since he was going to be living here, becoming one of the gang, they probably should all know who he was. Jack and Pete knew, of course, and he'd already given Laura the bare bones. "My family is what you could call wealthy. I didn't stick around and go into the family business, but I did sell part of my interest and made some investments that turned out pretty well. I'm not surviving on a pilot's salary. I own the plane and another one like it. The guys lease from me."

"Cool. What's the family business?"

Out of all of them, Ben would understand, once he made the connection. He was in the industry, he must already know the story. "Do you have a wine rack?"

Ben gave him an odd look. "Sure, why?"

Smoke stood up. "Show me?"

Ben led him back inside and into the kitchen. "Right there." He pointed at the wine rack on the counter, then dumped their beer bottles in the trash and pulled two more from the freezer. He handed one to Smoke, who was going through the bottles in the rack.

"This should give it away." He held up a bottle of the same red blend he'd had at Laura's place.

Ben's eyes grew wide. "You're kidding me?"

Smoke shook his head. "I kid you not."

"So, Smoke Hamilton, the pilot, is the son of Hamilton Groves Wines? Shit, Smoke! You could buy the entire frigging town, let alone Cottonwood Creek, right?"

Smoke shrugged.

"So, hang on. Your dad is the Cole Hamilton? And your brother is Cameron?"

He nodded, wondering how much Ben knew, waiting to see if he would piece it together.

Ben was squinting his eyes, apparently trying to remember details. "Then that makes you Cole Hamilton Jr.? The one that...?" He raised his eyebrows at Smoke now. "You know what they said about you?"

Of course he did.

"I always wondered what the real story was. I met Anabel Groves a couple of times at tourism fairs." He gave Smoke a questioning look. "She was beautiful."

Smoke nodded. "She still is, from what I hear. On the outside, at least."

"Was she as psycho as she seemed?"

That took Smoke by surprise. He'd always thought she'd had everyone else fooled, just as much as she had him—and his family. "A whole lot more than what she seemed. Yeah."

Ben shook his head. "Wow! I'm guessing you weren't really in rehab after all the scandal?"

Smoke shook his head. "No. But I agreed to go along with the story. It was better for everyone that way."

"Do you want to tell me what really happened? There were all kinds of rumors flying around for months."

Want to? No. Smoke didn't want to even think about it. Like Ben, he'd rather just forget, but part of him needed to. Like Pete had said, it was time for him to finally get over shit. He'd discovered that talking about it was cathartic somehow. "Some of the rumors were true. I did beat the crap out of the guy I found her with in Malibu. I'm not proud of that, but...."

Ben simply nodded, waiting for him to go on.

"You know the industry, so I'm sure you know that our engagement was perfect publicity and the perfect match for the Hamilton and Groves companies coming together. Our families had been friends forever. Anabel and I had dated on and off since high school. It was always expected that we would end up together. I'd never really questioned that. What I questioned was the expectation that I would go into the business. I had no interest. Cam was the one that loved all that, I just loved to fly. But since I'm the oldest the expectation was there. Anabel expected it too. And she hated me flying. She wanted to be married to the head of the new Hamilton Groves enterprise."

Smoke stared out at the water for a long moment. Remembering all the fights, all the manipulating she'd done to try to shape his life into what she wanted it to be.

Ben said nothing. Giving him the time to continue or not, as he chose.

Apparently he did need to talk about it. "She told me she was pregnant. So I asked her to marry me." He shrugged. "I wasn't even sure I wanted to be with her at all by then, but it was too late. You do the decent thing, right? After all the big fuss and announcements, after the engagement had been tied in to the whole publicity campaign about Hamilton Groves, she told me she'd lost the baby. I was devastated. I was hardly ready to be a father, but I'd gotten used to the idea, you know?"

Ben nodded, but still said nothing.

"I know now that she'd never been pregnant at all. But I didn't know that then. She thought she had me trapped, that there was too much on the line for both our families for me to walk away. She thought I was suckered and would have to marry her at that point. And I would have, too. If I wasn't a jealous, possessive jerk. She said she needed some time alone, to recover, come to terms with the loss. That she was going to stay at a friend's Malibu beach house. I offered to go with her, but she didn't want me along. The first time she went I thought I understood. Then she got over the so-called miscarriage real quick, and kept going back to Malibu. It was odd, but it seemed to be keeping her happy. She was still after me all the time about flying, though. She wanted me to give it up, to be around for her when she wanted me. She hated that I worked weekends. She hated when I had to change our plans and go fly. I thought her little Malibu trips were some kind of vengeance, as if she wanted me to feel the same about her going off and doing her own thing. I didn't, I was glad she'd found something she enjoyed doing that didn't involve me being responsible for her happiness. At least I was glad, 'til my little sister told me that Anabel was going down there to spend time with a guy. I kind of lost it."

"I can see why," said Ben.

"I flew down there. Found them out by the pool, messing around. I almost killed the guy, Ben. She actually fucking laughed in my face! She honestly believed I was still going to marry her. That I had no choice, because of the business. She wanted the status, she wanted me. She even told me, right there to my face that since I wasn't prepared to make her the center of my world, she'd need to have other 'friends' too. She knew I was a jealous bastard and she thought she could play on it. She found out she couldn't.

"I called the whole thing off. It nearly cost the merger, but she twisted everyone, including my family, into believing a bunch of horseshit. I went along with it—let them lay all the blame on me, say I'd gone into rehab. I took off. It seemed their business was more important to them than their son. They were disappointed in me that I wasn't stepping up to run it. It just seemed best for everyone that I disappear. My folks got the merger they wanted, my brother got to run the business like he wanted, Anabel got the sympathy and attention she wanted, was viewed as having had a lucky escape from marrying the useless heir to the Hamilton fortune."

"How was it best for you though, Smoke?"

Smoke gave a short laugh. "It set me free. It allowed me to make my own way in the world and not be a part of Hamilton Groves. It taught me that to be what a woman wanted I'd have to stop being who I am. So I learned that it's best to keep moving. And that when it comes to a woman it's best to give her what she wants in bed and not stick around long enough for her to want anything else. It was all for the best."

Ben nodded. "I guess so. But now you're talking about making this place a base, not keeping moving. And you've stuck around Laura for a quite a while now. What's the deal?"

"I don't know yet. All I know is I want to stick around to see what it might be. She's the first woman I've ever met who seems to get me. She understands how much I love to fly. She doesn't want to ground me so that I'll spend time with her. In fact she's as likely to fly away as I am. She doesn't want to be grounded herself. I just don't know yet. All I know is that I'm prepared to take the risk of finding out."

"I can see that. You two are good together."

"I hope so, thanks Ben. But what about you? I came here to give you the chance to talk, instead all I've done is talk myself."

"That's okay. You took my mind off my own stuff for a while. That's better than talking about it."

"Are you still going to go to the fundraiser?"

Ben shook his head vigorously. "No. Like I said. I'll probably end up needing to be here anyway. It sounds like you're moving on, Smoke. You're ready to put the past behind you, right?"

"Yeah. I guess I am, and it feels good. You might want to try it, too?"

Ben gave him a sad smile. "I might want to, bud. But I'm not ready to. But it's different, for me the past is the happiest place I've ever been. That's why I don't want to let it go."

Chapter Eighteen

Laura piled up all the pillows on her bed and snuggled up to watch TV. She loved British TV; they had such a weird sense of humor! And the commercials were so civilized and sedate compared to back home. She found it fascinating. She was enjoying just chilling out and doing something mindless, she was tired. It had been a long and fruitful day, touring the offices and warehouse, meeting the in-house design team. They were a great bunch, and she was looking forward to working with them.

She turned the sound down when she heard her cell phone ringing. Who on earth would that be? She checked the screen. Leanne!

"Hey! You do realize I'm in London and this will cost you a fortune?"

"Hey Laura. It's okay. My phone bill is ridiculous anyway, so it's not a problem. I just wanted to ask you something."

"What's that?"

"Who is Michael, and why is Ben not coming to the fundraiser?"

"Oh. He's definitely not coming then?"

"Apparently not. Dan called and told me there's been a change of plan. That I still have a date, someone called Michael, but that Ben can't make it. You know what Dan's like. It was obvious that something had gone down, but he wouldn't tell me what. At least it gives me an excuse to check in with you, see how you're enjoying London, if you've found yourself a cute Englishman—I just love an accent, and you're surrounded by them. I'm jealous!"

Laura laughed. "No, I'm too busy with work to be on the lookout for a cutie. But I'll tell you what, if you love an accent then you'll like Michael. He has an Australian accent, he lived there for years."

"Ooh, sounds promising, but do you know what happened to Ben? I've ogled him from afar the last couple of years when he's been there with Pete. I was hoping to get my hands on him." Her raunchy laugh rang its way across the Atlantic. "I mean, get to know him!"

Laura shook her head. "No, I don't really know. We were all talking about the fundraiser on Friday night and there was talk about some girl being over from England and maybe she could go. I can only guess she's an ex, because he went all quiet and said he wouldn't be able to make it, he'd be busy at the resort."

"Too bad. I could have helped him get over her."

"Maybe it's for the best, Lee. He didn't look like he wanted to get over her." Laura was a little relieved that Ben wouldn't be going with Leanne. Michael, on the other hand, would be more than capable of keeping up with her, and giving as good as he got. "I think you'll do better with Michael anyway. He's a lot of fun."

"What's he look like?"

"Brown hair, green eyes, nice. Good looking."

"Does he look anything like Ben? Ben's gorgeous."

"Not really, no. He's pretty hot, just in a different way."

"Speaking of hot, are you still screwing the smoking hot pilot?"

Laura frowned. She wasn't just screwing him...she wished Leanne would accept that. "Yeah."

"Oh, sorry, I didn't mean to touch a nerve. Don't tell me you're still wanting more than that?"

"Lee, it's complicated, but I assure you whatever we are doing it's a whole lot more than just screwing each other."

"Whatever you say, Laura. As long you don't say I didn't warn you."

"Lee, you'll see when you meet him, okay."

"Yeah, we will see."

"What does that mean?"

"Nothing. I'm just agreeing with you. Now tell me more about this Michael. Am I likely to need to keep him in LA for the week? Is he that kind of hot?"

Laura laughed. "He is that kind of hot, but I doubt you could keep him for the week. He has a son he'll need to get back to."

"Really? Ooh, I like it. There's something sexy about a single dad, don't you think?"

"I don't know, Lee. I've never dated one."

"Well, we'll have to find you one, after you're done with sexy-pants the pilot."

Laura had to giggle, she could just imagine Smoke's face if she called him that. "Let's just focus on Michael, can we? He's a good guy. A lot of fun. One of the few men I know who will be able to give you a run for your money."

"This gets better and better! Maybe I'll keep the weekend after the fundraiser free too, go up to Summer Lake for a second helping and finally visit Dan and Missy. Will you be up there then?"

Laura hoped so. "I don't know yet. Let's not get too far ahead of ourselves, shall we? You might scare him off on the first helping!"

Leanne laughed. "Yeah, that's true. Let's keep our options open. You might be done with sexy-pants by then too, and we can do some hunting in the Bay area instead of going out to the boonies!"

"Lee!"

"Okay, okay! Just keep your options open, girlfriend. This isn't like you. You're starting to worry me!"

"I know, it's a bit worrying to me too, but I like him enough to see where it goes. Anyway, I am keeping my options open. They've offered me the option of living here, if I want to."

"Oh, that could be cool! If you don't stay there for too long, and I can come visit. Just think, you'd be surrounded by all those accents, everywhere!"

Laura had to laugh. "I don't know that I'll do it." She couldn't imagine living here and not seeing Smoke anymore, but she couldn't imagine not moving because of him, either. "But if I do, you had better come visit." She had to remain open to the possibility.

"You can bet your ass I will, girlfriend. Hang on. Sorry. I've got another call coming in. I'll have to go. Enjoy London. Call me when you're home. Let's see if we can get together before the fundraiser, okay?"

"Okay. See you soon."

Laura hung up and turned the sound back up on the TV. Not so long ago she would have been thrilled at the prospect of living here and having Leanne come to visit her. Now all she wanted was to get back to Smoke, and to Summer Lake. What was happening to her? And what would happen to her if she followed her heart instead of her common sense?"

~ ~ ~

Smoke kissed his mom's cheek. "This was good, Mom. I'm glad I came."

"Not as glad as I am, Cole." She gave him a hug. "I hope we'll see you again soon?"

He nodded. "Yeah. It's not like I'm in Miami, or even Houston anymore. It's only a quick hop up here from Summer Lake."

"Do let me know how it goes with the house, won't you? I'll be keeping my fingers crossed for you. It looks such a darling little place." She smiled. "Although I wouldn't have dared imagine you with a picket fence!"

Wow. They really had come a long way, that she would tease him about that. For years it seemed all they'd wanted was to corral him inside a picket fence—with Anabel. "Laura told me I couldn't buy it, because I'm not a picket fence kind of guy."

His mom's smile was so gentle. "It sounds like she knows you well, Cole. I'll be keeping my fingers crossed there, too." She hesitated, then seemed to make a decision. "You know after everything that happened, I was afraid you would never let yourself get close to a woman again. I know we messed up back then, but I hope you also know how sorry we are, and that it was only because we thought we knew best. Obviously we didn't, you did. I need you to know that we will support you in whatever you choose now. If you choose this Laura, we'd love to meet her, when you're ready. She sounds wonderful."

Smoke nodded. "She is." He didn't want to say any more than that, because he didn't know that he really was choosing her yet. Part of him wanted to. Part of him thought he already had. But part of him still wasn't sure he was capable of it. More importantly, he didn't know whether she would choose him—

for anything long term. And bringing her to meet his family? That was a huge step. One he wouldn't take until he was absolutely sure.

His mom was watching him. "It seems to me you've already fallen, Cole. You'll catch up with yourself." She gave him another hug. "She's a very lucky girl. Now, shouldn't you get going if you're going to meet her flight?"

He nodded, still wondering if his mom was right. Had he already fallen for her?

~ ~ ~

It was such a busy airport, there was no way of knowing if the latest wave of passengers coming out were from Laura's flight or not. She'd texted him when she changed planes in New York, and this last flight had landed fifteen minutes ago. Surely she'd be out soon? Smoke was lurking behind the seating area, half hiding behind one of the pillars. Partly because he was hoping to spot her before she spotted him, and partly because he was in uniform and that always attracted attention—he'd just never thought of it as unwanted attention before. He avoided making eye contact with a pretty girl leaning on the next pillar who kept smiling at him.

There she was! Damn! Abso-fucking-lutely gorgeous really was the word. She was looking around, eagerly. That happy little buzz started up in his chest, because she was looking for him. The buzz faded out when the guy walking beside her put a hand on her shoulder. He was getting a business card out of his wallet. Screw that.

Smoke strode towards them, noting that at least she wasn't even really paying attention to the guy, she was still looking around. Her eyes lit up when she saw him. That gorgeous smile made his throat go dry, just like the very first time he'd seen her. She threw herself into his arms. He crushed her to him and claimed her mouth in a kiss that belonged in the bedroom, not a crowded airport. He didn't care. He'd missed her. By the way she kissed him back, she'd missed him too. He was vaguely aware of the guy walking away. Smoke was making it very clear there was no point waiting around to hand her a business card. Her hands cupped around his neck while his closed around her waist, pulling her against him so her body could feel how much he'd missed her, too.

Eventually he looked down at her.

"Hey gorgeous!"

"Who are you calling gorgeous, gorgeous?"

It made him smile. He liked that this was becoming their 'thing'.

"You! I missed you, lady."

"I missed you too, Captain Hamilton. Can we get out of here? Take me home?"

He grinned, taking hold of her bag and taking her hand. "I'd love to."

Once they were settled in the back of a cab he pulled her into his arms. "So how was it? Did you have a good time?"

"It was great. I think I'm really going to enjoy working with them. We kicked around some design ideas and I can't wait to get started."

He grinned. "Do you want to get started in that little workshop?"

She raised an eyebrow.

"At my house?"

She laughed. "You bought the place?"

"I'm working on it. It looks like it'll all go through quite quickly. So, what do you say? I was serious. I won't charge you any rent."

There was doubt in her eyes. "I'd love to. I just need to see how this works out."

Hmm. Not the response he'd hoped for.

She brightened. "And besides, you're a big meanie, buying it when you knew I wanted it too." She laughed.

He held her closer. "Well you know you can come stay anytime you want to." He rested his lips on her hair for a moment as he held her tight. "I'll even let you stay in my bed." He felt her tremble in his arms. Jesus! The things she did to him. When she went all soft like that it was all he could do not to lay her down wherever they were. The back of this cab was no place for it, but he might not be able to make it past the back of the plane.

They'd managed to keep their hands off each other while they got out of the cab, dealt with the guys at the FBO and rode the golf cart back out to Papa Charlie. Now Smoke was pulling up the steps, closing the door and locking the world out.

When he turned back into the cabin Laura was smiling at him. "What, lady?"

"Since you're in uniform, I know I'll have to keep my hands to myself."

Her faith in his ability to remain professional was the only thing that stopped him from heading for the long sofa in the back.

She was smiling. "Until we get there. But you have this strange effect on me. See, I don't even know where 'there' is. Where are we going?"

He laughed. He hadn't even considered that her apartment was right here. That they could have been there by now, even that that was where she had probably meant.

"We're going to Summer Lake, of course. Didn't you ask me to take you home?"

That smile slayed him. Damn! "Of course." She planted a little kiss on his lips. "Let's go home."

~ ~ ~

As soon as he cleared the runway at Summer Lake, Smoke called up the FBO. "We'll be taxiing to the ramp, can you have the guys put Papa Charlie to bed."

"You got it, Smoke. Jason's here, do you have time for a chat?"

No way. He was having the guys put the plane away in order to get Laura home sooner. "Sorry. No can do. We're running late."

"No problem. We'll catch up with you soon."

Laura smiled at him. "What are we late for, Captain Hamilton? You have another night out with the gang lined up?"

"I have not. It's just that I should have had you home hours ago." He shut down the engines and removed his headset. While Laura was taking hers off he reached across to unbuckle her. "Home and in bed, lady. Let's go."

She smiled and followed him to the door.

Inside the FBO, Jason greeted them with a wave. "Hey Smoke, how's it going? Did you hear they're reducing the number of guys they're giving single pilot waivers to?"

Smoke had heard, and right now, he couldn't care less. He just wanted to get out of here, in a hurry. He nodded. "Yeah."

"We'll both be alright though. They're only weeding out the incompetent. They want to keep the best."

Rochelle came out from the office and put an arm around Jason's waist. "Can you get your ego to shut up for a minute? These two are in a hurry."

Jason laughed. "Sorry guys." He looked at Laura, making Smoke smile. "But you need to know your man here is one of the best."

"The best, thank you!" said Smoke with a laugh.

Jason winked at Laura, "Second best, but we can let him believe whatever he needs to, huh?"

Rochelle shook her head at them then turned to Laura. "If you're going to keep hanging out with this guy, I should probably warn you about pilots and their egos."

Laura laughed, "Thanks, but too late. I already got the idea!"

"Oh, you may have an idea, but it's worse than you think. Do you know how many pilots it takes to change a light bulb?" Jason groaned.

Laura looked up at Smoke with that smile. He'd take the teasing just to see the fun and laughter in her beautiful blue eyes.

"Go on, how many?" she asked.

Rochelle laughed and poked Jason. "Only one. He just holds it up and waits for the whole world to revolve around him."

Laura burst out laughing. Smoke knew he wasn't going to hear the end of this one. "That's perfect! Thanks, Rochelle."

"Yeah, thanks a bunch," said Smoke as he took Laura's hand. "I need to get this one home. We'll see you guys soon."

"Call when you get chance," Jason shouted after them. "We want to start getting everything set up."

Smoke waved over his shoulder. He'd talk to them soon. It just wasn't a priority right now. Laura was still laughing. "So the huge ego is a pilot thing, not just a Smoke thing?"

He stopped next to a brand new Ford pickup and backed her up against it, needing to feel the full length of her pressed against him. He nipped at her lips. "You only need to concern yourself with this pilot. And right now he needs to get you home."

Her arms were around his neck, her body yielding to him. "I know we've had some wonderful moments up against cars, Captain Hamilton, but do you think we should maybe restrict ourselves to only using our own? This one's all new and shiny, I'd hate for us to leave any marks." She was laughing at him!

"This is my car, lady. I got around to buying one. Perhaps you'd better get in it, before it's too late. He thrust his hips against her to reinforce his point.

"So, you went on a bit of a shopping spree this week?" she asked as he pulled out of the parking lot.

"What do you mean?"

"You bought a house, you bought a car...you have been busy." He reached across and took her hand. "I had to do something to keep myself occupied. See, I have this problem."

"And what's that?"

"I met this beautiful woman. I think about her all the time. Last week she was gone and I missed her. I think I was trying to numb the pain by spending money, buying things to make myself feel better until she came back. Do you think I have a problem?"

"I think you may."

"And what do you think I should do about it?"

"I think perhaps you need a prescription."

"For what?"

"Sex. Lots and lots of great sex. It's the only solution I can think of."

He grinned. "And do I have to take this medicine every day, twice a day?"

She threw her head back and laughed. "Oh, no. It's much better than that, you can take it as and when needed."

When he pulled up at the cabin he didn't have time to open her door, she was already out. He grabbed her bag from the back and ran up the steps to open the front door. Taking her hand he led her into the kitchen, where he claimed her mouth as his hands raked through her hair. He backed her up against the cabinets while she fought with his buttons. He loved how eager she was to get him out of his clothes. He got rid of her top and bra and slid his hand inside her panties. She was soaking for him. He loved the little sigh that escaped from her lips. In just a few seconds they were both naked. He closed his hands around her waist and lifted her up to sit on the counter.

"Right here?" she breathed as he parted her legs and stood between them.

This was the perfect height.

He grinned at her. "I thought I'd try an over the counter remedy."

She shook her head at him, but he didn't give her time to speak. He closed his hands around her waist and thrust deep. This height might be a little too perfect. She wrapped her legs around his waist as he moved inside her. Her arms were around his neck and the feel of her mouth, her warm breath just under his ear, was intensifying all the pent up need rushing through his veins. He wasn't going to be able to hold back. He needn't have worried. Her legs went rigid as she bit down on his neck. "Oh, God, Smoke!" He plunged deep inside her and let himself go, crushing her to his chest as she carried him away. Gasping together, they soared high above the clouds. He really would never get enough of her.

Chapter Nineteen

Laura smiled as she wiped down the counter top, remembering Smoke's face as he'd lifted her off it last night. He'd led her by the hand into his bedroom and they'd lain there for hours talking. He'd told her all about his plans with Jason and Rochelle. About setting up a flight school, making sure they each still got to take some of the longer flights for Phoenix. He seemed so enthusiastic about it all. Apparently he used to be a flight instructor, but had some issues around it, something that seemed like resentment. He hadn't elaborated. She shrugged; he'd tell her when he was ready. She'd told him all about London. She frowned as she poured two fresh coffees—almost all about London. She hadn't yet mentioned the offer to live there. She would.

She took the coffees outside to where he was still sitting. He'd made them a wonderful breakfast and was now working on his laptop. Checking some details for flights he had next week. As she set the coffees down his phone rang. He gave her an apologetic smile as he picked it up.

"Jason! What do you need?...They are?...What time?...Hang on."

He put his hand over his phone and looked up at her. "Would you be okay if I ran over to the airport for an hour at noon?"

She smiled. "Of course. You go do whatever you need to."

He nodded and gave her that sweet little smile, the one that almost made her forget that the cocky Smoke even existed.

"Jason? Yeah. That works. I'll see you at noon."

He hung up. "You really don't mind?" He looked worried!

She laughed. "I don't mind at all! I'll give Missy a call, see if I can't catch up with her, maybe we'll find Em and Holly too, and have lunch. And take as long as you like, you've been commandeering far too much of my time when I'm up here anyway."

He scowled at her now, but she could see the smile lurking. "Well, excuse the fuck out of me! I wouldn't want to interfere with your girl time. And here I was worried about leaving you all alone."

"No worries there, Captain. I never get chance to be all alone. Whenever you abandon me there's always someone around."

The smile faded as the scowl became more real. "Yeah. Someone like the guy at the airport yesterday?"

"What guy?"

"The one who was about to give you his card when I found you."

She laughed. "You mean the little skinny guy who wanted to talk to me about an engagement ring for his soon-to-be fiancée? The one who ran away when this jealous, possessive jerk swooped in and stuck his tongue down my throat in the middle of the airport?"

Smoke hung his head, but she could see he was smirking. "Yeah, that'd be the guy. Sorry."

She went and straddled his lap. "That's okay. I was more interested in being swept off my feet by the jerk."

He closed his arms around her. "He's not that much of a jerk, you know. He's just not used to wanting a woman to be his. He hasn't figured out what to do with it yet, but he's working on it."

He looked so earnest. The poor guy did seem to be all over the place. He was the one who flew away at the drop of a hat and didn't care who he left wanting in his wake. Yet here he was trying to make sure she'd be okay before he went off to do his own thing.

"He's doing a really good job of it, Smoke. You know I'm only teasing you. It's very sweet of you and I appreciate it. But you go do your thing, I'll go do mine. And I'm happy to. Neither of us wants to live in the other's pocket. We'll figure it out as we go." She nibbled on his bottom lip. "And if you don't have to be there till noon, we've got plenty of time to give you some more medicine before you go." She rocked her hips against him. He was already hard.

She had to wrap her arms and legs around him and hang on as he stood up. "More medicine, huh?" his hands closed around her ass as he carried her to the bedroom. "I think this time I'd better lie down while you give it to me."

~ ~ ~

Missy waved from a table at the corner of the deck. "Laura! Over here."

Laura made her way over and Missy stood to hug her. "Hey, hon! So good to see you. How was London?"

"It was wonderful, Miss. How are you?"

"I'm great. I still can't quite believe that I'm engaged to your cousin and that we're going to be getting married!"

Laura smiled. "Neither can I! I'm so happy for you both. Have you made any plans yet?"

Missy wrinkled her nose. "No. We're still trying to decide what we want. Dan thinks it'd be cool have the wedding in Vegas."

"But you don't like the idea?"

"I do, but...."

"But what?"

"I don't know, it just seems like a cop out. I wouldn't have to do anything. They take care of it all, all the details, everything."

"And you want to do it yourself?"

Missy laughed. "I really don't. Just the thought of organizing it all myself exhausts me! But I feel like I should, you know?"

"Why? Why should you get into all the work and stress if you don't want to? I'll bet that's why Dan wants to go to Vegas, just to make it easier on you."

Laura loved the way Missy looked when she talked about Dan. "It is. If it was up to him I would never left a finger again, my whole life. He's so sweet, Laura. He keeps trying to make my life easier." She laughed now. "We're still getting the hang of each other though. I mean, he's been buying me gadgets for the kitchen? I don't know how the hell to work them!"

Laura laughed.

"He honestly believes that if you have to program something to do its job, then it's useful! I think I'm slowly getting through to him, that if I have to program it, it's not going to happen. He got this coffee pot that's supposed to let you sleep in an extra ten minutes because you set it on a timer. It wakes up by itself and grinds the beans and makes the coffee automatically. The first morning I tried it, I was creeping down the stairs with Scot's baseball bat wondering who had broken in and was making all that noise! You can imagine how stupid I felt when I got in the kitchen and remembered!"

Laura threw her head back and laughed. "Oh, Miss. You're too funny!"

Missy laughed with her. "That wasn't even the best of it. The next night I set it all up again. Just to show him I'm coachable, I can get the hang of it. Only I didn't...quite. The damned thing woke me up when it was grinding the coffee, but I lay there in bed, all proud of myself. I've got this. I went downstairs ready to be the perfect little tech-homemaker, but...not! I hadn't put the little cup in all the way so the damned thing had spewed coffee beans all over the kitchen and was sitting there grinning at me with a carafe full of warm water!"

Laura was giggling. Those two were so completely opposite they really shouldn't work, but they did.

"Anyway, enough of my domestic disasters. What about you? I'm glad you're here again, but I must say I'm surprised. I didn't think you'd be back up here for a while. Didn't you just get back from London on Friday?"

"Actually it was yesterday afternoon."

Missy gave her a knowing smile. "And you just couldn't stay away?"

"Smoke said he'd meet me at the airport and take me home. I was hardly going to refuse. Only he brought me here."

Missy grinned. "Sounds like he did bring you home, hon. You'll be moving up here like the rest of them soon."

Laura smiled. She did like the idea. But what about London?

"Or won't you?" As always, Missy didn't miss a thing.

Laura looked at her. "I don't think it's quite as straightforward for me as it has been for the others, Miss. I mean, Smoke isn't exactly the settling down type. And neither am I."

Missy laughed. "Sorry, Laura. But remind me who it was straightforward for? Jack and Em? With her 'I'm too scared to love anyone?' Pete and Holly? With his 'I can't allow a woman into my life yet because it's not in the plan?' Dan and I probably had the easiest path to getting together, and that certainly wasn't without its bumps in the road."

Laura nodded. "Yeah, but...you all wanted it. You didn't have something else in your life that you wanted more."

Missy raised her eyebrows. "What is it that you want more? Because when you were both out with us all last weekend, it seemed like neither of you could possibly want anything in the world more than you wanted each other!"

Laura smiled. "Well, that kind of want is hard to avoid around Smoke."

Missy laughed, "Yeah, I can see that, he's like sex-on-a-stick." She giggled. "Or at least, sex-in-a-pilot's-uniform! But no, that's not what I meant. He was so into letting everyone know that you were there together. It was totally obvious that he wants to be with you, not just in bed with you. And you were the same. Normally you're like Miss I've-Got-My-Shit-Together untouchable, but around Smoke you're all teasing, and flirty, and girly. What could you want more than the guy who makes you feel that way?"

Laura shrugged. She wanted her independence. She knew Smoke did to. But did either of them want it more that they wanted to be together? And did being together have to mean losing their independence? She looked at Missy. "When I was London, they suggested I should move there."

"Oh. I guess that puts a different spin on things. And you want that more than you want to move up here? More than you want to be with Smoke?"

"Honestly, Miss? I don't think I do. I'm just not sure that I could live with myself if I passed up an opportunity like that for a man. That's not who I am."

"Hey, ladies!" Holly plonked herself down next to Missy. "How are we? Sorry it took me a while to get over here. A certain CEO didn't want to let me out of the house."

"More like he didn't want to let you out of bed!" Missy rolled her eyes.

"No!" Holly laughed. "He had planned for us to go up to Four Mile and take a look around this afternoon. You know what he's like about changing his plans! And here's Emma." Holly pointed to a beautiful blue convertible pulling into the square.

"Why the hell does she drive that thing on these roads?" asked Laura.

Missy laughed. "Because it's her baby and she refuses to get rid of it."

Emma sat down after hugging each of them. "Isn't this wonderful? We should make it a new tradition that we get together for lunch without the guys, I don't know, every other weekend or something?"

Missy and Holly nodded their agreement.

Emma looked at her. "How about you, Laura? Are you up for it?"

Laura bit her lip.

"Give her time," said Missy. "She's not accepted the inevitable yet."

"The inevitable? What does that mean?"

Holly laughed. "That you're going to end up living here, just like the rest of us. Summer Lake is like this magical realm. Once you come here you are assigned your very own hot man, and you get to live here and have a wonderful little life."

The others laughed. It was certainly true for them. But one word Holly had used bothered her. She didn't want a little life. She wanted to live a big life. To travel, to experience the world, to keep growing in her career.

"What is it?" asked Emma.

Laura shrugged. "I can see how wonderful it is for all of you. But I'm just starting to build my career up, to really go places. That doesn't seem to fit with moving here."

"Oh, no?" asked Holly. "Do you have any idea what's happened to my career since I moved here? It's not just taking off, it's exploding. Just because I live here now, doesn't mean I've lost the rest of my life. It's helped me expand. It could do the same for you. You can have a base here and still travel to meet clients. You'll have the store once Four Mile is built, too.

And from what Pete said, your smokin' hot man is basing himself here. You could travel the world over, but you'll never find another one like him, sweetie."

Laura sighed. "I just need to figure out what to do for the best."

"But you..." began Holly.

Missy cut her off. "Leave her alone. We all got there in our own time. Laura will do the same, if it's right for her. And besides, I need to eat, so let's order now, can we?"

Laura shot her a grateful look over her menu. She did need time to think about it. She looked around at the others as they ordered. They did have a great life here. She had been considering moving here. But the offer of moving to London? How could she turn that down?

Smoke headed out of the FBO into the sunshine. He was glad he'd come over, it had been a good meeting. Becoming a certified flight center would help with marketing and credibility and would also provide the instructional framework he was used to. Or at least had been used to. It had been years since he'd worked as an instructor.

As he walked towards his truck, he recognized the one parked next to it, an old blue Toyota.

Jack! "Are you tailing me now, Benson? Cos, if you are, I think you're supposed to park on the other side of the lot and keep your head down."

Jack laughed. "Yeah, thanks. I knew I didn't have it quite right. But hey, since I've blown my cover, you may as well come have a beer with me."

Smoke wanted to get back to Laura, not hang out with Jack. What was he up to?

Jack grinned, apparently reading his thoughts. "She's gone for lunch with Em and the girls. They won't be done for a while yet. I told Em to text me before she leaves. So follow me into town, we can have a beer in the bar and you won't miss a minute with my little bitty cousin. I need to talk to you, okay?" Smoke shook his head. "Alright, but you know normal people just pick up the phone and call."

Jack laughed again. "We both know how little respect you have for normal. And besides, you would have blown me off. True or false?"

Smoke blew out a short sigh as he climbed into his truck. "True. I'll see you in the bar."

Chapter Twenty

Smoke was already seated at the bar when Jack came in. The same girl from the other day was working. Apparently undeterred by that conversation, the eyelashes were fluttering and the hair was being flicked around.

Smoke nodded when Jack spotted him. "What do you want?"

"Hi sweetie, good to see you too! Don't be such a grouch."

Smoke had to laugh. "I meant what do you want to drink, asshole! I know what you want to talk about."

Jack grinned. "I'll get them, since I dragged you in here."

Once they had their beers Jack headed for one of the high top tables in a quiet corner.

Smoke pulled up a seat and rolled his eyes. "Come on then. What's up?"

"I just wanted to see if you've talked to Laura yet?"

"Yeah, I've talked to her quite a lot these last few weeks."

"You know what I mean. Have you told her how you got to be as screwed up as you are?"

"I've started to. Unlike some people, she is rather understanding and patient. She says we'll get there in our own time. That it'll all come out little by little as we get to know each other."

Jack nodded. "Fair enough. You know I'm really not trying to be an asshole. I'd love to see the two of you work it out, but it worries me that it could all come around to bite you in the ass if you're not up front with each other."

Smoke nodded. "Thanks, Jack. No seriously," he added when he saw the look on Jack's face. "Thank you. I'm way out of my depth. I'm spending half my time buying a house and a car and setting up a life here that I can make her a part of. The rest of the time I'm wondering if I should just be wheels up and gone."

Jack was frowning now. "I don't know what she's told you about herself, but the one thing you will never be able to do with Laura is make her do or be anything. She'll disappear on you, go into hiding, if she feels her independence is threatened."

Smoke felt his throat go dry. That was odd. He'd grown to associate that reaction with being happy, with laying eyes on her. Now it was happening at the thought of losing her. As he stared at Jack it dawned on him—no way could he stand to lose her!

"I didn't mean it like that, Jack. I meant let her in. Let her be part of my life."

Jack held up a hand. "It's okay, bro. I know what you mean, but I'm not sure she would. You're going about setting up all the trappings of a normal life—the house, the car, changing your work life so that you'll be based in once place, be around more. Most women would be getting ready to drag you down the aisle with all the signals you're giving off. I just want to make sure you know that Laura doesn't work that way. Everything you're doing is more likely to scare her away than reel her in."

Smoke stared at him. "I'm not trying to reel her in, Jack. I'm..." He ran a hand over his eyes. "Honestly? I don't know what the fuck I'm doing. I just know I want her to be part of my life. I don't want to change the way I am, but that's okay, because she doesn't want me to. And I sure as hell don't want to change the way she is. It's her being the way she is that makes me love her."

Jack's jaw dropped.

"What? What's up, bro?" Smoke was worried.

Jack was recovering quickly, a huge grin spreading across his face, making the corners of his eyes crinkle. "Did you hear what you just said?" he asked.

Smoke frowned. "What? That I don't want to change the way she is?"

"Why not?"

"Because that's....Oh, fuck!"

Jack was laughing now. "I hoped that was where you might end up! Now you just have to find a way to make it work. I remember the day you swore you would never love a woman again your whole life!"

Smoke pressed his lips together. Rolling the thought around in his mind, barely hearing Jack. That's what makes me love her. It was true. Now he stopped to think about it. He did love her. He wouldn't have been able to make love to her if he didn't. But what the fuck was he going to do about it? He looked up at his friend. "What do I do, Jack?"

Jack slapped his shoulder. "You'll figure it out. My only suggestion is you talk to her. Tell her everything."

"Even tell her that I...." Smoke couldn't bring himself to say it out loud.

"Damned straight! Especially that!" Jack's phone buzzed. He picked it up off the table. "And it looks like you'll get your chance to, any minute now. They've finished and are about to head home." He tapped out a text then looked up at Smoke. "Or at least they were. I just told Em to bring Laura back here."

Smoke stared at him. Jesus! What could he do with this? Was he ready to tell her that he....? There was no time to decide. She and Emma came through the door from the deck. Her beautiful smile lit up her face when she spotted him. The happy buzz hummed loudly in his chest. He smiled back at her as she walked towards him. He might not be able to say it, but damn! He sure as hell couldn't deny it. He was in love with her!

~ ~ ~

Laura was surprised to see Smoke sitting with Jack in the bar. She smiled, loving the sight of gentle Smoke out in public. The way he was smiling at her had her heart racing.

Jack stood up when they got to the table. He put an arm around Emma. "We'll see you guys soon." He grasped Smoke's shoulder and gave him a shake. "Don't take too long about it."

Laura was even more surprised that Smoke turned the same gentle smile on Jack. Weird, he would normally have punched his arm or something, but he just smiled and said, "Thanks, bro. I'll call you."

Emma gave her a hug and then they were gone.

Smoke was by her side, taking hold of her hand. "Hey, gorgeous."

"Who are you calling gorgeous, gorgeous?"

"You. Let's go home, lady. We need to talk."

She let him lead her out of the bar. They walked down by the water's edge. "For someone who says we need to talk, you're being awfully quiet," she said after a while.

The way he looked at her melted her heart. That look didn't need words. It told her he wanted her. As Missy had put it, wanted to be with her, not just be in bed with her. If she had to describe that look she would have said it was full of love. But it couldn't be, could it? And what was she supposed to do if it was? Panic? That seemed like the only reasonable response. For some reason though, she didn't feel panicky. That look made her feel happy—so very happy. And she had a fair idea that the look on her own face was mirroring it. He stopped walking and pulled her to him. Cupping the back of her head with his hand, he brushed his lips over hers. As always, her arms reached up around his neck of their own accord, pulling him down into a kiss.

Standing there wrapped in his arms, his mouth exploring hers, the gentle breeze off the lake reminding her where she was, she knew in her heart there was nowhere else on earth she'd rather be.

When he lifted his head, his eyes were full of questions. "Did that tell you anything?"

Laura took a deep breath and nodded slowly. "I think it did. And I think you're right. We do need to talk."

Little furrows creased his brow as he took her hand and started walking again. "Let's take it home then."

Back at the cabin they settled on the sofa out on the deck. "So, what do you want to tell me, Captain Hamilton?" She tried to make her voice sound light, but it held none of its usual teasing tone; even she could hear that.

Smoke curled his leg underneath him to sit sideways on the sofa as he took hold of her hands. "Did that kiss on the way back tell you anything, lady?"

She nodded.

"What did it tell you?"

"I need to hear you say it, Smoke."

He shook his head. "I'm not sure I know how to make those words come out."

She was aware of that. Maybe it was best left alone anyway. Maybe it was best to stay away from the words she thought he meant.

"What do you want to talk about then?"

"I think it's time I tell you my story. See if you still want to stick around for those words. You might want to run before I ever say them."

"I doubt that, Smoke."

His face looked pained.

She reached out to touch his cheek. "You've already told me you're no saint—though that wasn't hard to figure out. It's the past. We all have one. Your past has made you who you are today and I...." Oh, God! What had she been about to say? He was looking at her, the pain in his eyes replaced by hope. No. She couldn't bring herself to say it, even while he was looking at her like that. "I really like who you are today."

His shoulders sagged, they both knew it was because of what she'd failed to say. But dammit, he'd refused to say it, too!

He nodded. "You're right. It has. I loved a woman once before. I was engaged to her. She loved me in the beginning too, but she ended up pretty much hating me." He shrugged. "It was mutual."

Laura said nothing. She didn't know what she could say.

"She wanted to be the center of my life, my world, my everything. She hated that I love my job so much. She thought I should turn my back on it, put her first whenever she wanted me to. I didn't. I couldn't." He looked up at her, his eyes sad. "I don't know how."

Laura wrapped her arms around him and hugged him close. He looked so sad, so lost. "I'm sorry, Smoke."

He pulled back to look at her. "What for?"

"That she didn't love you back like you needed her to."

The creases in his brow were back as he thought that one over. Then he shook his head. "That's not what I meant. It was me that couldn't love her the way she needed me to. I made her miserable, just by being me. I don't want to do that to you."

Laura let out a little laugh and shook her head. "You make me so happy by being you, Smoke. I love hearing the way you talk about flying. I love seeing you fly. I love the way you care so much about your work. I love that you have your own thing, something that's so important to you. I would suffocate in a minute if...someone...tried to make me the center of their world, their everything."

He nodded. "I'm starting to understand that. That's what we need to talk about. See, while I've been buying this house, setting up the flight school, laying the foundation for a life here...I'm doing it all with the hope that you'll be a part of it."

Laura held her breath. Waiting for the panic to kick in, for the need to run to take over and drown out everything else. She waited. But it didn't happen. She stared at him in shock, as her heart raced—happily!

"I can't make you the center of it, and I always thought that was what a woman wanted, what a woman needs, in order to be happy. But you really don't, do you?"

She shook her head. "I not only don't want it, I definitely don't need it, and more to the point, I couldn't stand it."

He nodded. "But could you stand to be a part of it? To see if there's some way we can be together that will let you be you, and me be me, but alongside each other?"

Laura bit her lip. London was hardly alongside Summer Lake. Oh, his poor face! "You don't need to answer right now. But would you think about it?"

"Smoke, I...."

He looked up at her hopefully.

Oh, God! She had to tell him. "When I was in London they asked me to stay."

His gray eyes bored into her.

"To go and live there."

His lips pressed together. "Oh. Sorry. I didn't know. You should have said." He shrugged and as if he'd flipped a switch, the cocky Smoke was back. "So, how about we forget everything I just said?"

"But, Smoke, I...." She didn't get chance to finish the sentence. He'd pulled her towards him and his mouth came down on hers. She put her hands on his shoulders to push him back—she needed to explain. He deepened the kiss, claiming her mouth, owning her body. His hand was inside her top, his thumb circling. She let out a low moan as his other hand pushed her skirt up and slid inside her panties. All thoughts of explaining what she'd meant were lost. She couldn't even think straight, let alone put a sentence together. Her skirt was around her waist now, she was on her back. Underneath him. How did he do it? His fingers only left her heat to unbuckle himself and push her panties to the side. It had become so familiar to feel his knees pushing at her thighs, opening her up so he could....Oh, God!

She clung to him as he filled her. There was a desperation in the way their bodies expressed everything they were too afraid to say. His arm around her waist, his hand in her hair told her she was his, she was where she belonged. Her arms around his back, and her legs around his told him she knew; she belonged to him. They told him what her words wouldn't—that she needed him. Each thrust of his hips demanded she let him in, into the deepest part of her body, into her heart, and into her soul. And she let him in, closing around him as he plunged inside her, holding him tight, begging him to stay. They took each other closer and closer to the edge. She felt him tense and knew that this time, when he said it, it would be true. She'd be his. He let go and she saw stars as he took her with him. But even as her body soared away with his, her heart hurt. Because this time he didn't say it.

This time there was no lying there, nuzzling and whispering. Even while he was still breathing hard he rolled off her and pulled up his pants. He gave her the cocky grin and disappeared inside. She straightened her clothes, since they hadn't made time to get out of them. This was horrible. She felt cheap, like someone he'd just fucked and was about to fly away from. He wasn't, was he?

She went inside and was surprised to hear the shower running. She knocked on the bathroom door. "Come on in. You've seen it all before."

She stepped inside. "Smoke. Don't shut down on me. Please?"

He grinned at her. "I'm not shutting down, I'm cleaning up."

"Talk to me."

"Laura, you know I'm not a big talker. We've talked enough."

"No we haven't! You told me what you wanted to say. You shut down when I started to tell you what I wanted to say."

He shrugged and turned away to test the water. "Doesn't seem like there's much left to say." He turned his back to her as he took his shirt off. "Talking is over-rated anyway. Do you want to join me?" He stepped out of his clothes and into the shower. "Can you close the door on your way in—or your way out?"

Laura felt the anger bubble up. He was deliberately being a pig. She slammed the bathroom door shut and got undressed. The shower was already full of steam as she stepped in, careful not to close that door quite so hard. He had his back to her as he worked shampoo through his hair. The muscles on his broad back rippled as his arms moved. He might be acting like a cocky pig, but the tension was rolling off him in waves. She put a hand on his arm and planted a kiss between his shoulder blades.

He spun around so fast she almost lost her balance. His arm snaked around her waist while he braced his other hand against the wall above her head. "It's been good, Laura. But I think it's time to call it quits."

Her heart stopped in her chest as her stomach tied itself in a knot. Had he really just said that? "What do you mean, Smoke?" She searched his face, unable to believe he could mean it.

He had her backed against the wall now. The water was hitting the back of his head, rolling down over his face, his neck, his shoulders. "I mean it's time to say goodbye." His voice cracked on that last word. Maybe it wasn't just water rolling down his face?

She felt her own tears sting and closed her eyes to keep them in. Her heart felt as though it was being ripped from her chest. She didn't want to say goodbye to this man, ever. She couldn't, wouldn't say goodbye to him. No god-damned way!

"You asshole!" She poked a finger in his chest. "You big, fucking coward!"

His eyes widened in shock. She was a little shocked herself at the words that were coming out, but she pushed on. She was all too familiar with the fight or flight instinct, and for the first time in her life she was prepared to fight—for what she wanted.

"It's not time to say goodbye at all. It's time to figure how the hell we're going to do this! You think it's okay to tell me your shit and then close up on me when I try to tell you mine? You're going to have to do better than that Mr. Cole Alexander Hamilton! You're going to have to grow a pair and work with me here!" She glowered up at him.

He shook his head sadly. "I'm not being a coward. I'm doing you a favor, Laura. You need to fly away from here. You need to be free. Free to go to London and wherever else life takes you. I'm not going to be the one who holds you down. I know

how that feels, and I won't do that to you. Because...I love
you."

Who'd have thought it would take calling him a fucking
coward to make him say it out loud? "Then you really are an
asshole, Smoke. Because I love you too! And you are not going
to be able to push me away or keep me out. You're going to
work with me, you big Neanderthal!" She couldn't believe he'd
just told her he loved her and she was calling him an asshole.

His lips were pressed together his face was still tense, but she
was relieved to see the tiniest hint of a smile lurking.

"You know you're gorgeous when you're angry, right?" He was
leaning his weight against her now, getting hard again.

"Don't mock me, Smoke! I'm serious!"

"I noticed." His hands closed around her waist. "So am I. I
will not hold you back from doing what you want to do."

"I know you won't. For one thing I wouldn't let you, but more
importantly I know you'd never try to, any more than I would
try to tie you down."

He nibbled her ear before his mouth moved down over her
neck, nipping and sucking.

"Smoke, listen to me!"

His mouth was working its way back up, his tongue moving
over her skin, tracing her jaw line. He bit her chin, then her
lips before leaning back to look at her. "I am listening, I heard
you tell me you love me. Did you hear me tell you I love you?"

She nodded.

"So you're telling me you want to find a way to make
something work? That you really want to be mine?"

She nodded again. "I want to be, but please, don't ever do
what you just did out there again?"

"I couldn't say it out loud, Laura. I couldn't hold you to
something you don't want. I said it in my head though.
Because even if you walk out that door. Even if you go to live

in London and I never see you again, in my heart you are mine. In my heart you will always be mine. And I will always be yours. I told you you were trouble, lady. You've broken down every wall I've ever put up. Busted through all the defenses it took me years to build. Now, whether you want me or not, I'm yours. My heart is yours and always will be."

"But Smoke, I do want you, that's what I'm saying. I don't know how, but we'll make it work. We have to."

His knee was between her thighs. "Then let's try this again shall we?"

He took her hard and fast. Their cries mingled as one when they came together.

Smoke slammed into her as he cried, "Mine!"

Laura knew she truly was as she gasped, "Yes!"

Chapter Twenty-One

If he'd thought he had a problem with always needing to be holding her hand or touching her before, Smoke knew he was even worse now. They'd dried each other down after the shower, fallen into bed and laid there talking. He'd held her hand the whole time, stroked her hair, touched her face. He was lost and he knew it. He still had that uneasy feeling, though.

"I love you, lady, but I refuse to hold you back. Whatever we work out, however we do this, I want you to spend as much time in London as you need. Do what you want to do, go where you need to go, for as long as you like. Do you understand me?"

She nodded and snuggled closer under his arm. "I will. I'll go to London, but I don't want to live there. I want to be able to spend time with you."

"We will." He planted a kiss on top of her head and stared out at the lake. "We'll see each other when we can. You can come stay with me. I'll come visit you if you want me to, but it won't work if you give anything up so you can be with me."

"I'm not talking about giving it up, Smoke. I'm talking about finding a way to do it all. You were the one who talked about how everyone else is managing, remember? Jack and Emma, Holly and Pete, Dan and Missy. We can do that too. We just have to figure out how." She turned to look up at him. "We can do it and we will do it. Because I love you. You were the one who said it could work if you found the right person. Well I know I have." The fun and laughter were shining in her eyes as she added, "I never would have guessed that my right person would be an ego-ridden, great big Neanderthal of a possessive jerk, but since you are we'll just have to make the best of it."

He laughed at that. "At least you know what you're letting yourself in for."

"I do, but will you explain something that doesn't make sense to me?"

Smoke tensed, knowing there was still so much more he had to tell her. Still, she needed to know it all before they really could go anywhere with this. "I'll do my best."

She pulled his head down and planted a kiss on his lips. "You don't have to tell me till you're ready, but I want to ask the question, okay?"

He nodded, feeling himself relax a little. She was so good about not pressuring him. "Ask away, I'll do what I can."

"I just don't understand where the jealous, possessive bit comes in. It doesn't sit right with the guy who will fly away at the drop of a hat. I mean I can see that it's true, but I don't understand where it comes from, what makes you that way?"

He squeezed her hand, which made him realize that he was holding it once again. He did know the answer to this one, he just hoped he could explain it. "Okay. First, you do understand why I take off rather than stick around?"

She nodded, "Of course I do. It's my natural instinct too."

"Yeah, to me, sticking around—feeling obliged to stick around—has always felt like I was being grounded. Having my freedom, my ability to fly, taken away." He paused. How to explain it? "You're right about my big ego. I do like to feel that when I fly away I'll be missed. That the people I leave behind wanted me and don't just forget me when I'm gone. When I choose to stick around, to not fly away, I need to know that I'm doing it for a worthwhile reason." He paused, knowing he had to stop talking in generalities, to be forthright and honest. "I need to know that you actually want me. That you want me enough that you're not interested in anyone else. I need to know that I'm not making a mistake, that I'm not grounding myself for no reason. I feel like I'm making this huge sacrifice and I need to know that it's as important to you as it is to me. I need to know that you want me, and only me. I need to know that you are all mine. It's no sacrifice if we're in it together, so I need to know that we are. I guess the jealous and possessive thing is my way of seeking reassurance—that you want me, love me, and trust me as much as I do you. Does that make any sense?"

She nodded, but her eyes were troubled. "But I don't want you to make any sacrifices to be with me."

"Like I said. If we're in it together, it's no sacrifice. It's what I want, so I'm not giving anything up. I'm gaining everything. I just need to know I'm important to you. With everything that happened, I ended up feeling like I wasn't important to anyone. I wasn't important to Anabel. She didn't want me, she wanted the package, the status, the influence that would come from our being together. When it all went to shit, I felt like my family didn't want me, that they had only wanted the son who would help make Hamilton Groves a reality and who...."

"What did you just say?"

"I felt like they didn't really want...Laura, what...?"

Her face had gone pale. "You said Hamilton Groves? Meaning wine? Meaning one of the largest producers and distributors in the country?

Oh, shit! He'd done more talking these last few weeks about his past and his background than he had done in years. He was getting used to the idea that he didn't need to hide who he was. What he'd forgotten was that he hadn't told Laura yet. He'd told Ben, but not Laura. "Yeah." He hugged her to him. "I told you I came from money? I told you I grew up in Napa? I didn't think the particular family made much difference." Apparently it did.

She was staring at him. "Anabel Groves?"

He nodded. "You know her?"

"I made her engagement ring."

He couldn't help the bitter laugh. "She's found another poor sucker then? I wonder if she told him she's pregnant."

Laura's eyes were huge now. "Is that what she did to you?"

He nodded. "It was a lie, though."

"Was everything else lies, too?"

"I don't know. What everything else are you talking about?"

"She told me that she'd been engaged once, a long time ago. That her fiancé had hit her for talking to another guy. That he'd beat the guy up and put him in hospital. That he made his family threaten to ruin her family if she went public with the truth. That her fiancé had gone to jail for what he did, but his family said he was in rehab. I just never made the connection that you were that Hamilton."

Jesus! Anabel was still telling people that? He looked at Laura—and she believed it? His heart refused to beat, if she could believe that of him, what was the point? "You tell me, Laura. Do you think that's the truth?"

She shook her head. "Not of the man I know. I can see you beating the guy up if they were sleeping together. But, you? Smoke—and certainly not the Cole I've seen, hit a woman? Never. I don't know who you used to be and I don't know about your family, but I do know you. You're not capable of that."

His heart restarted with a loud thud. He blew out a big sigh of relief. "Thank you. You're right. I did beat the crap out of the guy, and I'm not proud of that. I guess that fueled my jealous, possessive streak. I was sacrificing so much to try to make that woman happy, and she was using him to taunt me that I just wasn't good enough."

Laura wrapped her arms around him and hugged him. "I'm sorry. It just shocked me. I had no idea. Is that why it was such a big deal when you told me your name?"

He nodded. "Kind of. I figured if you knew the name we could talk about it. But it was more important than that. Smoke is the part of me that the world sees." He gave her an apologetic smile, but he needed to say it. "The guy that women want to sleep with. Before I made love to you I needed you to know....I'm not going to say 'the real me,' because Smoke is real. I needed you to know the rest of me. Cole is the part of me who felt rejected and betrayed, the part of me that, as a result, trusts no-one and stays hidden, stays safe. Telling you my name was my way of letting you in. My way of letting you know that I trust you."

She hugged him even tighter. "Thank you. That means the world to me."

He hugged her back. "You mean the world to me, lady. It's good to do this, to get it all out. We need to. So what else?"

"You don't have to go there if you don't want to, but...well, since we're being honest. This one is kind of huge for me. What's the deal with your family? You know my story with Dale. The thought of your family just being who they are terrifies me. Then the whole business with Anabel? What was the real story?"

Smoke didn't want to talk about it. It was too painful, but he understood why she needed to hear it. "My parents are good people. I didn't believe that for a long time, but they did what they did because they loved me, and they thought they knew what was best for me. They made some choices that they now acknowledge were poor ones. They took their business where they wanted it to go—and lost their son in the process. We're getting closer again now. In fact...how would you feel about going with me to see them?"

She looked terrified.

"I'd like you to meet them, Laura, but no pressure. We could do a real quick visit next weekend, on the way to the fundraiser? Real quick, like half an hour. I'll pick you up in Papa Charlie, we'll stop at their house and then go on to LA. What do you say?"

"I don't know, Smoke. There's no hurry, is there? I'd like some time to think about it."

"If you don't want to, we don't have to. But the more you think about it, the more scary it will be. You'll blow it up in your mind and relate it back to your ex's family. That's why I want to do it so soon. Get it over with, and do it in one quick visit."

She smiled at him. "You're right."

He grinned at her and swaggered his shoulders. "Of course I am! When have I ever been wrong?"

She laughed. "There goes that ego again."

"And why wouldn't it? The most gorgeous lady in the world just told me that she loves me. This ego is going to be flying high on that one for a long time."

~ ~ ~

Laura touched the flowers that sat on her desk and smiled. She re-read the note that had been delivered with them.

Birds of Paradise.

They remind me of you.
I love you, lady.
Cole xxx

Once he'd finally managed to say those three little words, it seemed like the floodgates had opened. These flowers had been waiting for her at the store this morning. Yesterday it had been a bunch of balloons at her apartment, a dozen airplanes and a dozen hearts with I love you written on them.

He'd brought her back to San Francisco on Monday morning so that she could start getting everything ready to sell the store. He had a busy week himself, flying Jack and Pete to some big meeting down in San Diego. He was hoping to be back by Friday night and come stay with her. Then they would go to the fundraiser on Saturday night—after stopping in to meet his parents. She shuddered at the thought. For all his reassurance that it would be a quick—literally a flying visit—and that his parents were good people, she was nervous about it. Dale's family had been good people too, but she hadn't been able to survive them, she'd had to escape. She had often wondered if they would still be together if it weren't for the pressure that came with his name. She was glad they weren't, or she would never have met Smoke. But now it seemed he came from a family that might bring even more pressure.

Her phone rang, startling her from her thoughts.

"Laura Benson."

"Good afternoon, Laura, or sorry, it will be morning with you, won't it?"

"Oh, hi Colin, yes. Good morning. How are you?"

"I'm very well indeed, thank you. I'm rather excited to tell you that we've had our first inquiry about your designs."

"You have?" Wow! She didn't even think they'd made it public yet. "Who from? What are they looking for?"

"It's a gentleman looking for an engagement ring. I thought you'd be pleased about that, as they seem to be your signature piece."

"Yeah, they do." She felt a little deflated. She'd hoped to start out with something else. She didn't want to become known for only doing engagement rings. She'd been hoping this line might help broaden her appeal, not lock her down.

"Father would like you to come here to work on it. I'm sure it won't give you enough time to make the move, but you can start looking at housing whilst you're here." She frowned. "What won't give me enough time? When are you talking about me being there?"

"The fifteenth. All of our designers come together for a monthly meet up. You can meet everyone and get down to work on your first Levy exclusive. What do you think?"

"The fifteenth is next Saturday?"

"Yes, that's right. We like to do it on the weekend. Keep it relaxed and informal, so that all you creative types can flow and not feel inhibited."

Laura bit her lip. "Okay, I'll be there. I'm really not sure about making the move though, Colin. Not to live there."

"Let's call this another reconnaissance visit then, shall we? I know it's short notice, but I'm sure once you meet everyone, we'll be able to persuade you."

Laura was pretty sure that they wouldn't. She was happy to fly back and forth as much as she needed to, but she wanted to spend as much time as she could in Summer Lake—with Smoke. "Do you see a move as necessary?" she asked.

"No, no, no! Not necessary, simply desirable. And there's no need to decide now. We can discuss it further next week. I'll have Ava call you to make travel arrangements."

"Thanks, Colin. I'll see you next week, then."

"And I shall very much look forward to it, Laura. Bye."

She hung up and stared out of the window. It could work, she knew it could. She didn't want to be greedy—but she wanted it all. She wanted her work, wanted to travel, wanted to be respected for her skills, and most of all she wanted Smoke.

Chapter Twenty-Two

Smoke's throat felt like it was lined with sandpaper as he took in the silky turquoise, full length evening gown. Laura's long dark hair fell soft and silky around her shoulders. She was almost eye-to-eye with him in another pair of sexy heels. Maybe later he'd have her leave them on, when he took everything else off her. He'd hated not being able to get back 'til this afternoon and having to ask her to meet him at the airport and be ready to go straight to the fundraiser dinner. Seeing her at the FBO looking like this made it worth it, though.

"Hey, gorgeous!" He meant it more than ever. Abso-fucking-lutely gorgeous, didn't even come close to describing the way she looked.

"Who are you calling gorgeous, gorgeous?" Her eyes where shining with laughter, and something that looked a lot like lust.

"You," he said as his arm snaked around her waist and drew her to him. "The most gorgeous lady in the world." He brushed his lips over hers gently, not wanting to mess up the juicy red gloss that was giving him all kinds of ideas about where he would like lipstick stains.

She cupped her hands around the back of his neck, his own hands instinctively closed around her waist.

"Why thank you, Captain Hamilton. I have to say that you are the most gorgeous guy in the world. I need to get you into a tux more often."

He rubbed his hips against her with his most wicked smile. "It's you getting me out of the tux that I'm looking forward to, lady."

He felt her body soften against him, her hands tighten on the back of his neck. Damn! "If we don't go now, we're not going to make it."

"I thought we had plenty time of time?"

"I'm not talking about time, I'm talking about need. You look so hot in that dress, I need to get you out of it. You are making me so damned hard, that I may not be able to fly the plane. And," he cupped her ass and pressed himself against her, "your knees are going weak...aren't they?" He loved the little pink stains on her cheeks as she clung to him.

"Yes, they are. We could always skip visiting your parents? I'm sure they'd understand, since you only just got back from San Diego. Then we can go straight to LA. Check in to our room early?"

Now that was tempting, but no. "If we go now can we still do both."

He didn't miss the disappointment in her eyes. "I really want you to meet them, Laura. We'll make it real quick. And then we'll go check in." He held her gaze. "Make sure they gave us a good bed before we go down to the dinner. No one will care if we arrive a little late." The things she was doing to him. Had he really just said it was okay if they arrived late? He didn't do late. For anything. He'd be quite happy to tonight though.

She bit her shiny, bright red lip. If she didn't stop doing that they wouldn't make it past the back of the plane! He took her hand. "Come on. Let's go do this."

~ ~ ~

He looked across at her as he taxied off the runway. She looked terrified again.

"You have a runway in your back yard?"

He nodded. "They have the space. It makes sense, with the business, for them to be able to come and go from here."

She nodded but said nothing.

"It'll be okay, lady." He reached across and squeezed her hand. "You'll like them."

"But what if they don't like me, Smoke?"

"They will adore you! How could they not?"

"I don't know, but what if they hate me?"

He'd pulled the plane around onto the ramp and shut the engines down. "They couldn't hate you. And if they did, then we'd leave and never come back. You are more important to me than they are!"

"Smoke, you mustn't say that!"

"It's true, Laura. You are. Yes, I love them, they're my parents. But you are the woman I love. In the short time I've known you, you have shown me the love, respect and trust that they didn't. If it ever came to making a choice, I'd choose you. But it won't, because they will love you."

Before he unlocked the door, he turned back to her. "Are you ready for this, lady?" He loved that she gave him a brave smile even though she was obviously terrified. He let the steps down and stood beside her. "Don't worry, I'll hold your hand the whole time."

~ ~ ~

Laura smiled as she shook hands with Mr. Hamilton.

"You have no idea what a pleasure it is to meet you, young lady."

"Thank you. You too." He seemed nice enough, and genuinely pleased to meet her. She would never have guessed he was Smoke's father. He had sandy hair, was dressed very formally for a Saturday afternoon, and had a very stiff air about him, but he had kind eyes.

She turned to Mrs. Hamilton, who was smiling at her warmly. "Thank you so much for coming, Laura. It means so much to us." Laura liked her immediately. There was no mistaking where Smoke got his looks from; he was his mother's son. Her gray eyes twinkled as she smiled. Her hair was black, with deep streaks of gray. "I know you can't stay long, but I wondered if I could borrow you for just a few minutes?"

Smoke squeezed her hand which, true to his word, he hadn't let go of yet. She looked up at him and loved him even more. He was letting her know she didn't have to if she didn't want to. She gave him a tiny nod and let go of his hand. "Of course."

Mrs. Hamilton took her arm and led her away. "I won't keep you, darling. I just had to get you alone for a little girl talk."

Laura looked at her, wondering what was coming. In Dale's family the women had 'girl talks' to strategize and scheme about how to advance their husband's careers and social standing. Her stomach tied itself in a knot. She couldn't stand any more of that. "What kind of girl talk, Mrs. Hamilton?"

They were walking into a formal flower garden behind the house. Although house was far too small a word for the grand Hamilton residence. Laura looked back to where Smoke and his father still stood, talking next to the plane. His stance said he was ready to come rescue her as soon as she gave the signal. She gave him a reassuring smile. She could handle this.

"Do call me Madeleine." The older woman smiled. "And don't worry, I'm not an interfering old witch, at least not any more. I learned that lesson the hard way. I simply want you to know that whatever happened in the past, whatever mistakes we made as parents, we love Cole. We only want him to be happy. It seems that you make him happy. I wanted you to know that you have our support. I don't imagine he will want us to be a very big part of your lives, and while that saddens me, I do understand. Please know though, that if ever you want us, or need us for anything, we'll be here for you." She handed Laura her card. "Please know you can call me if ever you want to."

"Thank you." Laura wasn't sure what to say. That was an awful lot to take in for a first conversation. Madeleine was laying it all on the line. Laura decided to do the same. "I know he does love you. And I know he's making some changes right now. He's told me that he's getting closer to you again and that he likes it."

Madeleine's eyes filled with tears. She wrapped her arms around Laura. "Thank you. Thank you so much. I wasn't fishing for information, I hope you know that. But you've made me so happy by confirming what I'd hoped was happening."

"You're welcome. Smoke...Cole and I haven't been together long. I do know he loves you. I don't know everything that happened in the past, but do I know he wants to leave it all behind."

Little furrows appeared on Madeleine's brow, just like her son's. "You don't know the whole story?"

"No. We've talked as much as we need to." Laura didn't like how worried Madeleine looked.

"I hope you don't hate us when you do."

"Cole doesn't hate you. I don't see why I would. We've all made mistakes in life. What matters is what we learn, and who we become from them."

Madeleine smiled. "I can see why he loves you. Can I offer you one piece of advice?"

Laura nodded.

"Always let him know that you trust him. Of all the damage we did to him, making him feel that we didn't trust him was what hurt him the most." She shook her head sadly. "Because we didn't, and we should have. I've noticed when he's visited these last few months, he's always testing out whether we trust him. It's still an issue for him. He doesn't trust many people himself. He doesn't trust us yet, understandably, but I can see that he trusts you. Please, don't ever break that trust?"

Laura smiled, realizing that he'd kept testing her out too. Did she trust him not to push her around? Did she trust him to give herself to him in bed? And he had trusted her. In his own words, he was exposing his soul to her. He'd let her in to meet Cole, the guy who hid behind the ego. "I will do my best to never break it and I do try, all the time, to let him know that I trust him. That I love him."

Madeleine nodded. "Thank you, Laura. I can already see you're good for him. I hope we will become friends. If you'd like to."

"I would like to." She had to say it though. Much as she liked Madeleine, Laura needed to make very clear where her loyalties lay. "It will be up to Cole how much we see of you, but I will look forward to it." She took out one of her own cards and handed it over. "You can call me if ever you need to, though."

The smile on Madeleine's face told her she understood exactly what Laura was saying. "I'll look forward to it too, darling." She took Laura's arm and started leading her back. "His eyes haven't left you the whole time, you know. He's ready to come slay the old dragon, if you give him the nod."

Laura laughed. "He doesn't think you're a dragon at all. He just knows how I nervous I was to meet you."

"I hope you can see there's nothing to be nervous about?"

"I can. Thank you."

They were back at the plane now. Their two men smiling at them. As soon as she was close enough Smoke took hold of her hand and squeezed it. She squeezed right back.

"I hope next time you might at least stay for a drink," said Mr. Hamilton.

"Cole! Leave them alone! Don't mind him, we're just glad you came at all."

Smoke punched his dad's arm. "Yeah, this was only ever going to be a flying visit. We've got to get down to LA. I'll call you, figure out when we can stop by again."

"You do that, son."

Laura watched the exchange, knowing that she was seeing Smoke very carefully take down some more of the walls he'd been hiding behind. She was pleased for him. His parents obviously loved him.

"We'll hope to see you again soon." Madeleine hugged her and pecked her cheek. She actually kissed it, not the air next to it, and there was genuine affection in that hug.

Laura hugged back and smiled at her. "I'll hope so too."

~ ~ ~

As they watched the plane taxi to the end of the runway, Madeleine squeezed her husband's hand. He squeezed right back.

"I think he's found the one, Cole."

"It looked like it, but remember all we can do is hope, nothing else."

Madeleine leaned her head on his shoulder as they watched Papa Charlie thunder down the runway and lift off into the blue sky above the rolling green hills. "Did you see the way he held her hand?"

Cole nodded. "Yeah. I thought we'd never break him of that when he was kid—your hand, my hand...he was always holding on."

Madeleine blinked away the tears. "What we did broke that part of him, Cole. It looks to me like Laura is helping him put it back together."

Chapter Twenty-Three

Smoke led Laura to the elevators, hoping they wouldn't bump into any of the others. He just needed to get her to the suite. She looked up at him, that sexy smile making him even harder, although he wouldn't have believed that was possible. He'd wanted her since the moment he laid eyes on her in San Francisco. The quick stop to see his folks, and then the flight down here had seemed to take forever. All he'd wanted to do was get to the Wilshire and get her out of that dress.

The elevator doors opened. He pulled her inside and stabbed at the button to make them close again before anyone could join them. As soon as they closed he backed her against the wall, needing to at least taste her lips and feel her against him, until he could get her underneath him. He raked his hands through her hair, thrusting his tongue between her lips. She opened up for him, her arms around his neck pulling him down to her. He ground his hips against hers, desperately needing to be inside her.

When the elevator stopped at the twelfth floor he reluctantly let her go. The pink stains appeared on her cheeks, but apparently they weren't only caused by desire. She was looking past him as she straightened her dress.

"Hi, Leanne!"

A blonde in killer white dress was standing waiting for the elevator. The look she gave Smoke made him wonder if he'd ever slept with her. She was sending him those kind of daggers.

She smiled as she looked at Laura. "Hey, girlfriend. I see you brought man candy?"

Jesus! What was that about? Checking her over, he was pretty sure he hadn't slept with her; he would have remembered that body. She was nothing next to Laura, but she was still a ten.

"Lee!" Laura looked decidedly uncomfortable and he got the sense it was about more than being caught kissing in the elevator. "You haven't met my boyfriend, Smoke. Smoke, this is Leanne Miller. A very good friend of mine. She's an IP lawyer, actually she's Dan's lawyer."

Smoke extended a hand and she shook it coolly. This one was a ball-buster by the looks of her.

"Nice to meet you, Leanne."

She gave him the once over, then apparently liking what she saw, she looked him in the eye. Right there, in front of Laura, who had just introduced him as her boyfriend, this woman, this so-called friend was giving him the brazen fuck-me-if you-dare stare. Jesus! Some friend!

"It's nice to meet you, too. I'll look forward to getting to know you."

Was she for real? Smoke looked at Laura. Apparently she was oblivious! He had to get them both away from this one. He wanted nothing to do with her. More importantly, he wanted to get back to where they had been. His desire had shrunk a little in the face of this...this...whatever she was. She was a hard-faced bitch, was what she was! No doubt she was one of those stunning women who thought every man she met would gratefully crawl into her bed, given half the chance. Well, not Smoke. He was in love with an even more stunning woman and all he wanted to do was get her into his bed. He smiled as a thought occurred to him—into their bed!

He simply nodded at Leanne, then turned to Laura. "We need to get a move on, lady."

Laura looked at Leanne. "We'll see you down there. Have you met up with Michael yet?"

"No. I'm meeting him in the lobby."

Poor Michael. Smoke felt sorry for the guy, having that as his date for the night. He slipped his arm around Laura's waist and walked her away. Aware that the elevator hadn't moved, he looked back over his shoulder. Leanne was still standing there, holding the doors open with her foot, watching him. She smiled and gave him that come-fuck-me look again! He shuddered. He hoped she wasn't a very close friend of Laura's. If she was he'd have to make damned sure to stay out of her way. He wanted nothing to do with that, and Laura probably needed to know what her so-called friend was really like. Apparently she had no clue; she was smiling up at him, eyes full of lust and even better yet, love!

He swiped the key card and let her enter the suite ahead of him. All thoughts of Leanne, and everything else, left his head as he followed her into the sitting area. His cock was throbbing inside his pants again. He couldn't wait any longer.

"Look, we've got a balcony!"

Smoke shook his head and smiled at her through pursed lips. "That's really what you're interested in right now?"

She turned to him, eyes shining. "No. I'm interested in getting something quick to eat before we have to go down there."

She couldn't be serious? They were about to sit through a seven course dinner—if they did make it down there. She put her hands on his shoulders and looked into his eyes. He closed his hands around her waist and pulled her against him. "Can you wait, lady? Because I really need to feel you naked under me, right now."

Her tongue came out to moisten bright red, juicy-looking lips, sending a tremor through him. She bit her lip, making him close his eyes and let out a sigh.

"No, I can't wait. Because, Mr. Cole Alexander Hamilton, I think you know what I want to eat." She led him through to the bedroom and stood facing him. She was biting her lip again. Her hands were on his zipper and he bit his own lip as she knelt down before him. She smiled up at him while she pushed his pants down and freed his aching cock. He drew in a sharp breath when her long slender fingers closed around him. Oh, Jesus! She ran her tongue over him, teasing, circling before she took him into her mouth. His hands tangled in her hair as she held his gaze. Her lips were moving up and down the length of him. He wasn't going to last more than a minute. She was totally and completely in charge this time and he willingly went where she took him. The blood was rushing in his veins. He couldn't believe how lucky he was as he looked down into bright blue eyes full of love and a bright red mouth full of his cock. She swirled her tongue over the tip of him then sucked him deep into her throat. She demanded his release and he let go, flying high on blinding waves of pleasure as her mouth demanded more and more. When he was finally spent he pulled her to her feet and collapsed back onto the bed, taking her with him. His legs were still trembling.

She slipped her hand inside his shirt and gave him a very satisfied smile. She looked so pleased with herself. "I've wanted to do that to you since I got to the airport and saw you in a tux."

He couldn't help the chuckle that rumbled up. "In that case, I'll wear a tux every day, lady."

She propped herself up on her elbow and smiled down at him. "No, because I love you in your uniform, too." "You do?" The way she was smiling at him had the happy buzz in his chest humming so loud she must be able to hear it. She nodded. "I do, and I love you in your sexy-ass old jeans." He chuckled again. "Is that so?" "Yes it is, Captain Hamilton. I also love you in cowboy getup, and I love you, well I just love you. I love you in everything and I love you in nothing." She dropped her sweet lips to his and kissed him softly.

When she lifted her head, he tucked a strand of hair behind her ear. "And I love you, lady." He rolled off the bed and got rid of his clothes, then pulled her up to join him. "I love you in this dress. You look abso-fucking-lutely gorgeous in this dress." He unzipped it and pushed it off her shoulders, letting it fall to the floor around her feet. "But for now I need you out of it." He unclasped her bra and stroked her nipples, loving how they responded to his touch. He took her hands and she stepped out of the dress. Seeing her in just those heels and her thong had him aching again, throbbing to be inside her. "I love you in heels. Do you know what all your sexy-as-hell heels do to me?"

She smiled that smile. "I didn't, but now that I do, you know I'll be wearing them all the time."

"You can leave them on for now, then," he said, pulling her back down onto the bed with him as his hand found its way inside her thong. She was so wet! He got rid of the thong and knelt back to look at her. Her gorgeous naked body was ready for him, and those god-damned heels were still on her feet. He propped himself on his elbow, looking down into her eyes as he pulled her towards him, underneath him.

"I love you in anything. I love you in everything. I love you in nothing." He wrapped his arm under her and lifted her to kiss him. When he let her back down, he shifted his weight onto her. "I love you, Laura."

He wasn't sure if it was her voice or her eyes that answered him. "And I love you, Smoke."

He was spreading her thighs with his knees, desperate now to get back where he belonged. "I love you in everything, but do you know what I love me in most?"

She shook her head, her eyes begging him now.

He took her hands and laced his fingers through hers, pinning them on either side of her head. "I love me in you." He thrust deep and hard, loving the gasp that escaped her lips as he filled her tight, wet, heat.

Their bodies molded together, moving as one. Smoke knew they were becoming one as he moved harder and faster inside her. Her hips moved with his, urging him on, taking him deeper. Her legs came up around his, the feel of those heels spurring him on. He let go of her hands and slid an arm underneath her, needing every inch of her pressed against him, as if they really could melt into one. Her hands came up around his back. His free hand tangled in her hair. He slowed his pace, moving in long deep thrusts as he looked into her eyes.

She whispered, "I love you, Cole."

That took him to the edge. "I love you, Laura. I love you with all my heart and soul." She was tensing around him, and he couldn't hold back. "You. Are. M-i-n-e!" The rush of white-hot pleasure coursed through him and exploded into her. She took him flying higher than he'd ever been, her body pulling him deeper, begging for more and more until they collapsed, exhausted, entwined, together.

~ ~ ~

Laura came out of the bathroom as he was adjusting his bow tie. He squeezed his eyes shut.

"What is it? Are you okay?"

He chuckled and peeked one eye open. "I'm trying not to look, because much as I love that dress. As soon as I see you in it, I need to get you out of it."

She laughed, her eyes shining. "I was about to ask if I look okay. You can't tell what we've just been up to, can you?"

He walked over to her, smiling through pursed lips. "The freshly-fucked look suits you!" He was laughing as he closed his hands around her waist and lifted her off the floor.

"Cole Alexander Hamilton! You big Neanderthal, put me down!" she laughed.

He let her slide down his front. "Well, you asked."

She checked the mirror. "Do I really look freshly-fucked?"

He put a hand on her shoulder and met her eyes in the mirror. "You're safe, lady. No one will know what you've been up to. You've got fresh lipstick on."

She gave him a mischievous grin and ran her tongue over the freshly applied bright red gloss.

Smoke bit his own lip and spoke through his teeth. "If you don't stop that teasing right now, we won't be going anywhere!"

She laughed. "Sorry. It's not a tease, it's a promise. But maybe I'll wait till we're all at the table before I do it again."

"You wouldn't dare!"

She threw her head back and laughed. "Don't dare me, Smoke!"

He shook his head at her. "Be warned. If you do, this great big Neanderthal will pick you up, put your ass over my shoulder and carry you out of there, lady! I'll bring you straight back up here and demand you make good on your promises!" He pulled her to him and brushed his lips over hers.

She brought her arms up around his neck and looked deep into his eyes. "I love you, Smoke."

"And I love you, lady. But I think we'd better get out of here and join the party while we still can."

~ ~ ~

Smoke checked the name cards and was pleased to find that they were seated on the other side of the table from Laura's friend and Michael. He was even more pleased when he saw that they were sitting with Dan and Missy. He really liked the two of them, and he knew Laura did too. Everyone was still milling around. They'd missed most of the pre-dinner mingling, but they weren't late by any means. Though, if their time up in the suite was anything to go by, he could learn to not mind being late.

He looked around. He came to Jack and Pete's fundraiser most years, but other than that he stayed clear of events like this. They brought back the past. Fundraisers, fancy dinners, balls and galas had all been part of his life once. He admitted to himself that he used to enjoy them. It wasn't the events that he'd hated, but having to attend them with Anabel. Now they could become a part of his life again. He spotted Laura—she was so gorgeous—chatting with Emma and Holly. They were all done up to the nines. They were some beautiful women, but none of them came anywhere near his lady. He loved that in the future he could look forward to attending these events with her—especially if they started off like this evening had. He pressed his lips together in an attempt to hide his smile at the memory.

"I'm not even going to ask what that look is about," said Jack as he grasped Smoke's shoulder. "But I will guess that it means you and Laura are doing okay?"

Smoke nodded, unable to hold back the huge grin he knew was spreading across his face. "We are."

Jack laughed. "That good, huh?"

"Even better! In fact, shall I tell you how good?"

"As long as you remember you're talking about my little bitty cousin and keep it PG rated."

"I don't mean that, asshole! I mean I took her to meet my folks on the way here!"

"Whoa!" Jack looked stunned. "Seriously?"

Smoke nodded vigorously. "Seriously. Like, major seriously!"

Jack was grinning now. "Congratulations, bro."

"Congratulations on what?" asked Pete who had just appeared at Jack's side. "What's happening?"

"Smoke and Laura."

Pete gave Smoke that weird little smile of his. "Excellent. Our little chat helped then, did it?"

Smoke nodded. "Yeah. It did. Thank you."

"Tell him what you just told me," said Jack.

Smoke laughed, "Nah, because then he'll gloat!"

"Now you really have to tell me, what do I have to gloat about? I love it when I get to gloat!"

"Yeah. I know you do, that's why I'm not going to give you the satisfaction!"

"You tell him, or I'll have to," said Jack with a laugh. "I know how irritating he can be, but this one needs telling."

"For fuck's sake. Will someone just tell me?"

Smoke laughed. "I just took Laura to meet my folks."

"Wow!" Pete slapped his back. "I'm so happy with that, I'm not even going to gloat!"

Smoke and Jack looked at each other.

Pete laughed, "But you know that means I get a free pass on something else down the line."

"Yeah, that's more like it," said Jack.

"So," Pete looked at Smoke, "where does it go from here? Are we talking wedding bells? Are you coming over to the dark side with the rest of us?"

That wasn't something Smoke wanted to talk about yet. "We've got a lot to figure out. She's going to be spending time in London and she hasn't sold the store in San Francisco yet. I just closed on the place up at Cottonwood Creek. I've got the flight school coming together with Jason, and I'm still talking to the guys in New York about what will happen there."

Jack nodded. "I like it. The two of you will always need things to do, and places go, but I reckon you'll be able to come up with something that suits you both."

"I hope so." Smoke was starting to believe that they would, that this was going to work out better than he'd dared hope.

Pete punched Jack's arm. "Come on, partner. We'd better get this thing rolling." He checked his watch. "It's almost time for us to do our thing."

Smoke laughed. "Yeah, you go be the gracious hosts. When you two get through with your charm offensive and emotional appeals there's never a dry pair of panties in the house."

Jack grinned. "We raise a lot of money for a good cause."

"That's right," said Pete. "It would be remiss of us not use every means possible to appeal to the giving nature of our audience, and you know women tend to be in control of the purse strings."

"I don't think sex appeal is in the standard fundraising manuals."

"Hey, if you've got it flaunt it, right?" Jack grinned as he swaggered his shoulders. "In fact, next year I say we get you up there hosting with us. Between Pete's blond good looks, tall dark and handsome me, and smokin' hot you, we'll have every female taste covered, and take in some mega donations!"

Smoke laughed. "Maybe. We'll, see." He watched as the two of them made their way up onto the stage to address their guests. Maybe he would join them next year. It was weird, but for the first time in his life it felt good to think ahead, to make plans for coming years. It felt good because he knew whatever he did, he'd be doing it with Laura. He set out to where she was still chatting with the girls. They'd need to take their seats in a minute, when Jack and Pete got started. He noticed Missy talking to Laura's so-called friend, Leanne. She fixed him with big round eyes and gave him another of those come-fuck-me looks. Smoke shook his head in disgust and turned away.

Chapter Twenty-Four

"I think we all look so beautiful!" exclaimed Emma. "You chose such lovely colors for us, Holly, and that turquoise is perfect on you, Laura."

Holly smiled, "Thank you, I seem to be your personal stylist these days, and you do so well in green. Dan asked me to get Missy something as a surprise, and she wears that blue better than anyone I've ever known." She looked at Laura. "You don't need any help. You have a better sense of style and color than I do."

Laura smiled. "Thanks. I do love this dress, and yours is a knockout."

Holly looked down at her own dusky rose-colored dress with a smile. "Yeah, Pete loves this color."

"It's like we're Team Slinky gone all rainbow!" exclaimed Emma.

Laura exchanged a look with Holly. "You know, Em. I wish you'd come up with a different name for us. I mean, I like the idea of us as a team, but every time you say that I think of those springy toys that walk down the stairs!"

Holly laughed with her as Emma blushed. "Oh." She looked at them both, crestfallen. "I never thought of that! It doesn't sound so good anymore."

Holly put a hand on her shoulder. "It never did, sweetie. I just didn't have the heart to tell you."

Emma laughed. "Oh, well. You'll just have to come up with something better, then."

Holly looked up to where Pete and Jack were climbing up onto the stage. "I don't know about us, but we definitely need a name for the guys! It's like drowning in a sea of hot tuxedos!"

Emma smiled. "And here comes your smoking hot man now."

Laura turned to see Smoke making his way over to them. Her heart raced as he met her gaze. There were a lot of hot men here tonight, but none of them came anywhere near her Smoke.

"I hope you've accepted the inevitable by now?" asked Holly. "Because you would be one crazy lady to let that one go!"

"I have," said Laura with a smile as Smoke reached her side. He took hold of her hand and she squeezed. "I have no intentions of letting this one go." She loved the way his eyes bored into her as he tightened his grip on her hand, telling her he wasn't letting go of her either.

~ ~ ~

The band was good. After listening for a while, Smoke excused himself and headed to the bathrooms. He'd enjoyed the dinner, enjoyed laughing with Missy as Laura and Dan had regaled them with tales of their childhood. He loved the feeling that he was beginning a new chapter in his life. A chapter where he would have a home, and a new take on his career. He and Laura would be together, in whatever way would work for them both, and they'd be surrounded by good friends, all the people at their table tonight. He shuddered as he crossed the hallway. All of them except Laura's friend, Leanne. She'd caught his eye whenever she could and had been giving him major signals the whole evening. He was giving her

a very wide berth. He wanted nothing whatsoever to do with
that woman.

When he came out of the bathroom, Leanne was lingering
near the Ladies room. She smiled and came over to him,
putting a hand on his arm. "You've been avoiding me, but you
don't really want to, do you?"

He looked down into big round blue eyes and shrugged her
hand off. "I've been avoiding you because you disgust me.
Laura thinks you're her friend and you're coming on to me like
a bitch in heat."

He saw the surprise register in her eyes. He was pretty sure
that men never spoke to her like that. He would never
normally speak to a woman like that himself. But this needed
to stop, right here, right now.

She recovered quickly and gave him a sultry smile. Stepping
closer to him, she reached up and straightened his bow tie.
"There's no need to act the innocent with me, Smoke. I know
you want it. I'm saying you can have it."

Smoke caught a glimpse of someone over her shoulder. He
looked up in time to see Michael turn on his heel and walk
back into the ballroom. Jesus! That was all he needed—
Michael thinking he was making a move on this one. The poor
guy was welcome to her. He stepped back, pushing her hands
away. "What will it take to get through to you? Watch my lips.
I. Am. Not. Interested!"

She was still smiling at him! "I watched your lips, but what I
want is to feel them...all over me. Come on, Smoke, be honest.
You want me, you just don't want Laura to find out. She
doesn't have to. I know your sort. You want as many women
as you can get your hands on. I'm saying I want your hands on
me, and no one else need ever know."

She was moving towards him again. Smoke was starting to think she might be crazy. No normal woman would act like this.

"You don't get it. I don't want you, or any other woman. I love Laura!"

He started walking, needing to get away from her and back to his lady.

"Smoke wait!" She stepped in front him and his momentum carried them both forward. He stumbled but managed to catch her and keep them both from falling. As he regained his balance and let go of her he looked up to see Michael and Laura in the doorway. Michael looked pissed. Oh, for fuck's sake! He'd had her in his arms to stop her from falling, nothing else. Laura looked...horrified? Smoke's heart stopped. Surely she wouldn't believe that he'd have his hands on another woman? He loved her and she knew it. She trusted him...didn't she?

~ ~ ~

Michael was the first to speak. "What are you doing, Smoke?"

Laura shook her head. No! It was Leanne! And Laura knew full well what she was doing.

"Listen, Michael." Leanne at least had the good grace to look embarrassed. "It's not what you think. It's not what it looks like."

"It's not what it looks like at all." Smoke's eyes were boring into Laura's as he spoke. He looked...what? Angry? Hurt?

"It's okay, Michael," said Laura. "It really isn't what it looks like."

Smoke stepped toward her now his face starting to relax. "You know that?"

"Yeah," Leanne was looking at her, her face a plea for understanding. "She knows what I'm doing. Don't you, Laura?"

Smoke stopped in his tracks, his face a picture of confusion, soon replaced by anger. He stared at her now, waiting for an explanation.

"I do," she nodded, sad that Leanne's misguided attempts to protect her looked like they might ruin everyone's night. She looked at Smoke. "She thought you were only using me, that you'd still make a move on other women if you could."

Smoke seemed to explode. "So you set me up? You and this," he gave Leanne a venomous look, "bitch. Set me up? To test me? Is that how much you trust me, Laura? Is that how much you love me?"

"Smoke, no! It wasn't like that! I didn't..." She couldn't believe it! He was turning around and walking away. Her heart hammering in her chest, she ran after him. "Please, Smoke. Wait. Let me explain!"

He stopped a moment and stared down at her, his face etched with pain. "No, Laura. Let me explain. You don't trust me. So this is me gone."

She stared after him as he strode across the lobby and out. This could not be happening!

"Laura, I'm so sorry. I...."

"Not now, Leanne. I know you were only trying to look out for me."

Michael put a hand on her shoulder. "I don't know what the deal is, darl'. But I reckon you've got one shot to go after him. Go do it."

Laura nodded and began to run across the lobby. She found him outside, pacing back and forth. "Smoke, please listen to me."

He shook his head. "There's no point. You don't trust me. There's nothing left to say."

"I do trust you, just let me explain. You can't go like this. I need you to stay, listen to me, hear me out." A cab was pulling up. The doorman held its door open. "Please don't go, Smoke. You can't go, I love you."

He stood beside the cab and looked into her eyes. "And I love you, lady. You have my heart, you have my soul. But you don't trust me. I can't live with that."

"Please, just stay, it's a misunderstanding. You'll see. This is you in fight or flight. I'm begging you to stay and fight. For us. Don't choose flight."

"Flight is what I do. You know that. This is me flying away. This is me, gone." He ducked into the cab and slammed the door behind him.

As she watched the cab pull out into the traffic, Laura felt the first hot tears begin to fall.

She pushed her way back through the lobby doors. She needed her purse, her phone. She needed to call him, talk him down.

Michael came and put an arm around her shoulders. "Come on, darl'. What do you want to do?"

She shook her head. "I don't know. He's gone, Michael."

"I'm so sorry, Laura." Leanne was white-faced. "What can I do?"

"It's alright. You meant well. I know that. Would you go and grab my purse? I need my phone. And Lee, don't say anything to anyone."

Laura stared at the entrance, hoping that by some miracle he'd come walking back through those doors—tell her he'd been too hasty and that it was all okay. She knew it wasn't going to happen, though. His mother's words echoed in her mind. Making him feel that we didn't trust him was what hurt him the most. And that's what she herself had just done to him. It wasn't true. She did trust him, but he felt like she didn't and it hurt him enough to make him run—fly away.

Leanne returned with her purse. "Here you go. Do you have your room key?"

She nodded. They'd taken one each when they'd checked in, just a few hours ago. When they'd been so happy together. She felt more tears well up. "You two should get back to the party. The others will wonder where you are."

"No way," said Leanne. "I'm coming with you."

Laura shook her head. She understood that Leanne had meant well, but she didn't want to be with her right now. "No. You're not."

Leanne nodded, understanding. "I'm so sorry."

Michael, who still had an arm around her shoulders, took charge. "You get back in there, Leanne. I'll see Laura up to her room." He guided her towards the elevators.

Once they got back to the suite, Laura couldn't hold it in any longer. The tears started to fall in earnest. Michael wrapped his arms around her. "It'll be okay, darl'."

She shook her head. "You don't know him, Michael. He feels like I don't trust him. He won't come back from that."

"He will. I can promise you that. I've watched the two of you together. It might take him a while, but he won't be able to stay away forever."

She wiped both hands across her face, not caring that she was spreading tears and mascara stains everywhere. "What makes you so sure?"

"I've been where he is. As much pain as he's in right now, feeling you don't trust him, it's nothing compared to the pain that'll come once he starts thinking about a future without you in it."

She shook her head. "I don't want him to be in any pain at all, Michael. He's known too much already."

"Give him time, darl'. It'll work itself out. Do you want me to stay or go? Want me to send one of the girls up?"

"No. Thank you. You go, you'll be missed. And please don't send anyone, don't say anything. Let them enjoy their night."

"Are you sure?" He raised his eyebrows. "You know you're setting me up for more grief from Miss when she finds out I didn't tell her."

Laura smiled. He really was a good guy, trying to make her smile even now. "You can handle it. Do me a favor though? Don't let Leanne come back up here. She truly meant well, but I don't want to talk to her right now."

Michael frowned. "Yeah. She explained to me while you went after him."

"Don't look like that, Michael. She really did mean well."

"I know. I just hate how it turned out for you. She should have stayed out of your business, no matter what she thought she was doing."

Laura shrugged. "It's done now." She went to the door and opened it, needing for him to leave—needing to call Smoke, and needing to lie down and cry on the bed where only hours before Smoke had been loving her.

Once she'd closed the door behind Michael, she dug her phone out of her purse. She dialed Smoke's number and listened to it ring. The tears started again when she heard his voice. It was his voicemail, but at least it was the sound of his voice, and his familiar message.

"This is Smoke. You know what to do."

"I'm going to keep calling, Smoke. So you may as well pick up."

She hit the end call button and stared at her phone, hoping against hope that he would call her back. After a few minutes she tried again. This time it went straight to voicemail. He must have switched it off.

"I'm not giving up, you big Neanderthal. I'm going to keep calling until you talk to me."

She hung up again and went to check the mini bar. Fresh tears came when she saw the Hamilton Groves logo on some of the bottles. She decided on a miniature bottle of whiskey. What had Ben said? Whiskey was for when serious stuff hit the fan. This was pretty serious stuff. It shouldn't be. It wouldn't be if Smoke would listen to her, let her explain, but he refused to. He was running scared and hurt. She took her drink through to the bedroom. Seeing the rumpled sheets, she wondered how they could have come to this after being so happy together just a few short hours ago.

~ ~ ~

When she opened her eyes, Laura squeezed them shut again. Her head was pounding. She lay there and winced as it all came back to her. Smoke's face when he'd thought she'd set him up to see if he would cheat on her—as if she would do that! The hurt in his eyes as he'd looked down at her. You don't trust me. His sad, lost face in the moment before he got in the cab. This is me gone.

She groaned and pulled the pillow over her head. She'd emptied all the little bottles of whiskey while she kept trying to call him. She reached for her phone which was lying next to her. Lying where he should be.

He'd sent her an email!

Laura
I'm not going to talk to you. It's best that we just walk away. This is the way it goes. It's all sunshine and blowjobs, until someone wants a commitment. Then it all goes to hell in a hurry. I wanted to make a commitment with you. I love you, but love is just a four letter word. I can do those. Commitment? That's ten whole letters and a whole different story. Not a story I can be a part of. I can't do it. I'm not capable. You have my heart. You have my soul. But I can't have you in my life. Not if you don't trust me. I'm sorry. Enjoy London.
Love you always, lady.
Cole
xxx
Go to the airport with the others. Jason will drop you in San Francisco.

As she read it the tears came. Why wouldn't he just talk to her? Listen to her? She closed her eyes and shook her head. He was giving up on them because he thought she didn't trust him. Yet he'd jumped to that conclusion—he didn't trust her enough to let her explain! He was a coward. He'd run. And she couldn't even be mad at him, because she understood why.

No way was she going to the airport, though. She couldn't face flying in the back of the plane with everyone. If she couldn't sit up front, with Smoke, then she didn't want to fly at all.

Chapter Twenty-Five

Smoke didn't trust himself to fly. He'd hardly slept. He couldn't focus, and that was no state to be in the cockpit. So he had left Papa Charlie at Santa Monica Municipal. The guys at the FBO there would take care of him. Smoke rented a car from them, told them it was a one week return, but he had no clue where he was going, or when he'd come back. He just needed to get out of here. That was all he knew.

When what was going on with Leanne last night had sunk in, he'd felt sick to his stomach. He still did. He'd rolled it around in his head all night. Laura hadn't said that she thought he would make a move on another woman. But she had said she knew what Leanne was doing. And what she'd been doing was setting him up and testing him. He shook his head. He couldn't think about it anymore. His head hurt, but not as much as his heart hurt. Why had he let himself fall in love with her? He'd broken his own rules, broken the promises he'd made to himself. It served him right. He pointed the car towards the San Gabriel Mountains. He might not know where he was going, but he was determined to get out of LA as fast as he could.

~ ~ ~

Everyone was quiet as they got off the plane at Summer Lake. It had been a great night, but this morning a cloud hung over them.

Jack waited at the top of the steps after the others had gone down. "What did he say to you, Jason?"

"Just that he'd be going dark for the week. Papa Charlie is still in Santa Monica, but he'll have it back here next weekend. He said you guys weren't flying this week, but if anyone needs to I can take you in this."

"And he just said he was going dark? Didn't say anything about where?"

"No. I asked but he said he didn't know."

Jack nodded. That sounded about right for Smoke. "Well, thanks for the ride. I doubt we'll need you, but I'll give you a shout if we do. Let me know if you hear from him, will you?"

"Will do. But I'm not expecting to. He covered everything that he and I needed to get into this week so that he wouldn't have to be in touch."

When Jack caught up with the others in the parking lot, Pete was frowning. "I don't like it, partner. What do you think?"

As usual, Jack knew Pete was thinking the same thing he was. "Let's give him today. What do you say we all meet up at the Boathouse tomorrow night? We can see if anyone's heard anything, and then decide."

Pete nodded. "Okay. Around seven tomorrow night? Does that work for everyone?"

They all nodded their agreement.

"I'm going to call Laura when we get home. See if she's made it back to San Francisco yet." Missy scowled at Michael. "She spent last night by herself and now she's driving home by herself too. I wish I'd known."

Michael hung his head. "Sorry, critter. But she asked me not tell anyone. She wanted to be by herself."

Missy nodded begrudgingly. "I know. You only did what she wanted. I'm just worried about her. I just wish I'd known. I'll get back in that damned plane and go up there if she wants me."

Jack smiled to himself, knowing she meant it, no matter how scared she was of flying. "If you get hold of her and want to go, Miss, let me know. I'll set it up, or come with you."

"There's nothing we can achieve all standing around here, though," said Pete. "And we need to get out to my folks place. Keep the grapevine open guys, and we'll see you tomorrow."

~ ~ ~

Laura wandered around her apartment. She felt as if she was in shock. She still couldn't believe that what should have been a little misunderstanding had led to this. She jumped and ran for her phone when she heard it ring, hoping it would be him. Of course it wasn't.

"Hey, Jack."

"Hey, sweetie. Are you home yet?"

"Yeah. I'm back now. Sorry I didn't pick up earlier. I was still on the road. Have you heard anything from him? Is he back there?"

"No, nothing. He's gone dark."

"Jack if you hear from him, please will you explain what happened? I do trust him. I didn't know that Leanne was going to do that. When she said I knew what she up to, I agreed because I understood what she was doing. But he thought I'd set it up!"

"It's okay, sweetie. I know. Michael explained what went down. If I can find him, I'll explain it to him. But don't be surprised if we don't hear anything for a while. When are you leaving for London?"

"Thursday."

"I hate to say it, but I doubt he will resurface till after you're gone."

Laura nodded. She was kind of expecting that herself. "He's a big coward, Jack! But I love him."

"I know, sweetie. He loves you too. I know that for sure. I talked with him last night before everything got started. He was one happy man."

Laura couldn't help but seek reassurance. "He actually told you that he loved me?"

Jack laughed. "He told me that a week ago, before he even told you!"

That surprised her, but it made her smile, too. "It was probably a whole lot easier for him to tell you than it was to tell me."

Jack let out a short laugh. "You know, you're probably right, and seeing how he struggled to tell me, I can only imagine what he went through with you."

The tears threatened again as she remembered what it had taken for him to finally say those words to her—in the shower. "Did you want anything, Jack, or were you just checking in?" She needed to get off the phone.

"I just wanted to make sure you're okay, sweetie."

"I wish you were being more reassuring. I wish you were telling me that it's all going to be okay. That he'll be fine when he's had chance to calm down and think about it."

"I wish I was too, but I've seen him hurt before. He shuts down, puts up walls. Even when he comes back, it's like the real him isn't even there. He just hides behind the cocky Smoke screen. I've never seen him as happy as he was about you. To fall so hard from that height is going have him hurting real bad. I just want to find him before he can build too many walls up and shut us all out."

"Not very reassuring, Jack."

"Sorry, sweetie, but at least it's honest."

"Yeah. Call me if you hear anything, okay."

"Will do. Keep your chin up."

"Thanks, Jack. See ya."

Once she'd hung up, she decided to try a text.

I'm not giving up because I love you.

I leave for London on Thursday.

Please say you'll see me before I go?

She really didn't expect him to reply, but she could hope. She put her phone in her pocket and jumped when it buzzed. Her heart raced. It was him! She held her breath as she opened the text.

No. Do us both a favor and stay there.

Her eyes filled with tears. That was just plain mean. She put her face in her hands and let a few tears fall before she pulled herself together. She knew he wasn't really mean at all, he was hurting. He might be a coward, but he wasn't an asshole. At least he'd sent something.

~ ~ ~

Jack had tried calling and texting Smoke, but had heard nothing, yesterday or today. He hadn't really expected to. He sat on the front deck looking out at the lake. Emma came out and planted a kiss on his lips before sitting beside him.

"Do you think it'll all work out?" she asked.

He shook his head. "I don't know, baby. I hope so, but I know Smoke. I need to talk to him soon. The more time he spends by himself, the more walls he'll put up. If I don't get to him soon it won't matter anymore. Even when he understands that Laura had nothing to do with Leanne's stupid idea, he won't risk letting her in again."

Emma nodded sadly. "He sounds like me when I saw you with Laura and freaked out. Even when I found out she was your cousin, I was too scared. What I thought I'd seen had already hurt me too much. I thought being with you would only leave me open to more hurt."

Jack wrapped an arm around her. "I know. I just hope I can find Smoke and persuade him he needs to be as brave as my little Mouse. I'm going to call Pete. I don't feel like going into town and sitting around with everyone tonight. I know he's thinking of calling Smoke's parents and I'm going to say we do it."

Emma smiled up at him. "I love that the two of you kept in touch with his parents all these years."

"Yeah. They're good people. They screwed up, but they were quick to admit it when they realized what they'd done. Smoke shut them out completely, but they reached out to us. We were their go-betweens for a long time. The fact that he took Laura to meet them says how far he's come—with them, as well as with her.

~ ~ ~

Pete hung up and looked at Holly. "Jack and Em aren't coming in to town tonight. He's going to call Smoke's folks. I'm going to call Ben, see if Smoke has shown up at the resort at all. I doubt it though."

Holly nodded. "I could throttle, Leanne. I could throttle Smoke, too!"

Pete laughed. "Don't be like that, sweetheart. Everyone wanted to throttle me not so long ago. We all get there in our own time and our own way."

"I suppose. I just hope Smoke and Laura do get there. It's so frustrating!"

~ ~ ~

Madeleine Hamilton went to find her husband in his office. "I just talked to Cole's friend, Jack."

Cole Sr. took off his glasses and frowned at her. "Why? What's wrong?"

"He called to ask if we'd heard from Cole. He took off from the fundraiser and no one has heard from him since. They were hoping that since we've been getting closer again he might have been in touch with us. Apparently there was a bit of a scene with one of Laura's friends and he ended up thinking that Laura doesn't trust him."

Cole Sr. stood up and walked around his big oak desk. "And what are you thinking?"

Madeleine wrung her hands together. "I need to call him. I want to call her."

"Remember what we said, Madeleine. Remember what we promised each other? No interference, ever again. No matter what happens. No matter what we think might be best. Good or bad, his decisions are his own."

"That's what I came to tell you, darling. I'm not going to be able to keep that promise."

He shook his head. "We could lose him forever if you don't."

She nodded. "I understand that, but I'll deal with it, if it means he doesn't lose her."

~ ~ ~

Standing in the check-in line, Laura couldn't help looking around. It was hardly realistic, but she kept hoping that Smoke would appear. Hoping that he would come striding through the crowded terminal and wrap her in his arms. She'd kept having these silly little hopes since Madeleine had called her and said she was going to try to talk to him. Laura was grateful that she wanted to help, but had asked her not to. She didn't want Smoke to cut them both out of his life if he thought they were ganging up on him, or worse, trying to manipulate him into doing what they wanted. Still she'd hoped and hoped for a miracle.

She checked her bag and made her way to security, remembering the last time she'd done this, with Smoke at her side. Holding her hand. Now he was gone, and as she took her shoes off to pass through the scanners, she had to face the fact that he was probably going to stay gone.

Maybe she should stay in London. Do them both a favor, like he'd said.

~ ~ ~

Smoke came around the side of the house when he heard a car approaching. Who the hell could this be? He seriously considered hiding in the garage until they left. Then he saw it was Ben's truck rounding the corner and heading up the driveway, and he waited for him to pull up and get out.

"Hey, Smoke."

He nodded, not wanting to even say hello. He just needed to be left alone.

Ben reached into the back of his truck and pulled out a cooler. "I thought this might be a good time to return the favor." He smiled and lifted the lid to reveal a dozen beers nestling in the ice. "And these ones are stinging. So, are you going to invite me in?"

Smoke pursed his lips. "How did you know I was here?"

"Joe was out this way checking fences. He said he'd seen signs of life up here, and since you've been playing the fugitive all week it didn't take much to figure it out. Don't tell me you're going to send me and my ice-cold beers away again? I let you in when I didn't want to."

"Come on then." Smoke opened the back door and led him inside.

Ben cracked two beers open and they sat in front of the windows looking out at the lake. "This is some view you've got here."

"Yeah."

"So what are you going to do?"

"I don't want to talk about it."

Ben nodded. "Fair enough. Mind if I tell you some of what I didn't want to talk about when you came to see me?"

"Go ahead." Maybe it would take his mind off Laura.

"I told you the past was the happiest place I've ever been?"

Smoke nodded.

"It's true. For the last fifteen years, there hasn't been a day when I didn't wish I could go back."

Smoke looked at Ben, but he was staring out the windows with a faraway look in his eyes.

"I made the same decision that you're making now. I thought it would be easier to live with loss than risk more pain." He turned and looked Smoke in the eye. Raising his bottle he said, "Worst fucking mistake I've ever made. Every single day I wish I'd had the balls to go after her, to choose love instead of self-preservation. But it's too late for me." He took a long swig of his beer and looked back out the window. "It's not too late for you, though."

Smoke blew out a sigh. "Are you ever going to tell me your story?"

"Maybe someday. For now I just sit back and watch the rest of you live out yours. I've seen the others all get there in the end. I knew they would, because I knew they'd all fight for it. You've got me worried though. I'm starting to think you're as much of a coward as I was. Don't join me in the losers club, bud. It sucks!"

Smoke stared at Ben. He'd never thought of him as a loser, but he could see the pain and regret etched on his face.

Ben gave him a sad smile. "If seeing all the happy couples around you doesn't motivate you to go after your girl, I thought maybe talking to this sad bastard would do the trick.

Motivate you to not spend the rest of your life living with a regret you can't get past."

Smoke nodded. It was the same thing his mom had told him this afternoon.

Hate me if you need to, darling, but I have to interfere, because you're my boy and I love you. When you were small you used to fight all the time to get what you wanted, whatever you wanted. And you always ended up getting it. You lost that after what we did. Ever since then you've always chosen what you call flying away. I think of it as giving up, Cole. Please don't give up. Don't give up on Laura, and don't give up on happiness. You can be happy. I know that, but you'll have to fight for it. If you don't you might always regret it.

He looked at Ben. "No offense, but I don't want to end up like you."

Ben let out a sad little laugh. "None taken. I don't want you to either, that's why I'm here. So what are you going to do about it?"

Smoke emptied his beer and reached for another. "I don't know yet."

Chapter Twenty-Six

Laura left the Levy store and put her umbrella up as she hurried out. London was certainly living up to its dreary reputation this time. It matched her mood. She hadn't seen the sun since the plane had descended through the clouds and landed at Heathrow on Friday morning. She'd hardly had time to notice though. Colin had met her at the airport and taken her to meet with Mr. Levy Sr. to discuss her new line. Saturday had been all about their 'monthly meet up' as they called it. She'd enjoyed the day, getting to know the team of designers—both the in-house team, and those who had worked on exclusive lines for Levy just as she was doing. Colin was right; they were a great bunch and all very welcoming.

One of the older guys was someone whose work had inspired her love of diamonds as a girl, and her dreams of one day designing herself. She'd been tongue tied around him at first, but he'd been a real sweetheart and soon put her at ease. He'd been genuinely flattered by her admiration. He and a couple of the others had insisted on taking her on a tour of London on Sunday. That had been fun.

She was starting to think that maybe she should stay here. There'd be nothing left for in her San Francisco once the sale of the store went through. She certainly couldn't consider moving to Summer Lake. She wouldn't be able to live in the same place as Smoke if he didn't want to be with her—and his continued silence was starting to convince her that he really didn't. Her heel caught in the cobblestones and she stumbled forward, just managing to keep her balance. It brought her back to the present, which was where she needed to stay, she reminded herself. There was no point longing for a man who didn't want her, no matter how much she still wanted him. Luckily it shouldn't be too hard to stay in the present. She had so much to do, and she needed to get down to work. They had really started the ball rolling on her signature collection and had already had a few more enquiries come in. She'd been relieved to see requests for earrings and necklaces. The thought of engagement rings made her feel sick. Especially when she stupidly allowed herself to associate the thought with Smoke, and everything that now would never be. She'd been stupid to even hope. Neither of them were cut out for that kind of thing, and he was doing a good job of proving it.

She would have to deal with the sick feeling for a little while longer, since she was on her way to meet with her very first Levy client: an engagement ring. After this she intended to do everything she could to become associated with other things— in her designs and in her life. For now she would get through this meeting and then get back to the hotel. Watch some mindless TV and try to get through the evening without thinking about Smoke.

She'd thought this job might have fallen through. After the initial enquiry Colin hadn't heard anything more, and didn't have any details on what the client wanted. He'd simply been interested in an engagement ring and had specifically requested that Laura design it. Yesterday Colin had informed her that the client had been back in touch. He'd been traveling and would be in London today. He'd asked to meet with Laura to go over his ideas. She clutched her purse with her portfolio inside as she pushed her way through the doors of the Bleeding Heart Tavern. Apparently it was quite normal to meet clients here. Not quite as glamorous as she would have hoped, but still.

She looked around, a little irritated that she wouldn't know the client even if she was looking right at him. He'd told Colin he would recognize her—apparently he'd read the piece about her in National Jeweler. He'd said she'd find him at a corner table. She scanned the edges of the room. There was a guy in the far corner reading a newspaper, but he didn't seem the type to seek out a designer for an engagement ring. She looked around, not seeing anyone who did seem the type. Her gaze fell on a table in the corner by the window. Her heart stopped as she gasped. Smoke! His gaze locked with hers, the biggest smile lighting up his handsome face. At the same time there was fear in his eyes.

But he was here!

Her feet were carrying her towards him before she even knew she was moving. She held his gaze the whole way 'til she was at the table and he was standing to meet her. He really was here! He smiled. The gentle Smoke smile. The Cole smile. She knew her face mirrored his, but she couldn't speak.

"Hey gorgeous."

She felt tears prick behind her eyes and spoke around a lump in her throat. "Who are you calling gorgeous, gorgeous?"

His arms were around her. She buried her face in his neck as she clung to him.

"You, lady," he whispered into her ear. "I'm so sorry. Can you forgive me?"

She lifted her head and looked into his eyes. "I already have." She just clung to him, wanting to never let go of him again. There was no need for more words. His lips came down on hers and told her everything she'd hoped to hear. He was sorry. He loved her. He'd missed her. And she was back where she belonged. When they came up for air she remembered where they were.

"Let's get out of here, lady."

"I can't. I'm supposed to be looking for a client." She looked around wildly, wondering what that client would think of the little display they'd just put on. It didn't really matter though, she still had her arms around Smoke and didn't plan on letting go.

She felt his chuckle rumble up through his chest and looked up into his eyes. "You found him."

She looked around, not seeing anyone that might fit the bill.

Smoke tightened his arms around her. "Right here."

Her breath caught in her chest as she understood what he meant. "You?"

He was laughing at her now. "Yes, me. I'm your client. What else would I be doing here?"

"I thought you came to find me."

"I did." He brushed his lips over hers and looked into her eyes. "I did come to find you, and to ask you if you will make a ring."

"For you?"

He smiled and bit her bottom lip. "For you."

She was finding it hard to focus over the sound of her heart hammering in her chest. She stared at him, taking in the happy smile and the question in his eyes.

"A ring for you, for me?"

"If you want one."

"What are you saying? Smoke?"

"I'm saying I don't want to be a coward anymore. I'm saying I want to do this. I'm saying I love you, lady." He took her hand. "Come on. Let's get out of here."

She loved the feel of his big hand wrapped around hers, squeezing tight as they emerged back onto the street.

"I didn't know where you were staying, but I'm at the Rosewood. Let's go there, can we? It's close." He snaked his arm around her waist as they walked.

Laura's mind was racing. He was here! That was all that really mattered. And he wanted her to make an engagement ring—for him, for her! Yet he hadn't said what that meant. He hadn't asked that question, at least not in words. He'd asked with his kiss, was asking her with his eyes as they walked. If a smile could speak, hers was telling him yes.

Smoke swiped his key card and let her enter the room ahead of him. She waited for him to close the door, then wrapped her arms around his neck. "I missed you, Captain Hamilton."

"And I missed you, lady."

His mouth came down on hers as his hands came up to frame her face. She really was back where she belonged. Backed up against the wall, trapped by his big body, his hips thrusting against her, his hardness making her moan with need. His fingers tangled in her hair as he tipped her head back. His tongue slid between her lips, demanding more. His knee pressed between her thighs, demanding the same. She was melting into him, helpless. He could do whatever he wanted with her and they both knew it. His hands ran over her ass, down over her thighs. She gasped as he lifted one and then the other and wrapped them around him. She clung to him as he walked her to the bed where he pinned her underneath him. In seconds they were both naked. His arm was around her, underneath her as he drew her underneath him. "You were right. I was a fucking coward, but I don't want to be one anymore. I want to be a better man, for you."

His knees were spreading her legs. "You already are the best man for me, Smoke. The only man for me. I love you."

She gasped as he thrust his hips and filled her. "And I love you, lady."

She gave herself up to him, moving with him in the rhythm that had become theirs. He moved deep inside her, claiming her, giving himself up to her as much as she was giving herself to him. Every thrust took her closer to the edge, her legs tensed as he grew bigger and harder.

"You. Are. M-i-n-e!" He let go.

As she soared away with him, she cried the truth of her heart. "And you're m-i-n-e!"

Her hips bucked under him as he pulsated inside her, taking her flying away with him as they became one.

When they lay still, he buried his face in her neck. "Say you'll be mine, Laura?"

"I already am, Smoke. I never stopped being yours."

"But say you'll be all mine."

"I already am."

He lifted his head and looked down at her, his face earnest. "I told you once that sticking around, feeling obliged to stick around felt like I was being grounded, having my ability to fly taken away?"

She nodded, wondering what he was about to say.

"This week I discovered something."

"What's that, Smoke?"

"I discovered that not having you in my life feels like being grounded. I can't fly without you, lady. Flying isn't just what I do, it's who I am. And since I met you—since I fell in love with you—I can't be me without you. I need you. I need you to be all mine." He dropped his head and planted the sweetest kiss on her lips. "I need you to make me a ring." He kissed her again. "And I need you to wear it. Laura, I told you you will always have my heart and my soul and it's true, you always will. So, please, say you'll marry me, and I'll do everything in my power to make sure you never regret it."

She felt the tears sting behind her eyes again. She cupped his head and pulled him down into a kiss, answering him with her lips and her tongue before she dared speak. When she let him lift his head he looked down at her, his eyes pleadingly uncertain.

"Yes, Smoke. Yes, Cole. Yes, you great big ego-ridden Neanderthal, I will marry you and I won't ever regret it."

His lips crushed hers in a long, deep kiss. Eventually he rolled off her and pulled her into his arms. "I love you, lady. And I'm so sorry I walked away last weekend. I shouldn't have done that."

She snuggled against him. "No, you shouldn't, you big coward." She smiled up at him. "But it's okay, because I love you. I understand." She brought her hand up to touch his cheek. "And I'm not even going to say, 'Don't ever do it again,' because I know you might, but someday you'll learn to believe that I trust you, and you'll learn to trust me."

"I do trust you!"

She shook her head. "You obviously don't yet, or you would have let me explain."

He hung his head, deep regret etched into his expression. "I'm sorry."

"It's okay. I'm saying I get it, I understand, but there will be times when you'll need to understand me too. Say you will, Smoke? Say you can love me like that?"

He looked into her eyes. "I do love you like that. And I'll work to get better at it every day."

"It will take work though, Smoke. For both of us. You were right. If we make a commitment, it won't all be sunshine and blowjobs." She couldn't help but smile as she said it.

He was chuckling now. "I know that. We'll make it work." He pulled her to him. "But I think for you and me there will always be lots of sunshine."

She nodded. "Yeah, I think there will."

He smiled at her through pursed lips and added. "And blowjobs?"

She laughed and pushed at him. "We'll have to see. The one night we started out that way didn't end too well did it? I might not want to risk it again!"

He gave her a wicked smile. "Do you think I should wear my tux to persuade you?"

"Maybe?"

He sprang from the bed with a chuckle. "Good, because I brought it with me!"

That had her laughing hard. "You brought your tux because I said I wanted to do that to you when I saw you wear it?"

He turned back to her with a smile. "No, I brought it so I could take you out for a candlelit dinner if you said yes to me." He took hold of her hand. "And you said yes. So do you think we should take a shower before we go out?"

She smiled as he pulled her to her feet. "Definitely."

~ ~ ~

Smoke stroked his thumb across the palm of her hand, their fingers were laced together as they sat on the porch swing. She rested her head on his shoulder as she stared out at the lake.

"Can we keep the picket fence?" she asked.

He chuckled. "I was never really going to tear it down, you know. I was only joking."

She turned to look up at him and he knew that her beautiful blue eyes promised enough fun and laughter to last a lifetime—as long as he was smart enough not to screw it up. He'd flown too close to disaster already to dare risk losing her ever again.

"I wasn't joking about you not being a picket fence kind of guy though. We both know you're not."

He lowered his head to her and gently nipped her bottom lip. "Any more than you are a picket fence kind of girl."

She laughed. "That's true."

"Maybe we'll learn to be, lady. When we're here. Maybe this place will become our sanctuary, the place we come back to. A picket fence to me has symbolized being fenced in, tied down. It doesn't feel like that here—with you. I think this place can be a base and not a burden. For both of us." He squeezed her hand. "Do you?"

She nodded happily. "I do. Remember when I tackled you up at Four Mile? You said there couldn't be two winners? What do you say about that now? I say I was right, we both win. We get each other, we both still get to live the life we want. You get to fly, I get to design." She laughed. "And I get to have my workroom out by the orchard after all."

"And I still won't charge you rent."

"Just you try!"

He laughed and pulled her closer. "Maybe I will. Get you good and mad at me, so you start pushing me around and calling me names again."

She shook her head at him. "It worked, didn't it?"

"Yeah. It did." He lifted his head as he heard a car approaching. "Are you ready for this?"

She nodded. "I'm looking forward to it. And you're sure you're okay with your parents coming?"

He hugged her tight. "I'm glad they're coming and I'm glad you suggested it. I don't want to shut them out anymore, if it's okay with you?"

She reached up and touched his cheek. "Of course it is. That's why I suggested inviting them. They love you, they're doing their best, and I know you love them too. And besides, if it weren't for your mom, I might still be in London right now, wondering how I was going to face life without you."

Smoke was aware that if it weren't for his parents—and Ben—
they probably wouldn't be sitting here right now, waiting for
their friends to arrive, to show off their new house and
celebrate their news. He nodded. "I feel like they gave you
back to me by interfering."

"They did. Your mom made the call, but your dad agreed that
she should. They were prepared to lose you again if it meant
giving you the chance of being happy with me. That's how
much they love you."

He nodded. "And now you're giving them back to me, inviting
them to be part of this new life of ours."

"Because that's how much I love you." She grinned at him as
Jack's truck rounded the corner and wound its way up the
drive. "So can you please stop pushing us all away now, and
just love us back? It's time for us to fly off into the sunset and
get on with our happily ever after. We've got a lot to fit in."

"We have." He stood and pulled her to her feet as he saw
Dan's Jeep round the corner. "We've got a whole lifetime to fit
in and it starts right here, right now—when we tell them all
that you're going to marry me." He planted a kiss on her lips
and led her down the steps to greet their guests. "And you
know, I love it that flying off into the sunset, for us, will mean
coming back here. We'll each go off and do our thing, but
when the sun sets on our adventures we'll come back to this
place. This will become home."

She cupped her hands around his neck to pull him to her, his
hands instinctively circled her waist. "It already is home,
Smoke, because it's where we are."

Everyone was arriving at once. They must have traveled up
here in a convoy. Pete and Holly climbed out of his truck.
Ben and Michael had come with Dan and Missy in the Jeep.
There were hugs and kisses, handshakes and slaps on the back.

Jack had driven up to the orchard to turn around. He pulled up and Emma jumped out to open the back door. Smoke felt an odd lump in his throat when his mom and dad climbed out of that old truck. He hugged them both, tight.

He took Laura's hand and led her up onto the front porch and wrapped an arm around her as he looked at all the smiling faces turned towards them.

"Thanks for coming guys. We wanted you all to see the place." He looked at his mom and dad, and had to swallow around the lump in his throat. "Wanted to invite you to our new home and let you know you're always welcome here. We wanted to thank you all for everything you did to get us here." He looked at Laura and smiled. "Even when I was being such a coward."

She smiled at him, her eyes full of laughter. He knew what she was thinking—big fucking coward!

They both looked out at all the happy faces. He figured this crew probably knew what was coming. "And we wanted to get you all together so we could tell you that this gorgeous lady has agreed to be my wife."

It seemed like everyone was talking at once. Laura was surrounded by squealing women. Smoke got lost in a sea of happy congratulations and man-hugs. He found himself face to face with his folks. His dad was smiling, his mom had tears in her eyes. The lump was back in his throat as he opened his arms to them. "Thank you." The three of them clung together in a hug that finally put the past behind them.

When he let go of them he looked for Laura. She came to him and he took hold of her hand. He finally knew what happy meant. It meant being here with his lady, surrounded by friends and his family. They might be inside a white picket fence, but he wasn't being grounded—he was flying higher than he ever had;

A Note from SJ

I hope you enjoyed visiting Summer Lake and catching up with the gang. Please let your friends know about the books if you feel they would enjoy them as well. It would be wonderful if you would leave me a review, I'd very much appreciate it.

To come back to the lake and get to know more couples as they each find their happiness, you can check out the rest of the series on my website.

www.SJMcCoy.com

Michael and Megan are up next in Laugh Like You've Never Cried.

Additionally, you can take a trip to Montana and meet a whole new group of friends. Take a look at my Remington Ranch series. It focuses on four brothers and the sometimes rocky roads they take on the way to their Happily Ever Afters.

There are a few options to keep up with me and my imaginary friends:

The best way is to Join up on the website for my Newsletter. Don't worry I won't bombard you! I'll let you know about upcoming releases, share a sneak peek or two and keep you in the loop for a couple of fun giveaways I have coming up :0)

You can join my readers group to chat about the books on Facebook or just browse and like my Facebook Page

I occasionally attempt to say something in 140 characters or less(!) on Twitter

And I'm always in the process of updating my website at www.SJMcCoy.com with new book updates and even some videos. Plus, you'll find the latest news on new releases and giveaways in my blog.

I love to hear from readers, so feel free to email me at AuthorSJMcCoy@gmail.com.. I'm better at that! :0)

I hope our paths will cross again soon. Until then, take care, and thanks for your support—you are the reason I write!
Love
SJ

PS Project Semicolon

You may have noticed that the final sentence of the story closed with a semi-colon. It isn't a typo. Project Semi Colon is a non-profit movement dedicated to presenting hope and love to those who are struggling with depression, suicide, addiction and self-injury. Project Semicolon exists to encourage, love and inspire. It's a movement I support with all my heart.

"A semicolon represents a sentence the author could have ended, but chose not to. The sentence is your life and the author is you."

- Project Semicolon

This author started writing after her son was killed in a car crash. At the time I wanted my own story to be over, instead I chose to honour a promise to my son to write my 'silly stories' someday. I chose to escape into my fictional world. I know for many who struggle with depression, suicide can appear to be the only escape. The semicolon has become a symbol of support, and hopefully a reminder – Your story isn't over yet

Also by SJ McCoy

Remington Ranch Series
Mason (FREE in ebook form)
Shane
Carter
Beau

Coming next
Four Weddings and a Vendetta

Summer Lake Series
Love Like You've Never Been Hurt (FREE in ebook form)
Work Like You Don't Need the Money
Dance Like Nobody's Watching
Fly Like You've Never Been Grounded
Laugh Like You've Never Cried
Sing Like Nobody's Listening
Smile Like You Mean It
The Wedding Dance
Chasing Tomorrow
Dream Like Nothing's Impossible

Coming next
Ride Like You've Never Fallen

About the Author

I'm SJ, a coffee addict, lover of chocolate and drinker of good red wines. I'm a lost soul and a hopeless romantic. Reading and writing are necessary parts of who I am. Though perhaps not as necessary as coffee! I can drink coffee without writing, but I can't write without coffee.

I grew up loving romance novels, my first boyfriends were book boyfriends, but life intervened, as it tends to do, and I wandered down the paths of non-fiction for many years. My life changed completely a few years ago and I returned to Romance to find my escape.

I write 'Sweet n Steamy' stories because to me there is enough angst and darkness in real life. My favorite romances are happy escapes with a focus on fun, friendships and happily-ever-afters, just like the ones I write.

These days I live in beautiful Montana, the last best place. If I'm not reading or writing, you'll find me just down the road in the park - Yellowstone. I have deer, eagles and the occasional bear for company, and I like it that way :0)

Made in the USA
San Bernardino, CA
21 March 2018